Better Than Safe

"This book was fun, sexy, feel good, with a sprinkle of angst on top. Highly recommend!"

—Gay Book Reviews

"*Better Than Safe* (Better Than #4) by Lane Hayes was both hot and funny with some sweet thrown in."

—Scattered Thoughts and Rogue Words

"My dogs were lying right beside me and were chewing up sticks all over the couch and I didn't even realize they were doing it. That's how engrossed I was with *Better Than Safe*, by Lane Hayes."

—Kathy Mac Reviews

The Right Time

"There was romance and a sexy soccer player mixed in with real life issues. The entire series is enjoyable and I look forward to what will come next."

—Joyfully Jay

"…thank you, Lane, for another great story."

—Prism Book Alliance

The Wrong Man

"The writing is excellent and the sex is really hot."

—The Kimi-chan Experience

"The characters are lovable and you really feel like you know the guys… A really good read that I'd highly recommend."

—It's About The Book

By Lane Hayes

A Kind of Truth

Published by DREAMSPINNER PRESS
www.dreamspinnerpress.com

A KIND OF TRUTH

Happy Reading
Lane Hayes

LANE HAYES

DREAMSPINNER PRESS

Published by

DREAMSPINNER PRESS

5032 Capital Circle SW, Suite 2, PMB# 279, Tallahassee, FL 32305-7886 USA
www.dreamspinnerpress.com

This is a work of fiction. Names, characters, places, and incidents either are the product of author imagination or are used fictitiously, and any resemblance to actual persons, living or dead, business establishments, events, or locales is entirely coincidental.

ISBN: 978-1-63476-803-0
Digital ISBN: 978-1-63476-804-7
Library of Congress Control Number: 2015950519
Published January 2016
v. 1.0

Printed in the United States of America
∞
This paper meets the requirements of
ANSI/NISO Z39.48-1992 (Permanence of Paper).

For Claire, because it's your turn.
Your beautiful heart is a gift I cherish every day.
May the music inside you inspire you to reach for your dreams.

Chapter 1

There is nothing like a dream to create the future.
—Victor Hugo, *Les Misérables*

THE DOOR closed with a quiet click that echoed through my skull as though it had been slammed shut. I listened to the happy chattering voices around the worn wooden table and even managed to nod a couple times with what may have passed for a smile, but I couldn't shake the feeling this wasn't a good idea. I knew to trust my instincts. I knew better than to nod my head and agree with the majority because it was easier than admitting we were making a mistake. But I kept quiet.

For ten seconds.

"It's not gonna work."

Tim cast his eyes at the cracked, discolored ceiling, then smacked his forehead on the table for good measure before turning to me in utter disbelief. I wanted to laugh. Tim was easily riled. His facial expressions and over-the-top slapstick reactions cracked me up. He was convinced I lived to torment him. I did. Most of the time. But I wasn't teasing anyone. I wasn't trying to be difficult. I just couldn't shake the feeling something was off.

"Please tell me you're fucking around," he begged, combing his fingers through his dark hair in frustration. He rested his cheek on his palm and gave me a sideways, pleading glance.

"No. I—"

"Rand, you are fucking insane! This is the fifth guitarist we've auditioned. He's by far the best of the bunch. You know it! We sounded pretty damn good together. Listen to the recording again. Listen to—"

I stood abruptly, accidentally knocking my chair over in my haste to move. I felt trapped. Like a caged animal. The room was too small, too cramped, and I was about to come out of my skin. *Trust yourself*, I thought before rounding on the two men looking at me with a combination of worry and dread. My bandmates, my comrades. I couldn't let them down by agreeing to keep the peace. I had to go with my gut.

"Terry's good. But that's all. He's not amazing. He's not special. I don't think he's the man."

Cory sighed heavily but managed to look slightly cooler than Tim, who was now scowling at the table. "Rand, we need a guitarist. We have studio time booked, and no offense, but you don't play well enough to make this work. Your strength is being the front man with a kickass voice and sexy moves that make the girls wet and the guys hard. You're great at the occasional rhythm guitar, but we need someone full-time to handle lead. You can't do it all. We know our roles. I play bass, Tim drums, and you sing. And write. And find us gigs. It's too much for one guy. You've got to start delegating."

"Delegating?"

"Yeah. You're trying to do too much, and nothing's getting done now."

Cory was right. I *had* taken on more than I bargained for. Moving to New York was a big fucking deal. But it was a risk we had to take if we were going to take our band, Spiral, to the next level. Cory, Tim, and I had worked our asses off to get this far. We had a small and loyal fan base. In Baltimore. In New York City we were nobodies. We were starting from scratch. This could be the chance of a lifetime, but it was going to take big fucking balls to make things happen. This was the place. And now was the time. If we could make it in this city, we could make it anywhere.

However, the lack of a steady, reliable guitarist was an issue. A big one. Our previous one was currently doing his third stint in rehab, and our backup guitarist was my best friend, Seth, who only agreed to play with us occasionally to help me out. He lived in DC with his boyfriend now and had kindly informed me there was no way in hell he was moving to the Big Apple to do me a solid. I was on my own. While Tim and Cory were invested in making a go of the rock-and-roll dream, at the end of the day, Spiral was mine. My band, my songs, my lyrics, and my vision. They were counting on me to lead the way, and for the first time in a long time, I was lost. I was caught between following my instincts and doing what was necessary to keep forward momentum.

"Look, we told Terry he's got the gig, so it's his for now," I said with a heavy sigh. "I'm just worried he doesn't have the drive. He seems like the type who'd like to drag out his adolescence for as long as possible. He takes pottery classes, works at Starbucks during the day, and likes getting stoned in his free time. That's not the résumé of someone who—"

"Are you kidding me?" Tim pushed his chair away. "You work at a fucking bagel shop! Were you looking for a NYU grad with an MFA in music?"

I snorted, thinking both Tim and Cory could pass as college students with their short-cropped hair and clean-cut good looks. Their preppy sweaters hid copious ink, but the conservative attire was in deference to the chilly January weather, not a fashion statement. My longer hair made me the odd man out. But like them, I was dressed in a thick black sweater and even wore a beanie on my head. The temperature outdoors hadn't risen above twenty degrees in a week. I couldn't remember the last time I'd felt warm.

"My bagel stint is temporary. And it keeps me out of trouble. Give me shit and I'll conveniently forget to bring home the oat bran with jalapeño cream cheese tomorrow, asshole." I waited a beat for the finger I knew he'd flash me before continuing. "A degree isn't necessary, but I want someone serious. I don't want the drugs, the nonstop parties, or people who are in the game for a quick thrill. I want this to be something important. Something real. I have to trust we're all on the same page. I know you guys are but...."

"Hey. I get it, but we have to keep the momentum going." Tim crossed his arms over his chest. "We're wasting time. Renting the studio to practice isn't cheap."

"Nothing in this city is cheap," Cory grumbled.

"Thus the bagel job." I swiped my hand over my stubbled chin in frustration. No one said the road to success would be easy, but it would be nice to get on the fucking path already. "Okay. We'll start practicing with Terry tomorrow, go over the contract with the new manager the day after, and somewhere in there, I'm going to take guitar lessons."

I ignored their shared eye roll as I reached for my coat.

"Actually, it's not a bad idea. It'll keep you from thinking too hard," Cory snarked.

"Why don't you ask the guy who referred Terry? The college kid. What was his name again?" Tim draped his red-and-black scarf over his neck and pulled his gloves from his coat pocket.

"Um.... William Sanders," Cory replied. "The girl we met at that bar on Delancey referred him. She said William was a maestro. Unfortunately he wasn't interested in playing with a band. He's working on his degree. Terry graduated last year, I think. Or maybe he dropped out, but he went to school with them too. Remember Holly? The hot chick with huge—"

"You're telling me we're taking referrals from cute girls with big tits to find our Eric Clapton. No wonder I'm skeptical." I shook my head in mock disbelief.

"You got a better idea? You didn't like any of the other guitarists. At least you didn't hate Terry. Step in the right direction," Cory said, opening the studio office door with a goofy grin on his face. "By the way, I said hot… not cute. I asked her out."

"Look at you, Romeo." I pinched his cheek hard and chuckled when he punched my arm.

"Yeah, yeah. So let's find you something to get you out of the apartment in case… you know." Cory turned a funny shade of red as he turned to walk down the narrow corridor to the elevator.

Tim and I wolf-whistled as we followed him. "No, I don't know. Spell it out. You hoping to get lucky?"

"Fuck off." He pushed the button hard, then made a production of pulling out his cell and typing a message.

"Aw. Don't get cranky. We'll be good roomies, right, Timmy? We'll find ourselves a nice little bar while you entertain your friend, and maybe you can return the favor."

"Gee, thanks. I just sent you William's info. I still had it in my phone. Call him. If he can teach you how to change chords without fumbling… hell, I'll blow him. And if he's gay, sexy, and unattached, all the better."

"For who?" I asked, rolling my eyes. "I told you I'm playing by new rules for now. I'm not looking for a man. Or a woman either."

"Well it wouldn't hurt for you to find something or someone to do to keep your mind off the fact New York City didn't open her arms and legs the minute she found out Rand O'Malley had finally arrived."

I smacked him upside the head as we jumped into the empty elevator. Cory was a shit, but he was right. I had to stay busy. And productive. My part-time gig at Bowery Bagels was mind-numbing at best, but I could only write and practice for so many hours a day. Taking lessons would be a good diversion for me. New York City wasn't short on things to do, but I had to stay focused. And if things with Terry didn't work out, maybe I'd learn enough to take Spiral from a quartet to a trio and put the never-ending guitarist search behind us.

LIVING AND working with the same two guys was a challenge. We were crammed into a tiny two-bedroom, one bath apartment in the lower East Village. It was a fourth-floor walk-up with low ceilings and paper-thin walls, and in January, it was a fucking icebox. I slipped on my thick leather gloves, zipped my coat up over my chin, and picked up my guitar case before pushing open the lobby door. I braced myself against the elements, keeping my head down to ward off the chilly wind as I decided whether I should splurge on a taxi versus riding the subway to New York University. At this hour, it was time versus money.

I hailed a cab. I was already running late, and my balls were shrinking at an alarming rate after I'd only walked half a block. It was a no-brainer. Usually I was all about saving a buck and soaking up the ambience. The people-watching in New York City was second to none, and the best way to experience it was on foot. Street by street, every neighborhood was eclectic and brimming with life. Sometimes they were tragically hip, other times they were just tragic. But they were never boring. The city's energy was invigorating and hypnotic. It made you think you might actually have a shot at being something special. Someone extraordinary.

Maybe it was all in my head, but I swear I could feel it. A pulse, a beat, an upswing in tempo. Something was driving me to keep moving, keep trying. I had a dream, and instinctively I knew this was where it would begin.

"You gettin' out?"

Oh. Right. I handed over the cab fare to the disgruntled-looking driver without making eye contact. It struck me as a funny thing how faceless people could be in big cities. Cabbies, waiters… hell, the guy working behind the counter at the corner bagel store. Manhattan was a "point A to point B" kind of town unless you were a tourist or an artist who hoped to get paid to catalog details of this diverse city. For those who lived here full-time, details were distractions. True, I'd only been here for two months, but I hoped I never became too jaded to notice how freaking amazing this place was.

I glanced over at the arch monument across the street in Washington Square Park. Snow dusted the ground and benches lining the pathways around the circular fountain. A couple of tourists took selfies under the arch, but otherwise the park was empty—and strangely inviting. A sudden gust of wind quickly changed my mind. I crossed the street and heaved a huge sigh of relief the moment I stepped into the university's blessedly warm Performing Arts Center lobby.

The center was a stunning contemporary masterpiece of undulating lines in glass and travertine. I set my guitar case at my feet and checked out my surroundings while I waited for my guitar hero, William. There were a few students milling around, but they didn't fit his description. Tall, skinny, brown hair, with glasses, wearing a plaid shirt. Hmph. I peeled off my gloves and stuffed them in my pockets, then pulled out my cell to make sure I hadn't missed any messages.

"Um, hi. Are you Rand?"

I eyed the shy-looking guy standing a couple feet away. His rigid posture made him seem taller, but when I stepped forward to shake his hand, I could tell he was closer to my own six foot two. He was perfectly pressed and put together in a designer-label plaid shirt and khakis. The glasses were a sexy addition. He had a nice face. Not super-hot by any means but… attractive. Sort of. I caught him giving me a thorough once-over and wondered if he regretted agreeing to help me fine-tune my guitar playing. The thought made me smile. On the surface, our height and the fact we were both on the lean side were all we had in common. We couldn't look any different if we tried. I had longish, dark brown hair that skimmed the collar of my sweater, brown eyes, and more tatts on my arms, chest, and back than he'd probably be comfortable knowing about. I was pretty sure the only name brand I was wearing were my Levi's. Oh and maybe my underwear too, if they counted.

"Yeah. Hey."

"I—I'm William. I just finished a class and well… I asked permission for us to use one of the smaller rooms to play. I—it's this way." He shook my hand quickly, then turned toward the bank of elevators before I could reply.

The guy was nervous as hell. His palms were sweaty, and his voice quivered anxiously. I stared after him for a heartbeat, then wiped my palm on my jeans, sighing as I picked up my guitar and followed him. Whatever. If this was a bust, at least I'd be warm for an hour.

Three students carrying jackets and backpacks jumped in the elevator with us. They were engaged in a lighthearted conversation about a professor. When we stepped inside, one of the girls fluttered her eyelashes at me, then turned a pretty shade of pink when I smiled back. She was cute, I thought, adjusting my guitar case. She was too young for me, but there was no harm in flirting.

"We're here." William tapped my arm when the elevator doors opened, then stood aside so I could exit first. The gesture was extraordinarily courteous. Or uptight. I waved at the blushing girl while I waited for him to lead the way. A flash of disapproval flitted across his face. I wondered what bugged him. Me flirting or me in general. Either way, I was instantly intrigued. I couldn't help it. I was one of those guys who got a weird thrill from pushing people's buttons. I didn't know William at all, but suddenly, I was interested. If only to know what it would take to make him come a little unglued.

He walked ahead of me, stopping halfway down the wide corridor to open the door to a small classroom. I shrugged off my coat and set my guitar on a long, rectangular table against the back wall. There were maybe ten chairs placed in a semicircle facing a podium at the front of the room and a piano off to the side near a smallish window. A couple posters featuring upcoming musical events at the university were the only décor in the space. I noticed two guitars on stands near the podium. One electric, one acoustic. Both were gorgeous. And expensive. Not the kind of instruments I would have expected a college kid to own. Unless his mommy and daddy bought them, I thought uncharitably. I forgot NYU was no ordinary college. It cost big bucks to come here.

Yeah, Daddy definitely bought that baby. Fuck. I was practically salivating when he picked up the glossy black Fender Stratocaster. Seth had a gorgeous candy-apple-red one like it. This one was equally spectacular. Sleek, shiny, and very fucking pretty.

"So… um. I'm not sure what you had in mind. I mean, I'm assuming you play a little."

I removed my less impressive electric guitar from its case and slung the strap over my shoulder. "Yeah. I've been playing since I was fourteen. My problem is I can't change chords fast enough. I can fake it if I'm playing rhythm behind someone else, but I want to do it myself. I want to lead."

"You're in a band, right? Didn't you guys hire Terry?" he asked, setting the Fender aside to reach for his acoustic guitar at the last second.

"Yeah." I tried for neutral, but he must have heard the indifference in my tone.

"He's not working out?"

"He's fine. Is he a good friend of yours?"

"No. I… I mean, I know him. We were in a class together last year. He's into rock, and when I saw him at the coffee shop recently, he mentioned wanting to play more often. I'm definitely not interested in being in a band."

"Hmm. What are you interested in?"

He smiled wanly. "Writing music. Playing."

"Same here."

"Cool."

"Hey, before we get started… I have a couple questions."

William sat on the plastic chair at the end of the semicircle and cocked his head expectantly. I joined him, keeping one seat in between us. It felt awkward to have to turn to face him, so I picked up the chair and moved it in front of him. When I sat back down I realized I'd misjudged the distance. We were so close our knees touched. I pushed back slightly but noticed a faint blush color his cheeks. I wished I knew him better so I could tease him. He looked so prim and proper, I wanted to shake him up. But he also struck me as shy and a little fragile. I had to curb my compulsion to forcefully assert myself. It worked wonders when I was onstage working a crowd or hell, even maneuvering around the city. People would mow you over in this town if you let them. I never would, but I wasn't so sure about William.

He pushed his glasses up his nose and bit his bottom lip as he strummed his fingers lightly over his guitar. I could tell he was nervous. My earlier thought of wanting to push his buttons and watch him come unglued flew out the proverbial window. It would be too easy. And possibly destructive.

He kept his head down when he spoke. "Sure. Ask anything."

"How old are you? You seem way younger than me. No offense, but how much experience do you have?"

His brown eyes twinkled with amusement when he glanced up at me. The look was boyishly sweet and innocent. He was kinda cute. Nerdy, but cute.

"I'm twenty-two. I've been playing since I was six. I've been told I'm pretty good." He grinned widely before giving his attention back to his instrument. I'd bet it was already perfectly in tune but he wanted something to do with his hands. "But I won't be offended if you decide

I'm not what you're looking for. I'm a music major here. I graduate in May, but I'm hoping I get accepted to the MFA program in the fall for musical theater writing."

"Cool. Do you do much tutoring?"

"Only occasionally. I'm kind of busy, but this time works out okay for me and"—he shrugged self-consciously—"I could use the extra money. I'm a perpetual college student."

"And I'm perpetually broke. If this works for both of us, I can probably only do it once a week."

"That's fine."

"Do you play other instruments too?"

"Yes, a few. I actually spend more time sitting at that piano bench," William said, angling his head toward the piano in the corner, "than I do with a guitar nowadays. But this is my first love."

He strummed his fingers lightly over the strings, coaxing a gorgeous melody that resonated throughout the small room. He smiled shyly, but this time I sensed a growing confidence in the gesture, as though holding the guitar worked as a physical shield with a secret magical component the moment it was played. Interesting.

I wanted to join in and maybe show him I wasn't a complete moron, but I didn't recognize the music.

"What are you playing?"

"Something I made up. So… um. Go ahead and plug in to the amp. Maybe we should start with a song we both know. I'll watch your finger movement and see if there are any quick tricks I can help you with, but to be honest, if you've been playing for a while, you probably already know the only thing that really will make a difference is practice. Lots of practice. Have you taken lessons before?"

"Some, but I'm mostly self-taught. I have a good ear and I picked it up easily, but lead guitar wasn't my focus. There was always someone else who did it better than me, so I didn't worry about it. Now I want to make a real go of this. I don't want to play in crappy dive bars for the next ten years, then wake up one day and wonder why I'm still struggling to pay rent. I want this to happen. Terry may end up being awesome, but the one thing I do know is you can't rely on anyone else to make things happen for you."

"True. What's your band's sound?"

"Rock and roll with a heavy blues vibe." I grinned wickedly as I launched into "Sympathy for the Devil" by the Rolling Stones.

My voice had a raspier quality than Jagger's, but that was fine by me. I admired Mick's soulful vocals, but I didn't aspire to mimic anyone. An original sound was vital to making a name people would remember. When I got to the electric guitar lick, I knew William or anyone with a decent ear would flinch. I faked it as best I could, then stopped and held out my hand to my new teacher.

"Pleased to meet you, Will. Have you guessed my name?"

He stared at my hand, then at me with his mouth wide open before stuttering and fidgeting in his seat like a kid, looking anywhere but at me.

"What's the matter? Don't you wanna shake my hand?"

He gulped audibly and bit at his lip again. "I—um… my name is William."

I chuckled and brought my hand back to the strings when I caught on he wasn't going to shake it.

"Well? Can you hear the problem?"

He nodded. "Yes. You're impatient."

I threw back my head and laughed. "Now that, my friend, is the understatement of a lifetime."

With a tepid smile in place, William held out his acoustic guitar. "Let's trade and take it from the top."

"Do you know that song or do you want to try another?"

"I know it well."

Maybe it was the confident timbre in his tone or the way he commandeered my electric guitar like a nurse who was going to show a brand-new momma how to take care of her baby, but the geeky dude with the glasses suddenly sounded like a kickass, no-bullshit maestro. I traded guitars with my brow raised.

"Show me your stuff, Will," I challenged.

I started midsong and did my best acoustic guitar rendition of the Rolling Stones classic, complete with vocals. This particular song was one of my favorites. I found myself in a zone, leaning into the instrument as I sang about wealth and taste only to be ripped back into the moment by his astonishing guitar solo. I stalled for half a beat, overcome with what I could only describe as awe, before I picked up his cue and continued.

I was so pumped I couldn't sit still. I jumped up and gave the song my all, lifting the acoustic guitar like it had some kind of power when in fact the magic was coming from the skinny guy in a plaid shirt and glasses calmly swaying into the complicated notes. When the song ended, I whooped and held out my hand for a high five.

"Will, don't leave me hangin' again. That was fucking unreal! You're amazing!"

Will straightened in his chair. I could almost see a haze clear from his vision, as though he'd been so immersed in his music he needed a second to adjust to speaking in words. When the moment passed, he smiled. A glorious, radiant-sunshine kind of grin that made me blink. Yeah... nerdy but definitely cute. Maybe even hot. And when he raised his hand tentatively to mine, I swear my jeans got a little tighter. Not good.

"Thanks. I'm a big Stones fan."

"Me too."

"I can tell. You really... emote. Do you do that onstage?"

"Yeah, I get into a zone. Kinda like you just did. That was cool." When he blushed furiously and started to sputter, I held up my hand, then pointed to the guitar. "So... what am I doing wrong?"

"You aren't doing anything wrong. Like I said, you're impatient. I can give you a couple tips, but your mechanics are decent. The only thing that will really make a difference is—"

"Practice. I know." I sighed dramatically, then grinned. "You gonna take me on? Or am I more than you bargained for?"

Silence.

I cocked my head and waited for him to respond as the quiet took on a charged quality, an energy I recognized but was frankly confused by. This guy wasn't my type. At all. How was I getting hard now? Must be the music.

"Sure. I'll take you on." Will's voice was soft and low. He sounded like sex. No doubt it was unintentional, but there was something about his shy, sideways delivery that made me do a double take.

"Um... great. Thanks." I winced when my voice cracked. I twisted my wrist to check my watch and hopefully pull myself together.

"I'm open Tuesdays or Thursdays after class. I should be able to wrangle this room or another one like it from my professor. He's pretty cool about—wow."

"What?"

"Oh. Uh... nothing." He swiped a hand through his hair and adjusted his glasses again nervously. "I—you have a lot of tattoos. I...

anyway, one thing you need to do is keep your fingers closer to the—what are you doing?"

"Nothing." I pushed both my sleeves back, revealing my somewhat colorful forearms, and kept my gaze locked on his. "Sorry, where do you want my fingers, Will?"

The rush of blood to his face was instantaneous. I smiled, unable to control my wicked sense of satisfaction. He liked me. Scratch that. He was attracted to me. Maybe he'd come to like me too. As a friend, I amended in my head.

"My name is William," he corrected.

I laughed heartily, then steadied the guitar on my knee before beginning another song. He joined in a beat later like the pro he seemed to be. This time when he caught my grin, he returned it with a megawatt smile of his own.

As the music swelled around us, my shoulders relaxed for the first time since I'd arrived in New York City with a guitar, a couple buddies, and a long-shot dream. Maybe it was the quiet confidence of the well-dressed, perfectly coiffed kid with a killer smile and insane skill on a six string. Or maybe it was simply being in a room with someone who didn't expect me to have all the answers. Either way, I had a good feeling about Will.

AFTER THAT first guitar lesson, my days took on a new cadence. I worked the early shift for a few hours in the morning at the bagel shop. If I'd been up late the night before, I'd go back to bed for a couple hours, then I'd practice. And write. We practiced as a group every afternoon, sometimes well into the evening. So far, Terry was working out fine. He didn't blow me away with his skill the way Will did, but I couldn't see my guitar teacher jumping at the chance to take Terry's place. He wasn't going to play to a crowd of screaming girls shaking their tits at us while their boyfriends played air guitar next to them. It wasn't his scene. It was mine, though. I fucking loved the rush of performing in front of an audience. And after hiring a manager with connections to some small club venues in Manhattan, we finally had a couple of shows on the calendar and the chance to prove Spiral was the real deal.

Everything worthwhile in the music business was driven by networking. A friend from Baltimore whose club we occasionally played at referred a talent agent to us. It took two months of haggling before

Mike Cochran even agreed to meet. I couldn't tell if he was playing hard to get or if he was just a dick, but as Cory reminded me, we knew we were good, but we still had to prove it. And we did. The day after Mike met us, we signed a contract largely based on compensation from potential later success. Mike was willing to take a chance on us and act as our agent and manager. A week later, we were scheduled to play at Karma, an East Village club with a maximum capacity of five hundred people. Not big but the biggest we'd played in the city yet.

As the date neared, I felt a growing concern about Terry's ability to handle the band's original material. He was a decent cover guitarist, but I didn't want to do all covers. We didn't aspire to be a wedding or bar mitzvah band. I did my best to curb my impatience with his slow learning curve, but it wasn't easy. I griped to Will and even jokingly offered to pay to have him give Terry a lesson or two. Will chuckled and shook his head as he ran his fingers lovingly over his guitar strings.

"Terry's pride wouldn't let him take a lesson from someone like me."

I slapped my hands over my own strings, abruptly stopping all sound. Will cocked his head curiously at the jarring noise and stilled his fingers. "What do you mean, 'someone like you'?"

He sniffed and shrugged nonchalantly. "Really? In case it isn't obvious, I'm not exactly a rock-and-roll type."

"What type are you?" I huffed in amusement.

I watched Will carefully. I'd only known him a couple weeks now, but there was something very fraternal about playing music. It was a soulful endeavor that gave you the feeling you were connecting on a different plane. Maybe it was one-sided. The truth was, I still didn't know much about Will other than he seemed to spend a lot of time at the Performing Arts Center or in the theater district at his internship. It wasn't for lack of trying, but every time I asked a simple personal question, he would distract me with a song, and before I knew it, I was lost in the music again.

He adjusted his glasses and rolled his eyes. "I'm a band geek."

"Gotcha. A total nerd, eh?"

"Yep." He grinned sweetly.

I laughed, realizing this teasing banter was a sign of a gentle thaw. For the first time since our initial lesson a couple weeks ago, Will was actively joking with me rather than looking at me with mild distrust. As long as we were playing, he was fine, but actual conversation seemed to make him uncomfortable. Unless it was about music.

"Were you in the high school band?"

"Yeah. I played the drums," he said, adjusting his glasses again.

"No way."

"Way."

"You play the drums too?"

"Yes." He shrugged and turned his attention back to his guitar. "You need to build your chords from the bottom up. If you…."

And that was evidently the end of personal-share time. His intent expression and the determined set of his shoulders acted like a reinforced barrier behind the acoustic guitar he held. I noted the way the light hit his brown hair, sending golden highlights across his forehead and—I reached out unconsciously and brushed at a smudge on his temple.

"What are you doing?" He jolted backward in his chair.

"Hey, relax. You have something on your face. It looks… sparkly. Like glitter."

The skin beneath my fingers instantly turned a bright shade of scarlet. I glanced at my thumb and then at the shocked man cowering away from me in confusion. So what if it was glitter? Why was he so freaked out?

"Uh… thanks." He swallowed hard, then sat back in his chair before clearing his throat noisily. "When you build from the bott—"

"Hey." I gently rubbed his chin. A soft touch only meant to get his attention. He gulped again and bit his lip. The gesture went inexplicably straight to my dick. I refocused, waiting until he looked me in the eye before pulling my hand away. "I like glitter. And geeks are cool too."

Will's answering smile was breathtaking. The sun seemed to break through a thick cloud and bathe the room in brilliant golden light. My face felt suddenly warm. I wondered belatedly if I was actually blushing.

"Um, so the chords…."

"Right. Chords." I offered a lopsided grin and bent my head in concentration. What the hell was wrong with me?

A few hours later, I was still trying to figure it out. I couldn't stop thinking about Will. Weird things. His hair looked longer today. Kind of messy. I liked it. And those golden highlights I noticed. Were they always there? They made his brown eyes take on a hazel tone with flecks of green and gold and—

"Earth to Rand. Hello. Anybody home?"

I stared straight ahead as though lost in thought, waiting for Tim to move in a little closer and do that wavy thing in front of my face again. *Bam!* I smacked his hand down flat against the table. Hard.

"Fuck, that hurt!" Tim glowered at me as he flexed his fingers dramatically.

I grinned wickedly and picked up my beer while Cory cackled across the table and Terry looked on in bemusement. It was like Lucy snatching the football from Charlie Brown at the very last second just as he was about to kick the shit out of it. Again. Same result, a different day. Tim was a little slow. And pissed off now. I mussed his hair good-naturedly and raised my bottle in a mock toast.

"Sorry."

"Hmph."

We were tucked into a corner table at Mickey's, a tiny Irish pub down the street from the studio on Essex. It had become a favorite place to congregate because it was a no-frills, inexpensive meal in a town that charged three times as much depending on location. Supposedly it was a gangster hangout in the 1930s. I glanced up at the low tin ceiling and old-fashioned brass chandeliers over the bar. Yeah, I could definitely imagine guys with fedoras, slick suits, and shiny shoes hunkered over one of these worn wooden tables plotting murder and mayhem. Modern patrons were more likely to carry backpacks and wear ripped jeans and beanies. Like me. I snagged my hat from my head and stuffed it in my pocket, shaking the lingering numbness from my fingertips. Between my lesson with Will and regular practice with the band, my fingers were aching. It had been a longass day. I should have been exhausted, but I was bubbling with excess energy.

I glanced up at the waitress delivering our order and greeted her with an over-the-top welcome. I was starving. She laughed at my effusive thanks and lingered a little longer than necessary to make sure we were "satisfied." Cory chuckled softly as he cut his burger neatly in half.

"What's so funny?" I asked around a mouthful of french fries.

"You. You're a charming fucker, Rand. You could sell ice to an Eskimo."

I grinned in response before picking up my giant cheeseburger. "She's cute, but she's wearing a big ol' ring on her left hand. No thanks. Let's go out tonight and check out the clubs."

"Can't. I got a date later."

"Later? It's…." I checked my phone for the time. "Nine. Where ya going?"

"Out with Holly."

"Oohh." Tim and I threw fries at him and whooped like a couple of morons. Terry grinned but didn't join in.

Times like this I really missed Seth. I knew he was happy with his man in DC and band life wasn't for him in the long run, but he was one of us. He knew our stupid jokes and would jump in to razz without hesitation. Maybe I wasn't being fair to Terry. I knew I had to be patient and give the guy a chance. It was harder than it should have been, which was strange. Physically he fit in with the band. He had shaggy brown hair, a scruffy beard, and usually wore old college T-shirts with Doc Martens and jeans. And he was a decent guitarist. Maybe spending time with a phenomenal one was making me realize it wasn't smart to settle for second best. If there was any way Will would join—

Whoa. I had to stop thinking about the guy. I was bordering on obsessive.

"We lost him again," Tim grumbled. "Are you writing a song in your head?"

I gave him a halfhearted smirk as I reached for my beer.

"Tell us about Holly. Hey, you know her, right, Terry?" I asked in an effort to move attention away from myself.

"Yeah. We had a couple classes together last year. One of them was with William, the geek with the glasses. He's the one who gave you my name."

I clenched my jaw and willed myself to behave. I tried counting to ten but only made it to five before I let him have it. "Hmm… you mean the incredibly gifted musician who turned down the job first. That guy?"

Terry tilted his head and squinted at me as though he couldn't tell if I was playing with him or just being a dick. Tim and Cory knew. They both started talking at the same time while I stared at Terry with an insipid smile. Geez, I was an asshole. I allowed Cory to redirect the conversation and let the wave of protectiveness subside before I attempted to rejoin.

They were talking about the bar where Cory was meeting Holly in SoHo. I took a long drink and turned to Tim.

"We should probably make sure he gets there safe and sound. What d'ya say?"

Tim chuckled. "Oh yeah. This is a tough town. We'll take care of you, Cor. Wanna come along, Terry?"

"Uh… I can't. I'm—"

"No one's going anywhere with me." Cory glowered across the table. "Assholes."

We laughed a little longer than necessary. They were all probably happy to move past a potentially caustic scene, while I was frankly wondering what my problem was. Will *was* a geek. He'd say so himself. Why was I making life difficult with someone I was poised to possibly spend a lot more time with in the future than my guitar teacher?

Tim wanted to know the same thing. We tortured Cory by taking the subway with him as far as Broadway. His look of relief when we didn't exit at the same time was comical. I tried to ask Tim what our plan was, but I could hardly get a word in edgewise. He was too busy giving me an earful about being a team player and suppressing my inclination to say exactly what was on my mind. He assured me my occasional silence was preferable. I pulled my scarf a little higher on my neck and let him talk 'til he ran out of steam. Which I hoped would be soon.

"What is your problem with him, anyway? He's nice enough."

"Oh for fuck's sake! Are you done, Mom? I left him alone. I promise to be sweet to the little fella from now on. Better?"

I glanced out the window as the subway approached the next station. I stared at the young couple with matching nose rings exiting the train and idly wondered if they'd ever gotten stuck when they kissed. My attention was diverted by a flash of blue sequins a moment later. I looked up in time to see a tall woman in a long black coat and impossibly high heels move past me. Tim noticed my wandering gaze and snorted.

"Maybe you just need to get laid."

"That's always a decent solution. Where are we going?"

"You'll see. In the meantime, answer my question. What's the deal with Terry?"

"There is no deal! He rubs me the wrong way. I don't know why. It pissed me off that he had the gall to say anything crappy about the guy who ultimately gave him a shot."

Tim shook his head in exasperation. "Gave him a shot at what? We're nobodies, Rand! Your ego is insane. He didn't say anything wrong, and you know it. Stop picking fights."

"Okay."

He cocked his head warily and elbowed my side. "Okay."

"Okay," I repeated with a grin. I threw my arm over his shoulder and kissed his cheek. Sloppy and wet. He batted me away and gave me a dirty look. "I promise to be nice. I'll try anyway."

"Please do. And back the fuck off. People are gonna think we're a couple."

I snickered and perused the sparse subway crowd with wide eyes. "God, that would be awful."

"It would be for me. Check out the hot guy in the Yankee cap to your left. Don't look at him, moron," he hissed when I turned.

I rolled my eyes and clandestinely turned in my seat to catch a glimpse of said hottie. The man in question stood a few feet away from us, leaning on one of the poles near the exit next to the woman in heels. Her gaze was focused on her cell, but I could tell even from my angle that she was pretty. Short blonde, spiky hair, long eyelashes, and red lipstick. I turned back to Tim, indicating with a subtle hand movement he should check her out. He shrugged.

"I can't really see her. The guy's hot, though. He looks Puerto Rican or—"

"You're cheating. I thought we agreed when we came to New York that you and I would keep our bi sides on the DL, Timmy."

"Looking isn't cheating. Besides, let's be honest, I'm the drummer. No one cares who I fuck. And until we have a recording contract, I think you're safe too. So… who would you choose? The Latin cutie or the blonde with the—oh. Never mind. She's a he."

"Huh?"

Tim yanked on my sleeve before I could turn. "Don't stare. The pretty girl is a pretty boy, that's all."

"No way." I turned to shamelessly gawk at the statuesque beauty. Tim was right. I was stunned, not because I was wrong but because there was something familiar about the man in drag, and I couldn't figure out what it was. Maybe his profile or his—

"Quit staring!"

I nudged him hard and turned to give him a dirty look when he retaliated. The train was pulling into the next stop, and evidently, it was a popular one. Three or four people walked in front of us on their way to the exit. I stood in frustration and craned my neck to catch another glimpse of the drag queen, who'd moved toward the door.

"This isn't our stop."

"He looks like someone…." The crowd parted for a brief moment before converging again. I saw him clearly in that second but still couldn't place him. Until he bit his bottom lip.

I froze. It was Will.

Or was it? I couldn't tell for sure. I started to move toward the now-open door, but Tim pulled me back.

"It's not our exit. Oh wait. Maybe it is. I think we change trains here."

I listened to my friend's commentary about taking the F to some other letter in the alphabet, but my focus was now on getting the hell out. I didn't care about whatever club he wanted to go to in Chelsea. Could that really be Will?

I elbowed my way off the subway and stood on the platform, trying to get my bearings. But there was no sign of the man in a long black coat and heels. I swiped my hand over my chin in frustration. I was an idiot. That guy couldn't be Will. Will was a serious musician with big goals. He wasn't a cross-dresser. Not that he couldn't be both, of course. But I just couldn't see it. My overactive imagination had probably conjured him. I was obviously spending way too much time thinking about my guitar tutor. I just couldn't figure out why.

Chapter 2

THE FOLLOWING morning I headed out at the crack of dawn to Bowery Bagels. My friends thought I was nuts for taking a lameass job selling bagels for minimum wage. The early-morning hours were not conducive to a rock-and-roll lifestyle. Partying until three and waking up at five to politely inquire whether a customer wanted their bagel toasted with cream cheese separate or on the side sounded... well, like hell. But there was a method to my madness. I knew myself. I was disciplined as long as I had perimeters. If I gave myself too much freedom, my friends would be fighting over whose turn it was to carry my sorry ass home from the bar.

My tendency to test limits was probably a by-product of my somewhat bohemian upbringing. My folks were awesome, but they didn't care about rules. They taught my sister and me to always question authority and push boundaries. Rules didn't apply unless they were a matter of life, death, or what they called "social harmony." I was a cocky bastard who was certain I had rights far beyond anything I'd earned or deserved by age fourteen. I was sure my opinion counted. There were far too many stupid adults on the planet. Period. I was convinced I was correct when Seth's dad beat the crap out of him after he caught us kissing in their basement when we were fifteen. Who the fuck did shit like that? I was enraged. Seth was placed with a foster family when it became clear his parents weren't going to accept their son and might in fact pose a physical threat to him.

If this was so-called adult behavior, I wanted no part of it. Seth and I rebelled in every possible way. We formed a band, stayed out way too late, took drugs, drank, and screwed like rabbits. My parents shrugged and handed me condoms and a key to the house, while Seth's first foster family complained until he was moved to the next. By age seventeen, even I could tell we were on a path to nowhere. I began rethinking my stance on rules, discipline, and what the hell "social harmony" meant. It occurred to me I could set my own boundaries with a goal in mind. Goal number one was to graduate from high school. If I didn't want to be a dropout, I had to study. And get some fucking sleep once in a while.

When Seth moved on to model in Italy after graduation, it was time for me to think about what came next. What was I going to do with my life? Easy… I wanted to be a rock-and-roll star. I wanted to have a voice in music. Sure, it was a lofty aspiration, but channeling my anger, fear, and a desire to right the world's injustice into something positive was a better plan for me than working at my parents' all-natural food store. Music was the key. I met Cory, Tim, and our previous guitarist, Perry, at community college, and the rest, as they say, was history. Well, sort of. Now we had Terry instead of Perry. And we hadn't exactly made history, but I was more determined than ever to keep focused. No crazy partying and no unnecessary distractions, which in my case meant no relationships. With men or women. Discipline and hard work with minimal complication was the way to go. It was up to me to mold the band's future if we were going to have one. So for now, going to bed at a reasonable hour and waking up early was a good thing.

I pulled my beanie over my ears and shivered at the sudden gust of icy wind. Who was I trying to kid? This wasn't good for anyone. No one in their right mind needed a fucking bagel at five thirty in the morning. I knocked on the back door and waited for my boss to open it for me before my fingers froze.

"Good morning, Randall! Wanna cup o' coffee?"

George was always so damn chipper in the morning. I curled my lips in what I hoped passed for a smile, then followed him through the back room into the store. "Sounds good. Thanks, Mr. G."

George Gulden was a sixth-generation bagel maker. The old man had an encyclopedic knowledge on all things having to do with carbs. Bowery Bagels was a successful family-owned chain with stores throughout the five boroughs. All but one of George's four sons ran or managed the other locations, but this store on Bowery, a few blocks from NYU, was his baby. The original. People, including gourmet food tours, came from far and wide to sample his odd blends of cream cheese with savory bagels. I honestly didn't get it. It was a fucking bagel. A good one, but geesh…. Only in New York, I mused as I donned my apron and washed my hands. The secret had to be the owner. George was one of the nicest men I'd ever met. He greeted his regulars by name and was sure to ask after family members and friends. I'd worked for him for less than three months but already felt like I'd known him forever.

He regaled me with a story about his granddaughter's ballet recital the night before with the joyful countenance of someone pleased with his life. Bagels surely wouldn't be my path, but I wanted a piece of that kind of contentment someday. It would be cool to look back on my life when I was in my seventies and be grateful for the journey rather than worrying about wrong turns or regrets.

"And what did you do last night?"

I gave him a mischievous grin as I filled the wire baskets with fresh-baked bagels from the kitchen.

He wasn't fooled. "What did you really do?"

I chuckled.

"Nothing much, George. I practiced, had dinner with my friends, and went to a bar for one measly drink before going to bed."

"Hmph. You need to find someone."

"I don't think so. Not now."

"Everyone needs a companion. There's a nice girl, just about your age, who comes in most mornings—maybe she'll come by today. I'll keep my eyes peeled," he said with a wink before turning to greet the tiny, white-haired woman buried in a giant North Face coat. "Hello, Mrs. Schaefer! Good morning. How are you today?"

I shook my head at the short, balding old man with twinkling dark eyes and a ready smile. Hopefully he'd forget his quest to find me a girlfriend. And hopefully this morning would go by quickly. Nothing sounded better than climbing back in bed right now.

AT TEN o'clock, I untied my apron and waved to George, who was deep in conversation about sightseeing in the city with a massive guy from Minnesota. My shift was over, and though I no longer craved sleep, I was ready to move on. I grabbed my coat and scarf from the stockroom and was heading back to the counter when George called my name. He stood in the doorway, gesturing for me to hurry.

"What's up? I'm gonna get going."

"I have someone for you to meet."

I rolled my eyes. "Mr. G...."

"She's here! The girl I was telling you about. Come say hello. That's all I ask."

I blew out a long breath and followed him into the shop. He was still talking excitedly as though he assumed I'd be anxious to meet some chick who was roughly my age and ate bagels every day.

"I want you to meet Kelsey…."

I held my hand out to greet the pretty young woman with long brown hair and a friendly smile but stopped short when I saw the guy standing just behind her near the front door. George motioned between the girl and me, giving a brief intro before turning to the next person in line. Will and I stared at each other in surprise. Seeing him here was out of context. I recovered first.

"Hey. Uh… did you order?" I asked Will.

"Yeah. I…. Do you work here?"

When Kelsey coughed to get my attention and asked to place her order, I was the one turning beet-red. That was a first.

"I'm so sorry. What can I get you?" I wrote down her order distractedly, but I kept an eye on Will. Damn, he looked good. He was wearing a navy beanie and a long, navy wool coat. He looked smart and professional in a collegiate sort of way. And those glasses. Very nice.

"William, your order is ready," Mr. G yelled from across the crowded store.

"Thank you, George," he said politely as he reached for his to-go order in a brown paper bag.

"Wait! I'm off now. Hang on a sec, okay?" My tone was a little manic. Will cocked his head curiously before nodding. I breathed a sigh of relief and glanced back at Kelsey. "Your order will be right up. Nice to meet you."

I raced to the back room to look for my coat and realized a moment later I was wearing it already. What was my deal? I was acting like a nervous high school kid. I sprinted toward the door in my haste to be on my way.

"Later, Mr. G!"

"I'll see you Monday morning, Randall. Have a good weekend!"

Will's mouth twitched slightly at the corner. "Randall?"

I huffed a short laugh as we stepped onto the sidewalk. "No. Just Rand. He likes Randall better, I guess. I go along with it 'cause it's too much work to correct him every day. Which way you going?"

"To campus. I usually grab something here before I head to class."

"So you live nearby?"

"Yeah, a block away." He gestured vaguely behind us but gave me a sharp sideways glance. "I didn't know you worked for George. I stop by Bowery Bagel all the time."

"Hmm. I thought I mentioned it," I replied with a shrug. "I'm there three or four mornings a week. You must come by after nine. By this time, I'm usually back in bed, trying to squeeze in a couple more hours of sleep. One of George's helpers was out sick today, so I stayed 'til the rush hour frenzy died down. What the hell is it with people and their bagels?" I furrowed my brow and made a funny face.

Will's winning smile was timed to perfection. A sliver of sunshine broke through the clouds, sending a golden glow over his rosy cheeks. I couldn't help returning the gesture, though I wasn't sure what we were smiling about. I looked for a trace of glitter or a hint of leftover makeup, but other than the fact the guy in the blond wig and the bright blue dress had a gorgeous mouth and bit his lip too, I couldn't find a connection. My overactive imagination had obviously been hard at work last night.

Now I was simply happy to be with Will. It was an over-the-top sentiment, but it rang true. To meet him unexpectedly in an environment that didn't require an instrument was surprisingly… nice.

"George's are legendary." Will raised his eyebrows as he opened the paper bag and peered inside. He made a show of smelling the contents before neatly closing the bag again.

I chuckled at his antics as I sidestepped around a large group of pedestrians crossing at Broadway. We continued up Fourth Street, making small talk about the weather, warmer today than it had been all week, and the merits of buying or making your own coffee—we both recommended purchasing a to-go cup daily.

"It gets expensive, but our coffeemaker sucks. That will be my first purchase when I make a couple extra bucks. One of those crazy machines that does everything but boot up your computer in the morning. For now, I'd rather buy it than drink sludge. And don't tell George, but I even prefer Starbucks to his." I pointed at the familiar logo on the window on our left. "In fact, I could use a latte now. Can I buy you one?"

I willed him to say yes, though I had a sinking feeling he'd turn me down. I could tell that even after a couple lessons, he still wasn't sure of me. I made him uncomfortable. Not something I cared about usually, but this time I did. For some weird reason I wanted Will to like me. He started to shake his head but stopped at the last moment and pursed his lips thoughtfully.

"Sure. I have an hour 'til my class starts."

My pulse skipped a beat and my head felt… woozy. I swallowed hard as I reached for the door, willing my cool to resurface. Geez. Was I nervous? This couldn't be good.

I waited for our drinks and clandestinely watched Will as I pretended to check my cell for messages. He stood near the front of the coffee shop, glancing around for an empty table. The messenger bag slung across his thin body was a nice accessory. He looked like a serious scholar. Not a guy who'd been dressed in blue sequins mere hours ago. I had to give myself credit for having an active imagination.

"Any seats open?" I asked, handing him his drink.

"Doesn't look like it."

"The sun's out now. We could sit in the park 'til you have to go to class."

When he didn't answer immediately, I braced myself for rejection and wondered why it mattered to me.

"Well, if you have time. If not, that's fine too. I'll see you next Tuesday for your lesson." Will's words ran together, making it difficult to discern his meaning. I understood "time," then the hurried rush of "see you next Tuesday." I laid a hand on his elbow and gave him a reassuring smile. His nerves made mine subside. Fuck, we were an awkward pair.

"I have time," I said, inclining my head as I opened the door.

We were back on the sidewalk being jostled by impatient New Yorkers a moment later. The perpetual cacophony of honking and distant sirens sounded like background music and was strangely calming. All the noise and people lent a casual element to our chance encounter. It wasn't until we reached the wrought iron gates surrounding Washington Square Park that I noticed Will had gone quiet. I led the way to one of the numerous empty benches facing the enormous circular fountain and the famous arch. The trees were bare, the fountain was dry, and the park was mostly deserted. And cold. I doubted we'd last more than fifteen minutes. Will nodded while I yammered on about the band's upcoming gig while madly wracking my brain for something to draw him out of his shell.

"You should come by tomorrow night." I stretched my legs in front of me and studied my boots as though lost in thought. In truth, I was more aware of him than I understood and was baffled by it. "I'll text you the info. If you feel like it, you'll know the scoop."

"Okay." He opened the paper bag, pulled out his bagel, and painstakingly unwrapped the foil. It looked like a plain toasted bagel with regular cream cheese.

"Do you get that every day?"

"Most days." He tore off a piece of his bagel and offered it to me with a shy smile.

"Thanks." I popped it in my mouth with a grin. "You should try the everything bagel sometime. It's the best one. Trust me. In the past couple months, I've become a connoisseur. George has thirty types of bagels and just as many cream cheeses. One of his grandkids tried to talk him into naming them. But thankfully that idea was a bust. She's five, so her suggestions were along the lines of Pretty Pony Poppy Seed and Beautiful Blueberry." I shook my head in mock disbelief as Will chuckled.

"Speaking of names… I'm curious. Is your name really just Rand? Or is it a stage name?"

"It's my real name. My parents are their generation's version of total hippies. I'll give you a buck if you can guess my sister's previous name."

"Previous name?" He furrowed his brow. "No clue."

"You didn't try." I turned sideways on the bench, hooking my right leg over my knee before giving him an expectant look. He shrugged and tore off another chunk of bagel. "It's Ayn, like the author. Get it? Ayn Rand."

"I thought you said your parents were hippies. Ayn Rand's philosophy was pretty conservative."

"It's classic O'Malley. We see or hear something we think is cool or want with a sudden passion and *bam*! Gotta have it. Then we get it and realize we were missing a major component. My mom just liked the way the name sounded. She hadn't read Ms. Rand's books and didn't know anything about objectivism or its intellectual repressiveness. It wasn't until I was a few months old that someone called her on her interesting name choices. It was obvious to anyone who looked at Mom with her flowy dresses and long, wavy hair that Stevie Nicks was more her style than some radical philosopher. So she did her research after the fact, like O'Malleys do, and was suitably distressed."

"I bet."

"Well, she fixed it by legally changing my sister's name to Annabelle and calling her Bella. Think about it. Sis was already two! She'd been called 'the name that could no longer be spoken' for two formative years!" I shook my head in mock dismay.

Will chuckled. "Why didn't she just change yours?"

"She liked it," I said with an eye roll. "That story is the stuff of legend in our family. It comes up at Thanksgiving or at random big family events, and everyone gets a big laugh out of my liberal momma naming her kids after a right-leaning Russian radical. Luckily she has a great sense of humor. I would love to say we've learned a little bit about thinking things through, but as you can probably tell, I tend to learn as I go, which means I end up apologizing... a lot."

"Hmm. Your mom sounds pretty cool."

"She is. My dad is too. They're nonconformist free spirits."

"Very much the opposite of mine," he said with a wry half laugh.

"Everyone comes from different places... and from people who've made some mistakes in life. Our job is to try a little harder. And make our own mistakes," I added with a laugh. "As my mom always points out, it could have been worse. Rand is a decent enough name—"

"Yes, except for the politician who—"

"Yeah, yeah. What's in a name? It's the individual that matters. You can share a name and have completely different levels of intellect and life philosophies. Not every William is William Shakespeare."

"True." His eyes twinkled merrily as he took another bite of bagel.

"Well, she's a big Tolkien fan too, and knowing Mom, I could have just as easily been named after a hobbit."

Will gave me a wide-eyed look before covering his mouth and bursting into a fit of laughter. "Sorry. It's not funny. It's clever actually."

"Hmph. I could have been Bilbo O'Malley. Poor George would have a rough time making that one sound a little more gentrified."

This time Will nearly spit out his bagel as he doubled over. I looked on in amusement as he laughed hysterically. It really wasn't that funny... and hell, knowing my folks, it wasn't far from the truth, either.

"I'm sorry. I don't know why...." He dabbed the corner of his eye with a napkin and let out a deep sigh. I watched him closely. Will had a nice laugh. The kind that made you want to join in, whether or not you knew what the joke was.

"Feel free to use my wacky family philosophy in one of your musicals."

Will smiled. "I write music. Not dialogue. I'm no good at words."

"I'm the opposite. I write everything down 'cause I'm sure I can use it in a song." I pulled out a scrap of napkin from my pocket and took a quick glance to make sure I hadn't written anything embarrassing on it before handing it over. "Here's an example."

"'Golden brown. Green flecks. And soul.' What is this?" He tilted his head quizzically and handed the napkin back to me.

"Nothing yet." He didn't need to know my silly scrawl had anything to do with him. I was still processing that information anyway. I gave him a self-deprecating smile before continuing. "I was eating dinner with my friends after practice, and I couldn't get this vision out of my head. I don't always know what my notes mean when I start writing, but it's a habit now. One of the teachers I actually listened to in high school suggested it as a way to deal with negative feelings." I shrugged self-consciously.

"What kind of negative feelings?"

"Teenage angst. I'd get so pissed off at all the injustice and hypocrisy in the world. I still do. The difference is I've learned how to temper my rage."

"Do you write from personal experience?"

"Yes and no. Any decent writer puts a piece of themselves into their work. My early stuff was about my best friend Seth's fucked-up family and all the bullshit he went through when they found out he was gay. That wall of uncertainty and fear is far too big for the average fifteen-year-old to take on. It was just… wrong. I hated what they put him through. His fear fed my anger. I railed against the injustice of those so-called good Christians like the Emo version of a holy roller with a microphone shouting the word of… truth. Reason. Seth would look at me like I was crazy too. I couldn't help it. I was consumed. But he wasn't. Not in the same way. He'd figured out on his own how to deal with his pain, and I realized in the last few months of our senior year in high school, I had to follow his lead or wind up doing time."

"In jail?" Will's eyes bugged out in horror.

"In summer school, genius." I sipped my latte and took the piece of bagel Will handed over. "Anyway, Mr. Jacobs, my English teacher, suggested writing freestyle. No rules. Just go for it. I still had to do term papers and try my hand at haiku when he assigned it, but he told me he'd give me extra credit to write random thoughts down. Whenever I got pissed or was really excited about something, I got in the habit of jotting down a couple words or phrases. I wasn't disciplined enough to keep a journal, but that little exercise helped quiet my mind, I guess. But because I was kind of an asshole, I'd write things to make the poor guy squirm." I chuckled as I shifted on the bench to face him. "One time, I handed him this napkin I'd used to clean up some spilled milk. I'd written something crude about tasting jizz and waited to see how long it would take for Mr. Jacobs's ears to turn pink. He dropped that crusty napkin so fast you'd have thought it was coated in anthrax. I laughed until I cried. Literally."

I chuckled at the memory as I straightened my legs in front of me, scaring a couple pigeons away. Will wasn't laughing now. In fact, he was staring at me intensely.

"Are you...?"

I took another sip of my now-lukewarm latte and waited for him to continue. He didn't. He bit his lip in what I was beginning to realize was a sure sign of nerves.

"Am I what?"

He swallowed hard and looked down at the industrious pigeons hopping at his feet. I shooed them with a sweeping hand motion. They fluttered away noisily, leaving him no further distraction. I childishly wanted all of his attention. Although a moment later I wasn't so sure.

"Are you gay?"

I was aware of his steady gaze and earnest calm. I shifted on the bench restlessly, wondering if I should be honest. Like Tim said, I wasn't famous. And I was beginning to realize turning off the gay wasn't so simple after all. What could it hurt to tell my guitar tutor the truth? I opened my mouth and—

"No," I lied.

But it wasn't a lie, I told myself. It was a half-truth. Or half-lie. However, it felt bigger than the average lie of omission or white lie. It was the awkward kind that made you instantly wish you could have a do-over.

Will seemed uncomfortable, and now I was too. The temperature may have been hovering around thirty degrees, but my face was warm with shame. I had to divert attention to him until I was back on solid ground.

"Hmm."

"What does that noise mean?" I plucked at his beanie and tweaked his earlobe to get him to look at me.

He batted my hand away and turned so our knees touched on the bench. "Nothing. I'm sorry. It was a stupid question. I figured you were straight anyway. With a girlfriend."

"No girlfriend." I pushed his beanie over his eyes, then cocked my head curiously before I made myself ask, "How about you?"

"Cool it," he said with a scowl, swatting my hand away as he pushed the beanie out of his eyes. "I'm gay. I thought you knew that. I was betting it would take Terry five minutes or less to out me."

"Why would Terry care if you're gay?"

"He doesn't care exactly, but he's a jerk. I could never tell if he was insecure or homophobic. I just knew I got a vibe I didn't like."

"Which is why you referred him to us. Thanks, asshole."

"He's a good guitarist," he sputtered, turning a funny shade of pink. "I thought he was working out okay."

"He's fine. But I don't want to talk about Terry. Tell me about you." I tapped my empty cup on my knee and eyed him expectantly. "I take it you're out and proud."

"I'm out." He scrunched his paper bag almost violently into a ball and stood abruptly. He walked a few steps to throw his trash away before turning back with a phony smile. "I've got to run. Thanks for the latte. See you next week."

I jumped up and grabbed his elbow. "Whoa! What's your hurry?"

"I have class soon. I should go."

I glanced at my watch and then at him, wordlessly letting him know I was on to him. "Wait up. What did I say?"

His lips turned up on one side of his mouth. It wasn't a smile because his eyes were definitely not involved in the gesture. No… it was an expression of acute sadness. Loneliness. I studied him for a moment, wondering if I was reading too much into it.

He sighed and looked at something in the distance. "You didn't say anything. I'm out, but… I—my family didn't take it well. Not quite as bad as your friend's parents, but they don't like it. So we don't discuss it. Ever. They aren't bohemian or cool, and frankly, they'd love the fact you were named after a right-leaning radical. They share those same rigid views and judgmental morals. The kind that don't leave room for debate or… family members who don't fit. I'm a nowhere man. It makes no difference if I'm out because the closet door isn't wide enough for me to get through. I don't even know if that makes sense, but being gay is a major distraction between my parents and me." He scoffed derisively. "It's a distraction to me most of the time too. The only thing that really matters to me is my music. I should be getting going. I'm cold."

I pulled his arm when he started to walk away. "Hey. I don't know your story but… you're crazy talented, Will. You can be or do anything you want. You're in the right place to make anything happen." Ugh. I hated those placating words the second they left my mouth. I struggled to come up with something meaningful. I couldn't let him leave like this, especially with my lie sitting between us like a giant elephant only I could see. "What's your dream? What's the one thing you want to accomplish while you're on the planet?"

Will gave a half laugh, but his eyes twinkled with reluctant amusement. "Are you for real? We're standing in the middle of a park on a freezing winter day and you want to talk about dreams?"

"It's warmer than it's been in days."

"Which isn't saying much."

"You're stalling."

"I have class in twenty minutes."

I grinned at him, then reached out and snagged his beanie off his head. I couldn't help myself. I wanted to play with him. Be silly. I wanted to make him laugh.

"I'm keeping your hat hostage."

His face was set in mock outrage as he held out his hand, tapping his boot on the ground impatiently. "How old are you?"

"Twenty-five. Hurry. Your ears are turning red."

"You're twenty-five going on five. Hand it over." He pursed his lips, then burst out laughing.

"I wish there was snow on the ground. Next time it snows, we have to come back here for a snowball fight. You on?"

"Are you cra—where are you going? Hey! Come back!"

I pulled his hat over mine and waltzed away wearing two beanies as I embellished my considerable snowball-making skills. "I'm from Baltimore. We get enough snow that I've been able to perfect my craft over the years. You gotta go to the mountains to get to the really good powder but—"

"I'm not chasing after you."

"Nah, you shouldn't. I'm a fast runner too."

"I'm not and I don't want to play around."

He started after me. He wasn't joking. He was slow and awkward. Outmaneuvering him would have been easy. Too easy. I stalled and gave him a chance to catch me. It backfired when he tripped over my foot a second later. I caught him by the arm and pulled him against me. We stood chest to chest, our breath mingling visibly in the cool winter air. I detected a trace of desire in his eyes and immediately backed off. I yanked the hats from my head and stuffed mine in my pocket before gesturing for him to come closer. He stared at me for a second, then reluctantly complied. I pulled the navy cap over his head, making sure to tuck his hair underneath. This was the closest I'd ever been to him. I tried to imagine him with a wig, a blue dress, and a long black coat again, but it was too hard to see anything beyond his golden brown eyes, dark lashes, and the sweet freckles on his nose.

I jumped back with a start. What was I doing? Straight guys didn't do things like this. They didn't stare into another guy's eyes or mess with their hats, unless they were stuffing them full of snow or tossing them halfway across the park for kicks. The rush of heat to my face was clawing. I plucked at my scarf and tried a smile I hoped looked somewhat confident.

"So tell me… what's your dream?"

"I want to be a musician." Will's voice was so quiet. I was moved by an undercurrent of emotion in those simple words, as though he was telling me something important and it was up to me to read between the lines. The barren trees, cloudy skies, and sparsely populated park somehow lent an aura of significance to the moment.

"You *are* a musician."

"I want to be the best. I want to make a difference through music. That's my dream. Nothing else matters."

I nodded. Yes, I understood all too well. "You're going to do it. I can tell. Just remember, this is your life, Will. Don't let anyone put limitations on you. Be happy."

"I *am* happy," he whispered.

"Good." I touched the end of his nose lightly and smiled. I made a small production of pulling my beanie from my pocket and putting it on my head. "By the way, I'm gonna guess you weren't on the track team back in… where are you from?"

"Indiana. And no, I'm not a runner. I'm not into sports at all."

"No shit." I chuckled, then gasped in mock surprise when he punched my arm playfully. "Ow."

"Hmph."

"I'm teasing. Sports weren't my thing, either. I ran track 'cause I was fast and I needed all the credit I could get, but I wasn't into it. If I wasn't listening to music or trying to learn how to play guitar, I was parked in front of the television watching *Battlestar Galactica*."

"You like sci-fi?" His tone indicated he was more interested than his carefully casual glance at his watch suggested.

"Yep! I'm a sci-fi geek. I love anything that takes you to another world. It could be wizards and dragons or starships on secret intergalactic missions. It's my escape from reality. What's yours?"

Will snickered beside me as we waited at the crosswalk. "I like sci-fi too. I don't go for the space stuff so much. I'm more of a *Harry Potter*, *Lord of the Rings* kind of guy."

"Magical powers, huh?"

"Exactly!" His grin was bright and beautiful. "Wouldn't it be awesome to have a magic wand and just… make things right?"

"Yeah. It would."

The light turned green. People bustled around us when we didn't move quickly enough, and an unfamiliar panicky sensation came over me. Once we made it to the other side, this impromptu twist in my morning would be over. I felt a strange compulsion to keep him talking. To make this moment last as long as possible.

"I heard there's a place in the Village where they show random movies like *Harry Potter*. We should go sometime. I mean, I don't know many people here and—" I didn't recognize my voice. I was trying to play it cool and failing miserably. I bit the inside of my cheek to stop myself from piling on any additional lameness.

"I'd like that." Will smiled and glanced toward the entrance of his building, then back at me. "Thanks for the coffee. I'll see you next week."

"Yeah. Hey… come to the show tomorrow night. I'll text you the info." God, I couldn't shut up. *Leave the guy alone already, Rand.*

Will stepped away from the revolving door with a confused look on his face. "I'm not sure if I can but—"

"Try."

He nodded and gave me one last smile before disappearing into his building. I stepped aside to avoid being jostled by harried-looking students. I was nowhere near where I needed to be, and I felt strangely out of sorts. I'd basically walked a boy to class for the first time ever. And I kinda liked it.

Chapter 3

KARMA WAS an extremely hip converted garage turned nightclub. Other than the cement floor, every surface was shiny chrome and steel or black. Single, vintage bulbs hung over the bar at the back of the club, illuminating the space with a retro-meets-contemporary feel. I'd admired the bar's sleek, modern vibe when we'd come to set up our equipment and run through a sound check earlier. This was a nicer venue than I'd expected. I wouldn't have been surprised by a difficult-to-find, tiny dive bar in a questionable part of town. Hiring a well-connected agent slash manager may have been the band's best move yet, I thought as I surveyed the crowd from a corner bar seat.

"Hi. Whatcha drinking? Looks like you need a refill."

I glanced over at the pretty girl with long, jet-black hair and a sultry smile leaning against the bar. She moved forward and pressed her ample bosom into my upper arm. She was wearing a tight, sleeveless white T-shirt to show off her tits as well as her stunning ink work. My gaze wandered to a red rose with lush green vines encircling her upper bicep.

"Damn. That's really cool." I pointed to the thorns as I scooted off the barstool and stepped aside for her to order.

Her heavily lined eyes sparkled with pleasure at the compliment. "Thanks. What can I get you? Is that a gin and tonic?"

"It is, but I'm done for now. We're going on soon and—"

"Oh my God! You're with Spiral. You're the lead singer! I can't believe I'm meeting you! I'm Leah," she said, extending her right hand.

"Nice to meet you. I'm Rand."

"I know. I actually have been following you guys for a year or so. I saw you in DC last year and—"

Her words ran together as she picked up momentum. I nodded a few times and grinned when it became obvious I wasn't going to get a word in. My healthy ego demanded I bask in her praise for a minute before joining my bandmates.

"Thanks. Hope you dig the show. I better get going."

"Oh right. Hang on one more sec. Holly!" She turned to pull a petite woman through the crush of people surrounding the bar. "I want you to meet my friend too."

I saw Tim gesturing for me near the stage. I signaled to him as I swallowed the last of my drink and turned back to say a quick good-bye to Leah. A pretty blonde was standing next to her now with her hand outstretched. I shook it and started to back away when she asked me to tell Cory she'd wait for him here after the show.

I quirked my head sideways, finally cluing in that she was the girl he'd been seeing. Holly. Which meant—

"Hey, you know Will too, right?"

Holly smiled brightly and nodded. "I think you mean William, but yes. He's a sweetie. We go to school together."

"Is he with you? Did he come tonight?"

"Here? No way! William isn't into clubs and bars. He's quiet. This kind of scene makes him nervous."

"Oh." I sighed and pasted a plastic grin on my face. "I invited him but—hmm. I'll give Cor your message. Nice to meet you guys."

"Break a leg. And come find me later. I'd really like to buy you that drink," Leah insisted.

I waved absently, then began navigating through the crowd to reach the stage on the other end. He wasn't coming. I didn't really think he would, but having his friend confirm it was… disappointing. God, I was making myself nuts. So I had a crush on my guitar teacher. So what? Will and I came from completely different worlds. A love of music was really all we had in common. If I were smart, I'd shake it off and move on. I wished I could stop thinking about him, but more than that, I wished I hadn't lied. It was stupid and unnecessary. But not something I could fix now.

I took a deep breath as I approached my bandmates with what I hoped looked like a sincere smile.

"It's showtime, boys."

MUSIC TOOK me to another realm. It always had. And that night, we were on fire. We rocked the tiny club like it was Madison Square Garden. I got lost in the blues. It seemed to take me to another plane where I could lose my frustrations and regain my footing. When you lived in the moment, you could make anything happen. I was never more certain of it than when I stood onstage, singing my heart out. We played some covers but made sure to fit original material in as well. My challenge was to make a happy, buzzed audience become a crazed, passionate crowd who sang along to every word of the songs they knew and swayed to the new songs with a quiet intensity that guaranteed they'd look Spiral up and buy any available tracks they could get their hands on.

I was in enough of a zone that I was able to overlook Terry's mistakes and miscues. They weren't glaring to anyone but me. I'd definitely bring it up later, but for tonight I let it all go.

We played for an hour and a half with no breaks and two encores. It was a successful show by anyone's standard. The four of us rode an epic performance high as we slapped high fives and whooped excitedly backstage afterward.

"That was sick," Tim yelled, punching his fist in the air.

I laughed as I pulled off my sweaty black T-shirt and reached for a fresh one. The cooler temperature in the small backroom felt invigorating on my damp skin. I had so much energy, I could barely contain myself. I didn't know where I wanted to go, but I wanted to move, dance, and yeah… sex sounded like the perfect way to top off an amazing night. A brief vision of Will flashed in my head. I wanted to back him against a wall and tear the buttons off his perfectly pressed shirt. In my manic brain, the image morphed into the man on the train in blue sequins. Suddenly it was Will with a dress pushed over his ass begging me to fuck him as I reached around to jack his thick cock and—

"C'mon, boys, let's get a drink or ten." Cory slapped my back as he moved toward the door, yanking me from my erotic daydream.

I shook my head to clear the clashing visions and grinned at my friend. It was tradition for the band to celebrate with a few shots or drinks after a big show. And this one was big. It heralded a beginning of sorts. I didn't have to wake up early the next morning, so if I felt like going a little wild, I could. We generally stayed for a round at whatever bar or club we played, and caroused with the other patrons. They were usually as pumped as we were, so the energy was palpable. On a night like this one, we'd been known to close the place down. And in a city that never slept, it meant our evening had just begun.

Three shots of tequila and a few margaritas later, I was feeling no pain. I leaned on the bar and set my glass down so I could use my hands to describe some wacky story I was telling. Truthfully, I wasn't sure what I was saying anymore, but Leah didn't seem to mind. She laughed as she trailed her fingernails up my arm. She'd been glued to my side all night. We'd made out for a while in a dark corner, and now she was giving me a hungry look I knew well. I was horny as hell, and God, it would be so easy to take what she was offering, but instinctively I knew a woman wasn't going to do it for me tonight. Not when all I could think of was a man.

I pushed away from the bar just as Terry walked up. When he offered to buy her a drink, I wanted to thank him, even though I got the impression he'd been waiting to jump in and stake a claim. Whatever.

"I'll be back," I mumbled with a wave.

I was bleary-eyed but still energized. Funny details stood out, like Cory and Holly making out at a nearby table. Terry chatting with Leah, who was staring at me like a piece of meat. And Tim… checking his phone for text messages.

"Timmy, who ya talkin' to?" I asked with a hiccup.

He gave me a blank stare but didn't answer. In the way an intoxicated mind latches on and won't let go, I had to know. I swiped his phone from his hands and tried to read the display. It looked like I was staring at two cells. Letters collided and blurred nonsensically. I frowned and handed it back to Tim, who looked like he wanted to clobber me.

"You're drunk."

"No shit. Where we going next?"

"*We* aren't going anywhere." He pocketed his phone and gave me a wide, shit-eating grin. "Don't wait up for me, sunshine."

"I wanna come."

"No, I'm—"

I tugged at his T-shirt and shook my head vigorously. "C'mon, Timmy. Let's get outta here. I gotta see other shtuff. You know?"

"Shtuff, huh? Rand, go home and sleep it off. I'm not babysitting you tonight."

"I'm a big boy. Don't worry 'bout me. I gotta move on. Ya know?" I put my finger to my lips and widened my eyes when I could see he was about to deny me. "Shh. Let's fade. No one will notice."

"You don't fade well and—oh fuck it. Fine. But I swear, if you—"

"I won't."

"You don't know what I was going to say."

"Does it matter?"

Tim took a deep breath and made a face. "No. You never stop until you get your way."

"Is that a bad thing, Timmy?"

"It's an annoying thing. C'mon."

HALF AN hour later we were in the West Village ambling along Christopher Street. I assured Tim I wasn't out to ruin his rendezvous with the hunky guy he'd met the other night. My focus was finding a gay bar with serious eye candy. I wasn't at my sharpest, but somewhere in my muddled mind, I knew tagging along with Tim would at least point me in the right direction. And maybe, just maybe, I'd see the boy in blue.

Tim bypassed the short line outside Boots and gave his name to the bouncer manning the door. I checked out the men patiently waiting for entry while the humongous man with a headset relayed our info to some mastermind inside. Tim was explaining something about the guy he'd met who bartended here on the weekends, but my attention was on the eclectic crowd. A tall, gorgeous guy with a sexy beard had his arm draped over a skinny young man dressed in denim shorts and an über-tight, sheer black cropped top. Poor guy had to be freezing. They were such an odd couple I couldn't help staring. Especially when I noticed how much makeup the smaller man was wearing. But it was the rhinestone-studded collar around his neck with a pink leash fastened and wrapped around the other man's wrist that made my jaw drop. Tim grasped my upper arm and dragged me inside the dark club before I had the chance to ask questions.

I shrugged off my coat and hat when we reached the far corner of the bar. Rainbow flags and disco balls hung from the low ceiling. The paneled walls were decorated with posters of drag queens and buff men in harnesses. In other words, there was no point in checking my belongings. I wasn't staying long. I'd nurse a cocktail before heading out to find a less… campy place to end my night.

"What's going on here? I can't decide if I feel underdressed or overdressed," I yelled above the din of a Sia remix.

Tim shook his head. "No clue. We're leaving as soon as Brad's done. Which is why I tried to tell you not to come. There are plenty of bars in the East Village too. You didn't have to follow me here to get laid."

"You mean you don't want me here?" I asked with faux confusion.

"Ugh. I don't get you. Why didn't you stay and soak up the rock-star love all night at Karma? That girl was all over you. If you're trying to shake the gay part of being bi, you should have stayed."

"I know but—I couldn't. This is harder than I thought. It might not be a mind-over-matter thing, Timmy. I don't want to fuck anything up but—"

"Relax. Believe it or not, you're safe in gay land."

"For now."

Tim shrugged. "What do you want to drink besides water?"

"I better stick to something with tequila. Surprise me."

I checked out the clientele while Tim ordered. There was definitely something going on here. Almost everyone appeared to be wearing a costume. This was a little like Halloween meets masquerade. No masks, though. Just lots of glitz and… chains. Weird.

Tim was back with our drinks a couple minutes later. He handed mine over and clinked our glasses. "To Spiral."

I grinned and took a healthy swig of what I thought was a margarita. I couldn't tell anymore, but the shock to my system told me it was strong.

"By the way, Brad said it's fetish night."

I threw my hand over my mouth to avoid spitting my drink on the guy in front of me. I coughed and sputtered while Tim chuckled and slapped my back.

"Fetish night? This could be interesting."

"I know. Check out the leashes."

"Would you ever play submissive?" I asked as we watched the guy in skimpy jean shorts on a leash.

Tim chuckled. "Never say never. You?"

I let my "yeah right" expression do the talking for me.

"Why not? I can totally see you wearing leather chaps with your ass on display."

"Have you been fantasizing about my ass, Timmy?" I leaned in to whisper in his ear and at the last second decided to torment him by licking his pierced lobe.

He pushed me away, scowling in irritation as I guffawed merrily. "What did I do to deserve you?"

"Good question. I think I—whoa!"

I did a double take as a tall, skinny guy in a blond wig walked by wearing a short pink dress, fishnet stockings, and high heels. No way. Could it really be him?

"Holy shit! I think that's him!"

"Who?"

"Wait. I can't tell. Hold my drink. And my coat. I'll be back."

I could hear Tim calling me back or asking a question, but I'd reached the level of drunkenness where everything sounded like an echo and nothing was clear. I couldn't trust my eyes or ears, but instinctively I moved forward, pushing through the throng of men huddled around the bar and in the direction of the guy in the blond wig. When I reached a clear area in the back, he was nowhere in sight. I was about to give up and head to the bar when a huge man dressed in flowing chiffon appeared out of nowhere from behind a wall.

"Are the restrooms down there?"

"Yes, sweetie. Be careful. The stairs are steep. I almost lost the heel on my Jimmy Choos."

I gave him a thumbs-up sign and skirted the wall to find the stairs. I carefully traversed the dark and shadowy steps, following the sound of voices to what I guessed would lead me to the bathroom. I pushed open the door and looked around. Two guys stood at a sink chatting, but there was no one else in the room. Huh. I heard a hitched breath like someone gasping for air coming from one of the stalls. I cocked my head curiously as the two men busted up laughing.

"No sex in the stalls, gentlemen," one of them admonished before flouncing out with his friend close behind.

I stood frozen in place in the middle of the tiny restroom. Sex? Nah. That didn't sound like sex. It sounded like someone… crying maybe. I squinted as though closing my eyes might help me hear better. Nothing.

What was I doing? I was wasting my chance. I should be upstairs checking out the odd eye candy or moving on to the next stop. Not playing detective in a creepy, dark bathroom looking for a guy dressed like a girl who kinda, sorta, maybe looked like my straitlaced guitar teacher. Note to self, no more tequila.

My reflection in the cracked mirror above the pedestal sink caught my attention like a shiny coin. I stepped forward to check myself out before turning for the door. My eyes were a little glassy, but I didn't look half bad. Or did I? I moved in closer and stumbled forward, catching myself on the rim of the battered, white sink before I smashed my nose on the mirror. Good save. I grinned like an idiot, pleased with myself in a stupid, drunken way that wouldn't make sense to anyone else. When the stall door opened, I turned to share my fortune with the only other occupant in the bathroom.

"Dude, that was a close call. Did you see—?"

The guy with the blond wig was standing two feet away from me. He looked at me in utter horror. I didn't understand why he'd be so freaked out unless....

"Will? Is that you?"

His bright red lips opened in a perfectly shaped O, then closed. He shook his head violently and wrapped his arms around himself as if to ward off a sudden chill. I looked at the tiny pink dress, but when I saw the fishnet stockings again, nothing else registered. My dick swelled in my jeans, making me feel even more light-headed than I already did. I struggled to process what was going on. Was the guy in the sexy stockings really Will? And what the hell was my problem? Fishnets and heels on men were not my thing. Were they?

He swallowed hard. I watched his Adam's apple move convulsively, but it was when he bit his lip that I knew. He did the same thing all the time when we played together. He did it when we were sitting on the park bench yesterday. It was a nervous habit. I made him nervous. But I didn't want to. I wanted to swim above this uncertain, foggy state and reach him somehow. Reassure him.

"Hey. It's me. Are you okay? Are you with someone or—?"

"Leave me alone."

He rushed for the door and grabbed the handle. I stepped in front of him, holding out my hand like I might to a scared animal.

"Don't! Don't go. Please. It is you, right? I don't—"

"Let me go," he whispered. "He's waiting for me."

"Who? Your boyfriend? I didn't think you had one." I studied him carefully. I couldn't make the puzzle pieces fit. This didn't make sense.

"I don't, but I have to go."

He batted my arm out of the way and slid past me effortlessly. I hesitated for a half second before following him. When I opened the door he was gone. I glanced up the stairs in wonder, unable to process that a man wearing high heels could move so fast. Especially when I remembered the same guy practically tripping over his own feet in the park yesterday.

Dance music reverberated through my skull when I reached the top of the landing. Disco balls and strobe lights cast a familiar glow I usually loved, like a seductive veil that threatened to pull me under and allow the night to make decisions for me. I shook off the feeling and strode with purpose toward the exit, craning my neck as I moved to see if I could locate Will amongst the mob. I glanced at the bar but decided not to stop. I'd text Tim later. If I remembered.

"You stayin' or goin'?" The bouncer manning the door gave me a suspicious once-over as I tried to focus. I couldn't decide which way to go. I was looking through liquid lenses and nothing made sense.

"I don't—did you see a guy wearing a blond wig? He had… um, those net-tight things and heels and pink! His dress was pink. Did you see him?"

The thick-browed, muscular bouncer nodded and gestured with his thumb. "He left with his guy. Do yourself a favor and grab a taxi, man. You're fucked up."

It was sound advice, but I was beyond help. I pushed my way through the plastic barricade shielding the entry from the bitter cold and stumbled out to the sidewalk. The blast of frigid air felt great. Then it didn't. It was freezing. I shivered as I tried to acclimate. The streets weren't as busy now, but people were still hanging out in front of the club. I glanced both ways. There was no sign of Will. I blew out a rush of air in defeat and turned back to the door just as a flash of pink caught my eye.

There he was. He was talking to an older man just beyond the line of revelers awaiting entrance. The man looked to be in his forties. He was slightly overweight, balding, and had the aura of a married man behaving badly. He was wearing pleated trousers and a long, expensive-looking cashmere coat. I skirted the people lingering near the entrance but stayed back to observe for a moment. Other than a never-ending conversation, I didn't detect any distress until the man reached out to caress his face. Will stiffened. It wasn't overt, but I noticed. He didn't want that guy. Maybe he was trapped.

All common sense fled. In truth, I didn't know what I was doing. I moved on impulse and instinct. My usual modes of transport. Add tequila and anything could happen.

"Hey, baby, is that you? I thought so but—oh shoot. Am I interrupting?" I wrapped my left arm around Will and held out my right to his oh so proper companion. "I'm Rand. Nice to meet ya."

The guy's eyebrows rose impressively in a look of sheer distaste. I chuckled at the affectation. It was over-the-top, and I'd reached the stage in the wee morning hours where everything off-balance struck me as hysterical. Like this douche in his designer duds giving me the stink eye. He had to be someone's husband and dad. He didn't look like your typical fortysomething cruising the gay nightlife with his boy toy.

"Rand—"

"You look familiar." I put my hand on my chin as though in deep thought. "I can't place it, but I know I've seen you before. Are you—?"

He turned his back to me and took Will's hand. "My driver's here. Get a taxi. I'll talk to you next week. Bye, Billie."

He kissed Will's cheek and walked briskly toward a waiting black Escalade idling near the corner. I stood at Will's side watching his friend's retreating form, wondering what to say now that we were sort of alone. I gave him a curious sideways glance and started at his withering once-over. He didn't look remotely like Will now. He emitted a no-nonsense attitude with flair. No wonder I was fooled. Will was like Dr. Jekyll and Mr. Hyde. Or William and Billie.

"Where's your coat?" He flung his hand out as a yellow cab appeared out of nowhere.

"Huh? Inside. I think."

"It's twenty degrees out here. Go get it."

He was right. As my adrenaline rush faded, a bitter chill settled in my bones. My teeth were chattering I was so cold. I turned to obey him but stopped in my tracks. If I left, he'd ditch me and I might actually end up convincing myself this was a dream. I was drunk and this was too improbable. I eyed him from the sidewalk while he stood near the taxi, waiting for the occupants to emerge. Once they'd paid the driver, he jumped in and closed the door. Fuck!

I sprang in front of the cab and ran to the other side just before the driver pulled into the street. I was lucky he didn't go heavy on the gas or I would have certainly lost my right arm when I reached to open the car door. I dove inside and closed it quickly, smacking my head on the seat in front of me when the cabbie screeched to a halt again.

"You fucking moron! What the fuck? You coulda gotten killed! This taxi's taken. Find another one, you fuckin'...."

I tuned him out and glanced over at my stunned-looking cabmate. "I'm coming with you."

"Do you know this idiot? Is he harassin' you?"

Will stared at me in the darkened interior, then out the window. My heart beat twice its normal rate while I waited to see if he'd literally kick me to the curb. The cold night air had a somewhat sobering effect. I was riding the last wave of a drunken, stupid high while on an adrenaline rollercoaster. I felt nauseous. Clueless. And I sure as hell didn't have a plan.

"It's all right. He's harmless."

He licked his painted lips and leaned forward to give the driver an address before looking out the window. I breathed a sigh of relief and settled back in my seat to observe him.

"Where we going?"

"*I'm* going home. You can have the taxi driver take you wherever you want."

I started to argue but let it go. Now that I'd finally found him, I was sticking to his side. We could haggle later.

"Who was the guy with the fancy coat?"

"Someone I know."

"Hmm. Why'd he call you Billie? I'm assuming that's spelled with an *I-E* like a girl. Am I right?"

He spared me a bored glance and reached for his phone, signaling he was done talking.

"He's kinda old for you, huh?"

Silence.

"Hey, whatever you're into is cool. It's just that I pictured you with someone different. Someone not so... married-looking."

This time his look was less friendly, but he still didn't speak. And suddenly, I was obsessed with cracking his cool exterior and getting some kind of reaction. I plucked at his fishnet tights and got my hand smacked a second later.

"Ow." I shook my hand and scowled dramatically. "That hurt."

"It did not. Can you do me a favor?"

"Sure, what is it?"

"Don't talk. Not one word. Go home, sleep it off, and forget you saw me tonight. Please."

I leaned forward and set my hand back on his knee. "That sounds like more than one favor, and I'm not—hey, did I tell you you're pretty? 'Cause you are. As a girl and a guy too."

Will removed my hand again and sighed. "Thanks. Now be quiet."

"But—"

"Quiet."

No matter what I asked or commented on as the driver sped along Eighth Street toward the East Village, my companion remained stubbornly silent for the rest of the drive. Ten minutes later we pulled in front of a nondescript brick building, somewhere near Bowery Bagels. I didn't recognize my surroundings per se, but I was in a familiar neighborhood. Maybe. I waited for Will to pay the driver, then hopped out of the taxi after him.

Fuck, it was cold. I shivered violently and wiped at my nose. This was miserable. I was dizzy and my stomach felt off. I hadn't been sick from alcohol in years, but I couldn't remember when I'd eaten last. This wasn't a good idea. Will obviously wanted nothing to do with me.

"What t-time is it?" I asked, staring over his shoulder as he punched in a passcode on the metal box next to the glass door.

He rounded on me angrily the second I stepped behind him inside the semidark lobby. "It's two. What do you think you're doing? I told you to go home, Rand."

"I—" I came up empty. My brain was buzzing and I couldn't stop shaking. "I'm cold."

"You're unbelievable." He sighed, shaking his head in disapproval. Somehow the blond wig and pink minidress under his long black coat didn't detract from the fierce vibe he emanated. "Follow me. You can borrow a jacket, and then... go home."

Will led the way to a narrow set of stairs. Funny details like his graceful carriage on those impossibly high heels stood out as we climbed three floors. I followed him down a dim hallway until he stopped in front of 3F.

"The lock sticks. Hang on," he muttered sleepily.

"Me do it?"

He gave me a sharp look. "You can't even speak in complete sentences. I got it."

He flipped a switch before opening the door into what felt like an icebox. It was as big as one too. Every inch of the small flat was visible from the middle of the room. There was a generous window on one end, and a red futon piled high with a stack of blankets and pillows against the long wall painted a dark blue. A tiny kitchenette with a minifridge, microwave, two-burner stovetop, and a sink was on the adjacent wall.

And an impressive array of guitars hung on the wall opposite the futon, with an electric piano nearby. I'd passed the tiniest bathroom known to man near the entrance, so I knew this was it. There's no way he shared the space. I couldn't see another person living here comfortably.

"S-so cold."

I sat on the edge of the futon and blew on my fingers. I heard Will moving around me, but I was too tired now to pay attention. He handed me a jacket and said something about me going home. I nodded and pulled the blessedly warm, down-filled coat over me, then collapsed backward onto the pillows. He pulled at me. My foot or my elbow. I couldn't tell. The second I felt the additional warmth of a blanket, I squeezed my eyes shut and let myself tumble completely into darkness.

Chapter 4

A COUPLE hours later I was wide awake. I had to pee, but I didn't want to get up. The room was too cold, and it was so warm under the covers. When my bladder insisted, I gingerly sat up and looked around. It was dark and I was in an unfamiliar bed. Someone was lying next to me, bundled under a pile of blankets, with a pillow stuffed between us. I pulled the edge of the blanket aside and froze at the sight of the mop of brown hair resting next to me. Jumbled pieces of my evening fell together in my mind. A great show, drinks, more drinks, another bar, and then…. Will. In pink. Holy fuck.

I swiped my hand over my jaw and observed his sleeping form for a minute. I couldn't reconcile Will, my shy tutor, with the diva I'd followed home. My brain was too hazy, and my bladder wasn't particularly interested. I climbed over him carefully and hurried to use the bathroom. I found myself staring bleary-eyed at my reflection in the mirrors abutting the tiny corner wall over the sink. I looked like hell. I moved in closer and opened the medicine cabinet, hoping to find aspirin to alleviate my imminent hangover and maybe some toothpaste to run over my teeth. Snooping wasn't my motive. In fact, I was foggy enough with exhaustion and the remnants of tequila in my system to be one-track minded. So yeah, I was surprised by the copious cosmetics inside the cabinet. Maybe I shouldn't have been, but again, it was unexpected. I picked up a tube of lipstick and uncapped it. Ruby red. Like last night. I put it back and closed the cabinet. Damn, Will was one interesting guy.

I tiptoed back to the futon, shucked off my jeans and the T-shirt I'd fallen asleep in, then climbed underneath the covers. The clothes were too restricting and uncomfortable to wear all night. I lay there lost in thought for a moment, more aware than ever of the man beside me than I'd been of anyone in a very long time. My attraction to him felt magnetic, like something beyond my control. As I pieced together the last part of the night, I felt a surge of envy for the old guy who'd caressed Will's cheek. He was all wrong for him. Too old, too slick, and too serious. Will needed someone to make him laugh. He was serious enough. I pushed the pillow he'd put between us to the end of the bed before ever so stealthily scooting closer to get a better look at him.

The first hint of body heat was sublime. It took every bit of self-control not to pull him against me and wrap him close. Something was definitely going on with me. Passing out in a guy's bed was one thing, but crawling back into bed and fantasizing about the most innocent press of skin was… well, it probably wasn't so innocent after all.

Will sighed in his sleep and then turned onto his back. I gulped, hoping he wouldn't awaken. I didn't want him to freak out. And for whatever weird reason, I wanted to watch him. My vision had acclimated to the dark. I could clearly make out his long lashes and full mouth. I couldn't believe I'd ever thought he was nerdy or plain. He was so… pretty. I felt a sudden urge to kiss him. It wasn't a bright idea. He'd wake up and kick my ass out so fast my head would spin. But the longer I stared, the stronger the desire to touch him became. I couldn't stop myself from brushing his hair out of his eyes. He flinched and twitched his nose, then turned on his side with his back to me.

I listened to his gentle breathing, a slow, even inhale and exhale. He smelled clean, as though he had scrubbed all evidence of the night from his body before climbing into bed. The reminder of his complex duality aroused me. I thought I knew him. At least to some degree. Obviously I didn't. I wanted to change that. I inched a little closer, laid my head on the pillow, and without thinking, draped my arm over his hip. He immediately shifted backward, against my groin. I swallowed hard, willing my twitching cock to behave. When he did it again, I knew it wasn't an accident. He was awake and aware. I bit the inside of my cheek and pressed closer.

I slipped my hand underneath his T-shirt, then went completely still to gauge his reaction. He sighed but didn't push me away. His skin was smooth and soft. I splayed my fingers wide and moved them over his lean stomach. I felt a hint of hair just under his belly button. I traced the narrow trail with my thumb and stopped almost immediately at the feel of his rock-hard cock through the thin layer of cotton. I felt light-headed with desire. If he were anyone else, I wouldn't hesitate to reach around to grip his swollen flesh. But this was Will, the guy who communicated best with his instrument shielding him from the real world. Sure, it turned out he was also a fishnet-stocking-, makeup-, and high-heel-wearing man with a certain amount of sass. However, I didn't know that guy. I had to proceed with caution, because now retreat wasn't an option.

I hooked my thumb under the elastic of his pajama bottoms and slid my hand inside his briefs. I waited for a signal from him. Stop or go. I couldn't tell if he was breathing. I couldn't hear anything over the sound of my heartbeat. I moved my hand lower, then swallowed hard and covered his rigid member. I sighed at the delicious weight. He was long and thick. About my size, I mused as I smoothed my thumb over the broad head and along his slit. A low groan and the slight tilt of his hips alerted me he was fully aware and better yet, he liked what I was doing. I pressed my aching cock against his exposed crack and kissed his shoulder. He didn't protest. In fact, he moved his hips backward, looking for friction. I complied. I angled my hips as I tightened my grasp and stroked him. A languid, slow slide with a subtle twist of my wrist from base to tip and back again. He moaned and writhed against me, then reached back to pull my thigh over his, silently requesting me to close any remaining distance. The wordless invitation sent me into overdrive. I hooked my leg over his and used the momentum to roll him on his back so we were facing each other.

Gone was my earlier reticence. We were two consenting adults under cover of the night. This felt too damn good to question. I couldn't convince myself this wasn't smart. Not now. I leaned forward and gently kissed his mouth. He hooked his arms around my neck and pulled me against him. The kiss was sweet. A gentle meeting of lips in the dark. Undemanding and almost tender. Until he licked my mouth in a request for entry. I groaned at the first feel of his tongue gliding alongside mine. When I tried to deepen the connection, he teased me with small licks, then a probing push until I growled in frustration and sealed my mouth over his. I rocked my pelvis into him, loving the slide of our erections through the thin barrier. But I was greedy. I wanted all skin. No obstacles.

I pushed his PJs and briefs out of the way before removing mine. We hissed in pleasure when our bare cocks touched. Will cupped my ass with both hands and spread his legs wide to cradle me between his thighs. He bucked upward, straining to find adequate friction. He was wanton and a little wild. His fingernails dug into my flesh as he licked my lips and sucked on my tongue. I pumped my hips against his, then propped myself up on one hand and gripped us both in a punishing hold. Will scratched my back and arched into my fist. He pulled me closer, fusing our bodies as he devoured me with kisses and bites. I gasped for breath, resting my forehead for a moment on his before pulling back to trace the shell of his ear with the tip of my tongue.

"Slow down, baby." My voice was low and hoarse. I hardly recognized it as my own.

"I can't. It feels too good." He covered my hand and squeezed.

The pressure went up a notch. I pushed into our dual-fisted grip with a renewed abandon. He was right. It felt really fucking good. I kissed his mouth, then pulled back to lick my palm before wrapping my hand around both of us and picking up the tempo. When I dipped my fingers to fondle his balls, he lifted his leg slightly to give me more room. And maybe permission to go further. I took a chance and slid one of my fingers over his hole. It was no more than a touch, but it was enough to send him over the edge. I felt him tense and then lose momentum. He pulled my hair and held me close as he fell apart, shaking uncontrollably. And I was right behind him. I saw stars. A veritable kaleidoscope of color as our warm release spurted between us.

We lay perfectly still for a moment, glued together with sweat and cum. It was heavenly. I could barely move, and Will didn't seem bothered by my extra body weight. I didn't want to surface to the real world until I had to. When he pushed my shoulder, I slowly rolled off him and braced myself for his reaction.

Silence.

I was beginning to wonder what the quiet meant when he sat up and grabbed his discarded T-shirt from the bottom of the futon and handed it to me. When I didn't take it, he reached over to wipe at the mess on my stomach before doing the same to himself. He tossed the cum-stained tee aside and burrowed under the covers, facing me.

"Do you want to talk?" I whispered.

Will huffed a half laugh and shook his head. "No. Go to sleep, Rand."

Unbelievably, I did.

A PLEASANT quiet filled the chilly room though far-off sirens sounded in the morning light. Muted noises of honking horns and people yelling seeped through the thin walls, but it was comforting rather than disturbing. The normal buzz of a city beginning its day. I glanced at Will sleeping beside me. He looked so young and innocent. If I hadn't woken up in his bed, I could easily convince myself I'd dreamt the latter part of my evening. And the middle of the night.

Will's eyes fluttered open. He sighed and stretched before turning onto his back. I watched his Adam's apple slide in his throat and wondered how this was going to go down. It had been a long time since I'd woken in a strange bed with no idea of what to expect. I had no problem with one-night stands, but I rarely slept over, and if I did, it was because we both wanted another round before we parted ways. This was a completely different scenario.

"Good morning," I ventured. "How'd you sleep?"

"Why are you here?"

"I just—" I couldn't think of a good reason that wouldn't scare him away, so I gave in to impulse, moving my hand tentatively over his stomach. He pushed me away and rolled over to climb out of bed. "Don't go. Please."

Will sat at the edge of the futon but kept his back to me while he pulled on his discarded briefs. "I have to use the bathroom."

I watched him retreat, willing myself not to speak and fuck anything up. At least he hadn't told me to get the hell out. Baby steps. I heard a door close, running water, then nothing. Patience wasn't my virtue, but I didn't move a muscle. I listened and waited.

I sat up when he came back in the room and walked toward a short bar of hanging clothes near the front door. "Don't."

He cocked his head curiously, almost as though he was surprised I was still there. "Don't what?"

"Don't get dressed. Come back to bed."

"But—"

"Please."

He hesitated, then huffed a short breath before crossing the room and scrambling under the covers. The sudden chilly blast of air sent shivers over my skin. Without thinking, I reached out to pull him into my arms. He stiffened and scooted away, turning on his side to face me.

"Sorry. It's just so damn cold." I smiled, patting the small space between us. "Sure you don't want to share a little body heat?"

Will wiggled his nose and closed his eyes for a moment. I could practically see the wheels in his head turning. "You're here because you passed out. I know that part. The question is, why are you still here?"

"I'm—not sure, but I'm glad I am."

He bit his bottom lip and flopped onto his back. "Rand, this is too weird for me. I don't get you, and I don't know how to explain me."

I let the silence linger for a moment longer, then reached out to trace his jaw with my forefinger until he turned his gaze to me.

"Can I just say I think you're pretty?"

Will's lips quirked in reluctant amusement. "You mentioned that last night, but… thanks."

"Can I ask questions?"

"Ugh! God… no! This was why you were supposed to just go away." He rolled to his stomach and planted his face in his pillow dramatically. "I'll see you Tuesday. We can pretend this never happened."

I chuckled and tugged gently at his hair. "I don't think we can do that. I'm too curious. Tell me about you… no, don't be shy. I bet I've got a story or two to make yours seem pretty damn tame."

Will rolled to his side and snorted. "I'm sure you do. Look, I don't think I'm ready to—"

"I know you said that guy isn't your boyfriend, but were you meeting him the other night?"

"The other night?"

"I saw you on the subway a couple nights ago wearing a long black coat over a blue dress. I just wasn't sure it was you until I saw you at the bar last night."

"What were you doing there anyway? You told me you were straight."

I sucked in a deep breath and released it in a rush. "Actually I told you I wasn't gay. I'm bi. I suppose it was a lie of omission. I'm sorry."

"A lie of omission," he repeated with a derisive snort. "I suppose that's one way to put it. But why? I told you I was gay. Why lie at all?"

"It's… complicated, but—" I pulled at his arm when he moved away from me. "I'll try to explain. First, tell me who the guy is."

"A friend."

"Do you work for him?"

"Kind of."

"Will, talk to me. I know I have some explaining to do, but I'm your friend." I wanted to add that I was younger and better-looking than the bald man, but I didn't think he was in the mood. I bit the inside of my cheek and considered how to plead my case. "I know a middle-of-the-night hand job isn't a major declaration, but the guy I hired to tutor me in guitar didn't strike me as A) the type to give them freely or B) the type to have a dress or two in his closet. I swear, you can trust me. Maybe you'll feel better if you talk about it."

He gave me a lopsided smile that wasn't particularly friendly. "I don't need a psychologist. I'm nuts and I know it. Explaining crazy is harder than being crazy."

"All right, then, I'll try to figure this out on my own." I pursed my lips and narrowed my eyes thoughtfully. "You're an escort, and that guy is your pimp or your customer or—well, am I hot or cold?"

Will stared at me for a long moment before answering. "Lukewarm."

"Huh? Which part was right? Are you an escort? Do you get paid to dress in drag? Is that guy your sugar daddy? Come on! You're killing me here!"

Will made a face of exaggerated discomfort. Or maybe it was real. A nicer guy might have backed off or assured him he didn't have to share anything that made him uncomfortable. That wasn't me. I was known only for selective bouts of kindness, and I was too damn curious to let this go. How could I? My mild-mannered, nerdy guitar teacher was a cross-dressing escort on the side.

"You're awfully dramatic."

"I thought you were a geek. A sexy geek, but a geek nonetheless. I wasn't prepared for the real you."

Will smiled. "A sexy geek? I'm flattered. I think. I'm not a mystery, Rand. Not really. I'm still the guy who wears glasses and would rather play guitar or piano than talk. But everyone has more than one side to them, right?"

"Not like that! If you told me you liked to sew in your spare time, I would have thought it was odd but not completely wild. This isn't a matter of having a variety of interests. It's more like having a split personality."

"Which do you prefer?"

His tone was low and provocative. I studied him for a moment, wondering if he was trying to throw me off track. He held my gaze with a quiet confidence that rattled me more than I wanted to admit.

"I like them both, but which one is the real you?"

He didn't speak for a while. I was beginning to think he wouldn't and that his silence signaled the end of our discussion. I was trying to think of something to change his mind when he finally spoke.

"Both. I'm kind of like an escort. Sort of. Martin isn't my lover, but we had an understanding. Kind of."

"Whoa, whoa! Hang on a sec. I'm not dealing with a full deck yet. Back up."

"Are we really going to dissect this?"

"Why not? We're just a couple guys hanging out in our underwe—oh." I made a show of checking my naked state under the covers to lighten the moment and hopefully coax a smile from him. I gave myself a mental high five when his lips curled in amusement. "Take it from the top. Speak clearly and try to leave out 'sort of' or 'kind of.' What do you mean by escort? Why do you dress up like a woman? Who was that guy, and why the fuck did he have his hands all over you?"

"You sound jealous," he noted irritably.

"More like hungover," I quipped, though in truth, I didn't know why I wasn't letting it go.

So Will was a closet drag queen. Not my business. So he had a sugar daddy. Not my business, either. I could safely blame my presence in his bed on alcohol, but I knew the reason I was still here had to do with something beyond a healthy dose of curiosity. Then again, this was juicy stuff. This shit happened in the movies, not real life. Only in New York City, I mused.

"I needed money." He shrugged and went quiet again, like those three words answered everything.

"O-kay…."

"Martin Kanzler is married. He lives in Jersey and—"

"I was right," I whispered.

"—he's loaded, and he's got a fetish or three."

"And you're the guy who gets tied up or wrapped in Saran Wrap by his lover?"

Will rolled his eyes. "I'm not his lover."

"What are you, then?"

"I already told you." He sat up in bed with his legs crossed, then cocked his head and gave me a funny look I had no hope of translating. "We had a loose… arrangement."

"Of the sexual variety."

"No. I told you I'm not his lover. I just… satisfy his quirks."

Gulp. "What kind of quirks?"

"He's attracted to men in drag. I dress up and go places with him. A bar or a club. Not a big deal."

"That's all he wants? No sex?" I asked incredulously.

"No sex. Sometimes it's a little more involved, but not recently. It's been a while since he's wanted to jerk off to my bare ass in fishnets."

"Holy fuck." I winced as my cock twitched at the mention of last night's hosiery.

Will's grin had a boyish quality, an innocence so at odds with the conversation. He seemed to have no clue how alluring and downright sexy he was with his messy bedhead and freckled nose, talking about things I would never in a million years have associated with the straitlaced musician.

"Anyway I—"

"Wait up! So he used to get off to your bare ass in fishnets, and now he just likes hanging out with you?" My skepticism was clear.

"Sometimes there's a little role-playing but—"

"Oh my God," I moaned. I squeezed my eyes shut and silently counted to ten, anything to avoid grabbing my now-throbbing penis. "What kind of role-playing?"

My voice sounded like a strangled whisper. Either Will was oblivious or he chose to let it go. He shook his head nonchalantly as though this was all so fucking normal.

"It can be anything from the boss and his wayward employee scenario to a daddy thing. He makes up a story and I play my part. It's kind of silly, but it's pretty innocent."

For once in my life, I was rendered speechless. It wouldn't last but... wow.

"Daddy," I choked.

"Yeah. He makes up a scene at the beginning of the night. Something I'm supposed to purposely disobey. Then he issues a couple warnings when I do or say whatever the script says and then...." He shrugged in a "doesn't everyone do that?" way.

"And then what? He punishes you? I don't get this. You must have been on the clock last night, so to speak, but he didn't seem jealous when I showed up. I know I wasn't exactly at my best but still."

"He's not my boyfriend, Rand. It isn't personal. At all. It's business. A consenting act between two adults. It's over now anyway."

"What do you mean?"

"Our arrangement is over. He took it pretty well. Maybe he has someone new in his life who actually will have sex with him. And doesn't mind getting spanked occasionally."

"Geez, that's...."

"Weird? Not really. The virgin and the married businessman. Everyone gets turned on by different things," he said with a shrug. "He's not a bad guy. He's just not for me. I ended it last night. I'll just add the money I owe him to my mountain of student loan debt."

"Good. Not the part about the student loans, and no judgment, but... we'll think of something else. Escorting isn't for you."

He looked astounded. "We? Rand, I—"

I set a finger on his lips to stop his speech. I didn't know what I meant. Not in any depth. I swiped my hand through my hair in agitation. "I'm having a hard time with this. Pun intended. I have another question." He stared at me blankly, no doubt willing me to shut the hell up. "You said virgin. Does that mean you never did anything sexual with Martin or *any* guy besides me? Last night we—"

Will closed his eyes and let out a low groan. "I wish I wasn't waking up now. I have a feeling I'm going to regret this conversation. Borrow the coat. I'll get it back from you Tuesday. If you still want lessons," he added with a worried frown before scooting toward the edge of the futon. "Can we please forget everything else?"

"Why? It was awesome. Will, look at me." I held his elbow and pushed the covers over him as though that might keep him in place. I licked my lips nervously when he didn't budge. Stubborn little shit. "Please. I admire you. It takes serious balls to dress up like someone of the opposite sex. It's not easy being one of eight million people in this city trying to make something of yourself. Don't stop believing that—"

"You aren't going to start singing Journey songs, are you?" He gave me a teasing grin.

"No." I chuckled. "I'm serious. You rocked the heels and fishnets last night. I'm not gonna lie, there's a part of me that is really fucking turned on by this kinky stuff. And I mean... really turned on. I want...."

I bit the inside of my cheek, wondering how to proceed as I took in the cautious set of his shoulders and his wary gaze.

"What do you want?"

"I want to spank you."

"Share time is officially over," he proclaimed, tossing the covers aside.

I grabbed at his arm, relieved he looked more amused than angry when I pulled him back to my side.

"I'm kidding. Well, maybe not. Look, I get inappropriate when I'm nervous, and fuck, you make me strangely nervous. I can't figure it out, but I want to get to know you. The *real* you."

Will's smile was slow to begin, just a tiny curl of his lips. It quickly turned incandescent. My nostrils flared slightly as I reached out to tuck a stray piece of hair behind his ear. I needed any excuse to touch him. With his twinkling eyes and pink-stained lips from the leftover red lipstick, he was extraordinarily appealing.

"But you're not even into men," he whispered with one brow raised in challenge.

I barked a quick laugh. "Obviously that's not true."

"Obviously. Explain why you're naked in my bed after letting me believe you were straight. I know it was dark, but you seemed to know your way around another guy's dick pretty well."

"I told you I'm bi. I know my way around both sexes pretty well." I shook my head, feeling ashamed for the lie all over again. "I'm sorry I wasn't honest. I made this deal not to—whatever."

His no-bullshit expression made me anxious. "You made a deal not to what? I just told you I dressed up to pay off a student loan debt. It's your turn, so what is it? You made a deal not to tell anyone you're bi, or you made a deal not to go the gay route?"

I swallowed hard, hating how that sounded. "Yes. To both."

"Then I repeat… why are you here? Is it because I was wearing a dress? Do you get turned on by blurred lines of masculinity and femininity?"

"No. I never have before, anyway. I think it's just you. Look, I'm not proud I lied. It was cowardly. Especially after you were honest with me. But I'm telling the truth now."

"How novel," he snarked, pulling a corner of the covers over his shoulder like a cape.

"I'm sorry. I hate it when people aren't honest. I'm really torn about this. I didn't think it would be a big deal. In my head, I figured I could treat it like a mind-over-matter thing, and then I *wouldn't* be lying."

"But why was it important to be straight? There are plenty of gay or bi musicians."

"Think about it. The ones you hear about are the ones who've already made it in rock and roll. Either people assume they're straight or they admit they're bi, but every picture is with them and someone of the opposite sex. An agent we tried to hire when we first came to the city told me being bi wasn't an issue, but having a boyfriend was. When I admitted I tend to gravitate more toward men than women, I was advised not to reveal my sexuality at all. It's distracting, he said, and a losing strategy. According to him, established acts can reveal those things but not newbies. Supposedly my looks are part of the package, but if listeners hear buzz words like *bi* or *gay*, they won't hear or see anything else." I gave a half chuckle but wasn't surprised it sounded hollow. "It's turning out to be much harder than I thought. Having to push down a major part of who I am to sell the other major part of me is… exhausting."

"I know the feeling. Remember when I told you I was standing in the closet door? Sometimes I think it would be easier to take a step back inside and close it for good."

"Why? I get that it may take time to embrace your gay side, but why go backward? Geez, how could you do without the sex? I love dick. I can't imagine not having—"

"What? Everything? You're greedy, Rand. You want it all. You're even willing to conform to someone else's rules to satisfy your gluttony." There was no mistaking his scorn this time.

"Gluttony? Look, I know it sounds bad, but when I'm wrapped up in the music, the business side doesn't matter to me. Whatever gets us heard is what I'm focused on. It's when I'm… just me that it's claustrophobic. I'm not straight and I'm not gay. I'm somewhere in between. My so-called conformity is a—"

"Business decision. Got it. That's how it started with Martin and me. I wish I'd never agreed to it, but I suppose I understand why you're lying."

"I'm not lying. I'm just not telling the whole truth." I immediately winced. "I mean I'm not telling anyone what isn't their business in the first place."

"Not much better, but in a weird way I get it."

"Where does that leave us? Last night was a game changer, Will. You know who I am, and I know you're a—"

"A freaky cross-dressing escort?"

"You're extraordinary. You're a beautiful man… and a sexy woman. I'm very attracted to you." I traced a circular pattern over his knee and massaged his inner thigh. He smacked my hand and lay down beside me, propping his head on his elbow.

"Oh please! I'm ordinary—"

"I hate to break this to you, but ordinary guys don't have lipstick of their own in their medicine cabinets. If you're ordinary, I like ordinary. Let's put it this way, most guys are like Velveeta. You're like Gouda."

"Cheese?" His eyebrows knit comically in confusion. Who could blame him? What the fuck was I talking about?

"Bad example. Can I kiss you?"

He blinked a couple times but didn't move. I inched closer so our knees touched, then reached out slowly to run my fingers along his earlobe. When he leaned into my hand, I cupped his neck and drew him forward and felt his breath on my lips. The urge to crash my mouth over his and twine my tongue around his was powerful. I breathed in his peppermint-and-sleepy scent before licking his bottom lip and tenderly pressing my mouth to his. His low groan echoed in the cool room. I heard a noise I belatedly realized was me whimpering for more. More contact. More Will. I tilted his chin and licked at his lips again, this time requesting entrance. He obeyed wholeheartedly.

The air was thick with possibility and an almost innocent wonder I hadn't known in years. I relished the feel of his soft lips and the enthusiastic push of his tongue. There was more need and raw desire in the kiss than skill, and somehow it made every little sigh and moan sweeter. I moved my hands through his thick hair, over his shoulders, and down his back, stopping just above the elastic waistband of his briefs. I didn't want to ask for more than he was willing to give. But the second he hitched his weight forward on one arm and inadvertently slid his hard shaft alongside mine, I thought I might pass out. We groaned in unison as the passionate fusion of lips was accompanied with a steady thrust of hips. Even with a thin layer of cotton separating us, it felt really fucking amazing.

Will bit my lip, then kissed and licked a path along my jaw and down my neck. Our morning stubble added a sexy, abrasive element. But it was the sway of his hips that drove me insane. If I didn't stop him now, my tenuous hold on my control would snap.

"Will, slow down, baby. We—"

"I want it to be you."

"Huh?" I pulled back in confusion.

"My first time. I want you to be my first," he blurted.

I was stunned into silence.

"If I go back in the closet in May, I don't want to be a virgin. I want it to be you."

My brows rose in surprise. "What's happening in May that's going to make you close the closet door?"

"I graduate." He huffed when I gave him a blank look. "It's too hard to go into detail, but the gist is my family would like me to keep my sexuality mum for a while."

"Starting in May?"

"Yeah, or summertime."

"So you want to get it on with me once or as many times as possible between now and then?"

Will chuckled. "Something like that. I don't want to get married and start a family, but I'm… I'm attracted to you too."

We let the silence speak when it became clear neither of us knew how to proceed. Until I couldn't take it anymore. I pulled back the covers to expose myself.

"I'm naked and hard. Are we proposing action now or at a later date?" I asked in a deadpan tone.

Will chuckled softly and reached for my cock. "I'm not sure. I've never asked anyone to—I mean, this isn't normal for me."

"I didn't think so," I said, gently stilling his hand. Not an easy feat when my body was humming with excitement at the promise of release. "But I can tell from last night you've had *some* experience."

"Some, but I haven't… you know."

"Gone all the way?"

"Mmm-hmm." He arched into me, purring with need when I grabbed his ass and pulled him against me, sliding my aching cock alongside his. It was so tempting to push the cotton barrier away and take what he was offering.

"So you and Marty never—"

Will sat abruptly and gave me a dirty look. "No. I told you I've never had sex with Martin."

"What do you call bending over in fishnet stockings, then?"

"That wasn't sex!"

"Sex isn't defined only by inserting your dick in—"

"Do you have to be crude? I didn't blow him or give him a hand job, either. The most I ever did was kiss him. That's not sex," he insisted.

"Kissing is fine, but baring your ass is crossing a line, babe. Acts of intimacy and sexual favors are forms of sex, just like—"

"Do *not* give me another cheese analogy. Why does it matter, anyway? We can look at it as a business arrangement of our own. We can take it slowly, see if we're even compatible. You're pretty irritating. This might not work, but if it does, we have until May."

"Compatible? What does that have to do with anything? I hate to point this out, but will you really solve any problems with your parents by going back in the closet? You're only twenty-two. Things will change. You'll meet someone and—"

"If that happens, I'll reconsider. I think it's the right thing to do for now. Maybe I can repair our relationship."

"By denying who you are? You'd be lying."

"Like you?" He gave me a smug look that made me instantly uncomfortable. "Think about it. This is a win-win. You'd get to keep your secret and still get—"

"Your ass?" I asked, unable to keep the disapproval out of my voice. The whole thing felt wrong and yet….

"Are you turning me down?"

"Hell no!" I sat up and planted a hard kiss on his lips. "Let's get some coffee and talk about this."

Will pulled back in surprise. "Don't you want to… you know."

"Yes, I most definitely want to… you know. But not all at once. I'm setting the pace. Usually that means you better hang on to your hat and hope you land in Kansas, Dorothy. But I'm going to try to curb my impulsive nature for you. You're far more reckless than me, and you're grossly unprepared to deal with the real world."

"Excuse me?" His forehead creased in disbelief.

"C'mon, Will! What do you really know about that guy? You can't be so trusting. Married Marty could turn into Marty the Murderer. That jerk could have gotten his kicks from beating the shit out of you, then fucked you senseless and left your stupid ass in a janky hotel room in Hell's Kitchen. Your claim to fame would have been a tiny segment on the eleven o'clock news instead of your name in lights on Broadway. Not pretty. I'm all for taking chances, but basic caution is essential to survival, babe. Especially when your street smarts are somewhat… questionable."

"Questionable?" he huffed. "I've lived here longer than you. I know how to take care of myself, Rand. And I've known Martin for years. He wouldn't hurt me."

"Years?"

"Yes, he's a friend of my parents," he said, casting an irritated glance over his shoulder before heading toward the rack of clothing in the corner.

I reached for my discarded jeans as I watched him slip a plaid button-down shirt over a *Harry Potter* T-shirt, then set his glasses on his nose.

"The creep factor just went through the roof. And don't be naïve. You don't know shit. Good thing you met me."

He rolled his eyes and pointed toward the jacket I'd left on the futon. "Right. Lucky me. Except your reasoning is off. How are you any more trustworthy than the average guy? How do I know you aren't Velveeta… or worse?"

I gasped theatrically, then waited a beat before asking with mock seriousness, "What's worse than Velveeta?"

"A cheese ball. The kind with nuts," he answered smugly as he pulled a red beanie over his head. "Let's get coffee. Your treat."

I grumbled good-naturedly as I zipped the coat he was loaning me and leaned in to kiss him. "Fine, but no fucking bagels."

I followed Will's melodic laughter out the door, equally as aware of the dopey grin on my face as I was that my life had taken a strange but interesting turn within twelve short hours. I wasn't sure this was a smart idea, but hey… that had never stopped me before.

Chapter 5

By Monday, I was sure I'd imagined the entire episode with Will. It was surreal. I ran the details through my head like scenes from a memorable dream. I wanted to stay in my head, making up silly songs about a boy dressed like a girl rather than dealing with real life. Real life was too unpredictable. General consensus was our first show had been a success. Our new manager was thrilled, and the guys were still floating on a post-show high. Sure, the venue had been modest, but the audience loved us. It was good news, but it was a small step in the overall scheme of things.

I listened to Mike's excited chatter about putting together what he called a "summertime series." He leaned on his elbows, then shifted back again as he outlined his plans to take over the small-club circuit in Lower Manhattan and Brooklyn. Tim, Cory, and Terry wore matching grins, oohing and aahing in all the right places while I sat tapping my fingers restlessly on my thighs. I wanted to get to work. All this talk made me antsy and only served to remind me I didn't want to play crappy clubs forever. One good show did not equal success.

"That's awesome! What do you think, Rand?" Tim gave me a sharp look, indicating he was aware of my flagging attention.

"It's cool, but we have a lot of work to do. The show was good, but it wasn't perfect by any stretch. We have to practice our asses off and get technically cleaner." I glanced at my phone distractedly. I was done here.

"What do you mean 'technically cleaner'?" Mike asked. He was probably in his early thirties but looked ten years older. He'd gone prematurely bald and had opted to shave his head. It was a good look on some guys, but I wasn't so sure about Mike. He was a pound or two shy of being painfully thin and had a nervous habit of bouncing or swaying in his chair like a kid on a sugar high. Whatever. His job wasn't to look pretty and not bug me. "The audience doesn't notice technicalities, Rand. They go to bars and clubs to get tipsy and listen to some good music. Look at this review."

Mike pushed his iPad toward me but didn't seem particularly bothered when I didn't reach for it. He picked it up and cleared his throat before reading aloud.

"'Nothing beats the winning combination of a bluesy rock-and-roll sound and a charismatic front man who oozes sex appeal. Spiral is a new band with classic style. Lead singer Rand O'Malley knows how to work a crowd. He's got moves that rival some of rock and roll's best, a commanding presence, and damn, can he sing!'"

"I won't go on, but the point is they loved you guys. That one is from Leah Fletcher's *Inked Rose Beat* blog, but there's another from—"

"Stop feeding his ego. The guy has a big enough head as it is," Cory scoffed good-naturedly.

I ignored Cory and gave Mike a serious look. "Look, I appreciate the positive feedback, but a couple good reviews doesn't mean we've made it. The goal is bigger, better venues and a record deal. No one will take us seriously if we aim low and don't clean up the stupid mistakes we make onstage. Shall we practice, gentlemen?"

"I'm just saying, you guys sounded pretty damn good Saturday night. I wouldn't sweat the small stuff if I were you," Mike said with a grin.

Talk about saying exactly the wrong thing.

"Oh boy," Cory and Tim groaned under their breath.

Tim made a funny face, silently pleaded with me to shut up. I ignored him and stood. I shook my head in an attempt to let the first wave of irritation subside before I gave Mike a detailed list of all the things wrong with "not sweating the small stuff." It didn't work.

"Gee, Mikey, I think somebody better sweat the small stuff, the big stuff, and every fucking thing in between. I think when Timmy goes too hard on a medium drumbeat or Cory flubs the backup harmony on a Muddy Waters classic, somebody better notice. Or when our guitar wizard Terry has ten miscues and forgets the bridge to an original piece? Holy crap… I hope someone has the balls to say 'That sucked, dude.' Anyone else want that job, or is it mine? 'Cause I'm not afraid to tell it how it is. We had a good first gig in an average-size club in Lower Manhattan. But stringing together a bunch of dates to do more of the same shit isn't how we're gonna make it big. Don't try to sugarcoat reality, Mike. If we're going places, it's because the blinders are off and we're fixing whatever doesn't work. You know the saying 'No one rises to low expectations'? Mediocrity is shit in my book. We can do better."

Tim and Cory shared a look. I'd bet their silent communication was regret they hadn't warned Terry and Mike about me. Spiral wasn't recreation to me. It was bigger than all of us, and the potential for greatness was out of this world. If we worked for it.

"Uh. Right. I get it. I do. I'll get some spring dates set up and contact a couple recording execs. I still like the summer series idea, but maybe we can go a little bigger on the clubs. I'll work it, man. No worries." Mike stood and extended his hand toward me. I shook it with a wry grin, proud I didn't roll my eyes. "I'll let you guys get back to practice. See you soon."

The room remained quiet after the door closed. I glanced around the table at my bandmates, then clapped my hands together like a schoolteacher.

"Come on, boys. Let's do this." I lowered my voice to sound like a concerned parent. "Or do we need to have a discussion?"

"Please no." Cory shoved his chair back and elbowed me in the stomach as he passed. "By the way, I never mess up Muddy Waters, asshole."

"You did Saturday night. And it wasn't pretty." I chuckled when he flipped me off and moved toward the door.

Terry was right behind him. "It was a good show. I may have missed a couple cues, but not ten and—"

"Ten may have been lowballing. It was probably closer to fifteen. You made mistakes, Terry. We all did. It's not the end of the world, but it will be if we don't get it right." I shrugged, confident I'd been as kind as I could be.

He started to walk by but stopped at the last second, giving me a pointed look with a sneer on his mug as he leaned in and hissed in my ear. "I fucked her. She didn't want to wait for your ugly ass, and I think she digs me more anyway."

"Huh? Who?" I was totally confused. Obviously I was supposed to be pissed by his news flash, but I had no idea who he was talking—oh. "The cute girl with the tatts?"

"Yup. She digs sucking cock too. Your loss, fearless leader," he snarled.

I stared after him. Yeah, I wanted to kick his ass. However, not for the reason he thought.

Tim looked up from his phone when Terry stormed out of the room. "What was that about? Don't tell me he was offended you basically called him a hack in front of the band and our new manager. Jesus, Rand! Can't you say things... I don't know... nicer?"

"No. I can't. That guy is wasting our time."

"What did he say?"

"He told me he banged the girl from the bar." I snorted. "As if."

"The girl from the bar is the one who wrote that review. Leah. He's probably jealous."

"Whatever. I don't have time for stupidity."

Tim furrowed his brow. "You know I was thinking... maybe we should tell Mike and Terry about us. You, me, and Cor are like brothers. We need to trust them and—"

"About us? You make it sound like we're a couple," I said testily. "I don't trust him, and I'm not telling him anything. I'd like to see how big a hole he can dig first."

"That's not very mature. The only way this works is if we're completely transparent."

"Or careful. Just relax. I'm not going to worry about Terry, and I'm not having any heart-to-hearts with him. I'd rather watch him squirm. He's a bad idea. I don't care about transparency with someone I know is a short-term fix. I've got to find a replacement for him."

Tim sighed heavily. "Why can't you just get along with people?"

"I'm trying, Timmy. Come on. Let's get to work." I tweaked his cheek and gave him a goofy grin to break the tension.

"Cut it out." He swatted my hand but didn't bother hiding a sly smile when he continued. "Or I'll start hounding you again about Saturday night *after* the gig."

I made a motion to zip my lips, then gestured for him to keep moving. He huffed good-naturedly, and he regaled me with a funny story from the bar after I'd left. He hadn't teased me much about not coming home, but I had a feeling it was because he hadn't, either. I wasn't going to volunteer any information either way. I trusted Tim, but I felt a strange protectiveness toward Will. His naïveté and lack of pretension were refreshing, but they made me nervous too. I wasn't ready to share him until I figured him out. I didn't want to hear anyone's thoughts on whether or not seeing a man was a good idea either. We'd had plenty of discussions about potentially being labeled and pigeon-holed before we were given a fair shot. It was best to concentrate on the music.

TUESDAY AFTERNOON couldn't get here soon enough. Other than sending random text messages, I hadn't talked to Will since Sunday. Two days wasn't much, but I was desperate to assure myself the whole thing hadn't been a figment of my imagination. And God, I wanted to touch him again.

We agreed to meet in the lobby of the Performing Arts building as usual. Only authorized students and faculty were granted use of the elevators and access to the classrooms. I gave my name to the receptionist and observed the students coming and going. College settings intrigued me. I loved the energy and excitement of educated expression and free thought. There was a hopeful vibe in the air that made me sorry for the jaded sensibilities of real life beyond these hallowed walls.

"Hi. Sorry, I had to talk to my professor and...." Will stopped in his tracks and smiled shyly when I handed over the coat I'd borrowed the other morning. He looked like his preppy self in a pair of khaki pants and a navy V-neck sweater. "Thank you."

"Thank *you*. My balls were seconds away from freezing off. I wouldn't have been any good to you then." I smirked playfully.

"Does that line actually work in the real world?"

"Not at all."

Will let out a soft chuckle before gesturing for me to follow him. "Right. Come on."

Two giggling girls in coordinating striped sweaters jumped into the elevator with us. I shifted my guitar case out of their way with a brief apology. They smiled in return and whispered something to each other. Elevator rides could be so awkward. No one wanted to speak candidly in front of people they didn't know in a confined space. So yeah, I was a little surprised when Will spoke up.

"I think you left a couple other things at my place." His tone was nonchalant, kind of like he was telling me what he ate for breakfast. "I found your hat under the bed."

I felt my brow rise dramatically. "You don't say."

"Mmm-hmm. I forgot to bring it. Sorry."

"No problem. What else? My underwear?"

Watching Will's face turn pink, then red was extraordinarily entertaining. I nudged his elbow playfully and tried to gain control of my smile before it threatened to take over my entire face. When I couldn't take the building pressure of emotion, I winked at the girls, then leaned in and kissed his lips, loving that I took him by surprise. The elevator doors slid open a moment later. Will stepped into the empty corridor and gave me a wide-eyed, incredulous stare.

"I cannot believe you just did that," he said as the doors closed.

"What? Kissed you on an elevator? It's not like farting, ya know."

Will huffed a sigh that clearly said he thought I was hopeless before turning to walk down the hall. "I was talking about the underwear comment, but yeah, the kissing part was awkward too. No one wants to watch two people going at it in a confined space. And besides, we're supposed to be playing this strictly straight while we're in public."

He stopped to unlock the door to the classroom, pausing to give me a perturbed look before he moved inside ahead of me. I barked a quick laugh as I set my guitar on the back table and shrugged my jacket off.

"First of all, that was hardly going at it. It was a peck. You were the one advertising I left my clothes at your place in front of a couple cute girls. And who said anything about playing straight?"

"Were we not in the same room two mornings ago talking about this?"

"We were. In fact, we were naked in your bed. Decidedly unstraight. But the way I remember it, I was the one who was holding back the gay while you were the one going for it. Let's go back to the elevator. I think you purposefully blew my cover back there with those girls. Were you jealous?"

He snorted and rolled his eyes. "You're unbelievable."

"Thanks."

"It wasn't a compliment," he quipped as he made his way to the piano.

"Well, the next time you announce you're holding my underwear hostage in a crowd, all bets are off, baby." I gave him a lascivious once-over and waggled my eyebrows.

Will chuckled. "I'll keep that in mind. But I'm pretty sure your tighty-whities never came up. My comment was perfectly innocent. There's a big difference between hats and underwear."

"I'm on to you, Will. You wanted those girls to know something's going on between us. They're probably talking right now. Bet they're wondering if we're in here having sex. Hell, they could be outside that door listening. Maybe we should give 'em something to talk about." I made a show of unbuckling my belt and the top button on my 501s. "Is there a camera in this room?"

"Keep your pants on. I've got two months left 'til graduation, and I'd prefer not to get kicked out of school, please," Will said primly, smacking my hand away.

"You won't get kicked out. I doubt we'd be the first anyway."

I rebuttoned my jeans and started to back up, but at the last second, I reached out to cup his chin between my thumb and forefinger. I traced his jaw and let my thumb roam higher to caress his cheekbone just under his glasses. His eyes fluttered shut. I loved the contrast of his fair skin and darker lashes and eyebrows. He was so damn pretty. And those lips. They were sensuous. That was the word. I leaned in and brushed my nose against his. I could feel his breath on my lips. The urge to plunge my tongue inside and take what I was very sure we both wanted was strong, but I waited for his permission.

When he didn't respond, I let my hand fall to my side and started to pull back. Maybe he really was serious about propriety in the classroom. I wasn't used to curbing my impulses to suit someone else's sensibilities. I'd spent twenty-five years doing only what I wanted. Screw anyone else. Now here I was, attempting to hide my gay side publicly while trying to follow Will's lead in private. It felt strange, I thought, just as Will launched himself at me.

I grunted in surprise when he wrapped his arms around my neck and crashed his mouth over mine. He softened the connection and tilted his head as he raked his fingers through my hair. I responded but let him control the tempo. Until he tentatively licked my lips. Fuck, he tasted sweeter than I remembered. Like peppermint candy or hot chocolate. I pulled him flush against my chest and slid my tongue alongside his, twisting and colliding in a passionate fusion. When he gasped for air, I pulled back, only to have him grind his hips into mine and lick my jaw. He swayed into me with a moan and lost his footing.

"Steady there."

I kept my gaze locked on his as I inched away. I couldn't figure him out. Will was sexier than he knew, which spelled potential danger for me. It was better to let the music take over for now.

I picked up my guitar and dragged a plastic chair over to the piano when he turned to take a seat at the bench. "What are we learning today, Teach?"

"Up to you. Do you want to play something you've already written? You could run through it, and maybe I can help you tighten it up."

"Good idea. If you can perform any minor miracles, I'd appreciate it. I need to become a master guitarist sooner rather than later."

"Trouble with Terry?" he asked distractedly as he ran his fingers over the piano keys.

I strummed the first few chords of a song I'd just written before answering. "I can't stand the guy. Being in the same room with him is a challenge to my already thin patience."

Will smiled sheepishly. "Sorry for the bad referral. You know, when you first called me about tutoring, I was afraid you'd be kind of like Terry. He's the adult version of the guys I avoided in junior high and high school. He always looked like he wanted to stuff me in a locker. You may be overly confident and a tad conceited at times, but you're nothing like him."

"Gee thanks. You probably wouldn't have liked me much in junior high, though. I wasn't a bully but I was always looking for trouble. I couldn't wait to do things to piss everyone off. I must be softening in my old age." I sighed as I stood and bumped his hip to take a seat beside him on the bench.

"Must be. I was the opposite. I always tried to please. I was careful not to rock the boat. I still am to a degree, but the best thing about being in a place like New York is the feeling you can lose yourself and start over."

"Lose yourself to find yourself?"

"Exactly. I haven't taken advantage of it yet, but still.... People rarely notice what you look like or how you act here, unless you're outlandish. Even then they're more likely to applaud your daring. That's not the case where I'm from. It's hard to blend in a small town with a gay population of one," he commented with a frown as he raised his hands over the keys again.

I adjusted the guitar strap, then pushed my instrument over my shoulder before turning on the bench to get a better look at him.

"I doubt you were the only gay kid."

"Maybe not but it felt that way. People didn't talk about being gay where I'm from. If homosexuality came up in conversation, it was spoken about in hushed tones like they were discussing an unfortunate and possibly contagious disease." He let out a humorless half laugh before sliding off the bench from the opposite side and picking up his acoustic guitar.

"Why did you come out, then?"

"I didn't. I was outed." His voice was so matter-of-fact. He kept his gaze on the fretboard as he twisted his wrist to form a complicated chord.

"Who outed you?"

"Huh? Oh. A concerned cousin who saw me at the theater sitting a little too close to a boy who was widely thought to be 'one of those.'"

"One of those what?"

Will smiled, but it went nowhere near his eyes. He didn't look haunted or upset. More like resigned. I didn't like it.

"Faggots. I'm from a small Midwestern town and people talk. It's like I told you, if you thought someone was... different, it was best to stay away from them. No one wants to be associated with undesirable types. Like gays. The short story is my dad's cousin, Agnes, saw me with Sean Ingersoll, town queer, and decided to warn my parents. Cousin Agnes was also the town librarian, and she already had me on her radar because of my peculiar reading habits. She thought it was odd that I always seemed to choose books by gay authors," he scoffed. "She thought she should warn Dad that people would start talking and maybe jump to conclusions about me being one of those 'homos.' Especially if I was spending time with Sean.

"So like the selectively concerned parent he is, Dad pulled me into the den after dinner one night and told me he was alarmed. He must have said 'they're all gonna think you're a faggot' five times before I finally snapped and said, 'I am a faggot!' Needless to say, he wasn't happy. And he was probably confused. Up until that moment, I'd always tried to please him. He expected me to cower, deny it, and renounce my friendship with Sean. But I wouldn't."

"What did he do?"

"He slapped me," he said. His voice was devoid of emotion. He sounded like he was reading the ingredients from a box of cereal and wasn't particularly impressed with the contents.

"Jesus."

"It wasn't the worst reaction ever. He didn't kick me out or beat the crap out of me. He hit me, then he just... stared at me like he was willing me to tell him I was joking. When I didn't say anything, he told me the conversation never happened. I was banned from seeing Sean, banned from the library and a host of other things I can't remember anymore. One of them may have been speaking to him 'cause I don't think we've said more than a handful of words since then. 'Pass the pepper' and eventually 'maybe you're better off going to New York' were about it."

"How old were you?"

"Sixteen. It was almost six years ago exactly. I survived those last two years living at home by avoiding my dad whenever possible. He did the same. He remembered I was around when I started applying for college. He made it clear I was expected to attend the private university in Pennsylvania where he and Mom met, but I'd lobbied for NYU and even applied against his wishes. It really pissed him off. I started leaving brochures around the house to make him nuts. But the final straw was when I left one in a copy of E.M. Forster's *Maurice* and highlighted the line 'You confuse what's important with what's impressive.' The next day my mother told me I could go to NYU."

"Passive-aggressiveness at its finest," I commented with a laugh as I adjusted my guitar in front of me. I ran my fingers over the strings but kept my gaze focused on Will.

"Yes and no. He didn't mention that he wasn't willing to pay for it or support me at all. He paid for the first semester, then pulled the rug out without letting me know. I should have known something was up at Christmas that year. He hardly looked at me. I didn't find out until I went back to the city and was met with a bigass bill I had no way of paying. My mom tried to help, but in the end her suggestion was to call Martin Kanzler. The rest, as they say, is history."

"Marty the Molester? Does she know about him?"

"No, of course not! He's not a molester, idiot. He's just… quirky, kinky, or whatever you want to call it. My parents went to college with him. They're friends. My mom thought he might agree to lend me the money to get through my second semester. It would give me time to apply for loans for the next year or give her time to talk my dad into not being a prick. Or for me to take back my words and tell him I was just going through a phase."

"You decided to go a different route, eh?"

"I took the money for that second semester because I felt like I had no choice. It was that or go home. I think my dad wanted me to fail and come crawling back for help. I met with Marty a couple months ago to discuss the 'terms' of the loan. Since I'm graduating and am about to take on even more debt in grad school, I was hoping he'd give me a slight reprieve and let me begin paying him back in another two years. He said he was open to that, but he had another idea."

"What was your initial reaction? It's a little outside the norm to be propositioned to dress as a chick. Even in New York."

"You'd be surprised," he said with a short laugh. "I thought it was… different, but after I got over the initial shock, I didn't think it sounded so bad. I've always loved—never mind. Dressing up to go to a few clubs and bars wearing heels and a dress sounded like a piece of cake. My friend Benny is in theater. I knew he'd help me with the makeup. It seemed like a sweet way to pay off thirty grand fast."

"Thirty grand?" I repeated with comically wide eyes.

Will nodded solemnly. "Yep. It was an unconventional choice that some people might find… distasteful, but I'm not sorry I tried it. It amounted to a few 'dates,' and I learned something about my own limits. I can't decide if the best or worst part was that I got a strange thrill doing something I knew would make my dad apoplectic if he ever found out. I don't know what that says about me. Probably nothing good. No one in my story is sympathetic. My dad is a homophobic prick, my mom is cold but she tries… I think. And I'm… an opportunist. A spoiled kid who got what he wanted, then made some unorthodox adjustments when it went sideways instead of doing the honorable thing."

"By 'honorable' you mean go into debt?"

"Oh, I'm in debt all right. I owe Martin thirty, but I owe close to two hundred thousand dollars in student loans."

"Two hundred thousand? Holy shit," I yelped, jumping to my feet.

"I know. I'm in debt up to my eyeballs. And I'm in music and theater. Jobs out of college in my field don't pay great, so chances are good it will take years for me to crawl out of this hole. No, the honorable thing, according to my parents, would be to renounce my words. Deny my gayness."

"Is that why you're thinking of going back in the closet? Is it to please them?"

Will shrugged and looked out the window for a long moment. "I thought things would be different here. It's a great city, but it hasn't changed me. Not really. Once upon a time, I at least had a family I

could count on. Now I'm alone, and whenever I see my family, it's…
uncomfortable. It's hard being alone all the time. But that isn't the only
reason. My dad asked me to do it. As a favor."

"Recently?"

"At Christmas. I told him I'd think about it. That's what I'm doing.
I'm thinking about it."

"But why? I don't get it. You haven't given yourself a chance. I
haven't known you long, but c'mon, Will, you barely go out! You won't
go to clubs or bars unless you're in disguise. How will you meet anyone
else like you?"

"You've got a lot of nerve to tell me I should step out of the closet
when you're in your own. Bars and clubs aren't my scene. It's not—"

"Because you haven't tried. There's part of you that's still the
little geeky kid from a Podunk town who wants to do what Mommy and
Daddy say. I have my own reasons for not blasting my sexuality to the
world… and I'm not saying they're noble by any means, but—"

"Then don't say anything! You don't know who I am or where I'm
from. Don't judge me until you're ready to tell the world who you really
are, Rand. Not that it matters. Being bi is nowhere near the same."

"You mean you think being bi makes me closer to straight than gay?"

Will shrugged. "Doesn't it? I'm nowhere close to straight. I could
never even pretend to be interested in a woman."

"Well, if you ask the average straight man, he'd probably say
the fact I love sucking cock makes me closer to gay. The thing about
being bi is it's hard to explain. It's the gray line in between that gay and
straight people don't trust," I commented with a shrug as I looked out the
window. Only the tops of barren trees in the park and the muted pewter
sky were visible. There was no real diversion to offer from uncomfortable
conversation twists.

"So that's why you decided not to come out as bi?"

"Initially, yes. I didn't want to waste time talking about sex when
I'm trying to sell music. But I changed my mind. I don't think fracturing
myself to appease anyone's sensibilities for the sake of a sale is a good
thing. Not in the long run. I haven't had the opportunity to tell my buddies
or our manager, but I will. I can't see myself making a giant statement
immediately. No one knows us on a bigger stage, and I want the music to
speak for us. But if someone asks… I won't lie."

"So you've changed your mind about us?" His voice was so low I might not have heard him if I wasn't standing close.

"No. Nothing has to change. I understand things aren't so simple for you. I may not have come from the same place, but that doesn't mean I'm naïve about the measure of tolerance and acceptance so-called good people dole out like currency. I've seen it. The playing field isn't equal no matter what the laws say. People will always look at the surface and judge without knowing the real story. I hate the unfairness of it all. It's a bullshit world sometimes. Don't speak too loud, don't upset the balance. Fuck that. Honesty isn't always pleasant, but it's better than ignorance. I don't want to be a hypocrite. I don't want to sell my soul by sharing the 'accepted' part to make a buck. I'll regret it. I'm speaking only for myself now. You'll make your own decisions. I'm nobody… yet," I said with a wicked grin. "Nobody cares who I sleep with. But when the time comes, I'll be honest. I'm a terrible liar, anyway. I should have known denying myself wouldn't work. It's been three months since I swore off guys for good. And then you came along."

"What will your band say? Terry won't like it."

"Now I'm coming out for sure," I exclaimed, rolling my eyes. "Terry won't be around by then. In the meantime, I'll stay on the DL for your sake. In case you decide the closet is your home," I teased, reaching out to tweak his ear.

"We'll see what happens," Will responded, swatting my hand away. "So we're still on?"

I nodded, strangely turned on by his bashful smile. My dick twitched in my jeans, and suddenly I needed more. I pushed my guitar behind my back again and cupped his neck to bring him close to me. Our noses brushed and our lips touched. Not a true kiss, more of a whisper. His instrument between us did nothing to sever the connection. I felt in sync with him. We weren't playing music and we weren't naked. But the moment felt intimate.

Until I opened my mouth.

"Right. Lipstick, fishnets, and sequins optional."

Will threw his head back and laughed. "You want me to dress up?"

"Just be yourself. If you feel like it, it's cool by me."

"Thanks." His eyes sparkled with a sort of gratitude that made me feel ten feet tall. "Come on. Let's get to work."

"All right. I started something new, but it's pretty raw." I strummed a couple chords and sang a line I'd memorized from my notes. "'Golden brown, green-eyed boy or a platinum blonde with a....' What's next? I could add fishnet hose and a—"

"Is this about me?"

"Maybe. Yes. Probably."

"Hmph. My eyes are brown. Not green. Why not write about the city or—?"

"Too predictable. And your eyes aren't just brown. They're golden and green, like a cat's. My words. No arguing. Anyway, I'd like to keep it upbeat, kind of like—"

"Like 'Brown Eyed Girl'? You aren't writing a same-sex version of that classic, are you?" he asked, obviously amused. I had the feeling he wasn't sure how he got stuck with me and was surprised to find he didn't mind so much after all.

"Hey, that's not a bad idea." I pointedly ignored his amused snort as I strummed a few rough chords.

Will smirked and playfully improvised a catchy hook. It was eerily close to what I was trying to inexpertly play.

"Exactly! That's it!" I paced while I tried a few new chords and hummed along.

He immediately reworked them and added the first portion, then played the short melody from the top. I tried to keep up with him, but he was further ahead than me. Will could hear things I couldn't, and he wasn't afraid to bend the notes to fit. He was musically fearless. I listened in awe for a few minutes, then struck my hand over the strings on my guitar to get his attention. He was becoming consumed, and I had to ask one more question before he got lost in the music and took me with him.

"Hey, stop for a second. I was gonna ask if—"

"If what?"

"How about a redo? Let's go to the movies. Two guys, no shame. Take back the night your folks found out you were a gay boy and make it yours. What do you say?"

Will stared at me with his mouth open. When I set my hand on his chin, he smiled, then looked down at his strings to hide the faint pink blush on his cheeks.

"I'd love to."

I nodded with a nonchalance I didn't feel and willed the heat on my own face to subside as I listened carefully to him coax a new sound from his instrument. I couldn't say why, but the moment felt like a beginning. A blank page, no words, no music, no real expectation. Anything could happen… or nothing. Starting now.

Chapter 6

"WHAT DO you think about changing the drums at the end of 'Lost Boy' to something like this? Hello? Earth to Rand."

"Oh. Sorry. Sounds good." I glanced up at Tim from my perch on a stool in the practice studio to indicate I was listening, then back down at my guitar. The band had been together all afternoon practicing. Maybe the meeting a couple weeks ago had helped because I thought we sounded pretty damn good. We weren't making as many mistakes on songs we should have been able to play in our sleep, which left us time to work on newer material. I loved the creative process. I wrote most of the lyrics, but everyone in the band collaborated musically. It was invigorating to hear my friends' interpretations to my words. Tim and Cory laid the backbeat while I worked on rhythm, and Terry…. Well, he tried.

Tim set his sticks aside and crossed the room to straddle the stool Terry had just vacated. He and Cory left together to hang out with Holly and Leah. The girls had come by earlier to hang out. I never minded playing to an audience, even if it was tiny. What I did mind was the weird way Terry baited me when they'd walked into the studio. He made a point of fondling Leah's breasts and cupping her ass while he checked her fillings. I wasn't a prude by any means, but there was something more there than a guy simply greeting a girl he liked. It seemed contrived.

And then there was Leah. She was always somewhere near me. It was innocent in a way. Her conversation was never overtly flirtatious, but there was something in the way she looked at me with slightly parted lips and meaningful stares that made it clear she wouldn't mind having *my* hands all over her ass. Maybe Terry noticed and hoped taunting me would get under my skin. I wanted to say it wasn't working… but it was. Not because I was jealous, but because I hated the distraction. As long as we were playing, I could tune out the background nonsense. When the music stopped, I knew it wouldn't be long before I went bat-shit crazy. Hopefully I'd find a replacement before then.

"What's on your mind?"

I refocused on Tim's concerned frown and offered my friend a sly grin. "Are you worried about me, honey?"

"I always worry, shnookums. Whatcha doin' tonight? Want to come to Boots with me later?"

I snorted and shook my head. "No thanks. I'm busy."

"Doing?"

"Something."

"Mystery isn't your style, Rand. What's going on? Did you meet someone?"

I ran my calloused fingers over the strings of my guitar softly as I tried to think of a riff to make Tim laugh and get him off my case. Nothing came to mind. My fingers ached and my head was elsewhere. I snuck a peek at my watch and stood up. I had plenty of time to go home, shower, and get across town to meet Will, but I was antsy.

"Let me rephrase. I know you met someone."

I set my guitar in its case and looked up. "Oh really. How?"

"You're distracted. Not in a bad way, though."

I huffed a short laugh and started to brush him off with a flippant reply, but I stopped. I could use a little perspective from a friend I trusted.

"Have you ever been on a real date before?"

"Of course. Remember Jenna? She was super old-fashioned." Tim cleared his throat, then pitched his voice in a woman's falsetto, "'Pick me up at six. Our dinner reservation is at six fifteen, so we can make the nine p.m. movie, and maybe if I'm up to it, I'll pencil you in for sex.' Geesh, by the time it was eleven, I was barely interested."

I chuckled appreciatively. "Poor Timmy."

"Who's the lucky girl who got Rand O'Malley to agree to a date? She must be hot."

Oh. Right. I hadn't gotten around to talking to Tim or Cory without Terry or Mike around, but... now was as good a time as any.

"He is."

Tim stared at me with his mouth wide open. When the incredulous silence went on two seconds longer than I could stand, I reached for my jacket. So much for share time.

"He? What the hell?"

"It's not serious. Don't get excited."

"But you're going on a date?"

"Kinda. Yes. What do you know about dates? Like dinner, movies, and stuff. I've never really done it."

Tim threw back his head and guffawed merrily.

"Never mind." I grabbed my beanie from my pocket and pulled it on before picking up my guitar.

"Wait! Sorry, but you sound so... serious. And maybe a little nervous too. Who is he, Rand?"

I let the silence stretch before answering. "Will. My guitar teacher."

"Oh. I thought he was a band geek. From what I've heard, he doesn't seem like your type."

"What you've heard from whom? Whatever. Forget I asked. See ya." My hand was on the doorknob when he came barreling at me.

"Whoa! I'm sorry. He must be special if you're this nervous about going out to dinner or—"

"The movies."

"The movies? You never go to the movies. My seven-year-old nephew can sit still in a theater longer than you can. What's up with you? This must be one bigass crush for you to sit two hours in the dark when sex isn't part of the equation."

I leaned against the door and observed Tim for a moment, deciding to let his teasing remark slide. "I like him. A lot. He's... sweet. Different. Kind of innocent but interesting. And he's easily the best musician I've ever met in my life."

"Oookay. But the movies?"

"It's a long story. Do you have any words of wisdom to add to 'it's boring as hell 'cause you may or may not get some at the end'?"

Tim stared at me for a second before shaking his head. "Uh... no. I mean, it can be nice too. I've never dated a man, though. I guess I always assumed guys don't date. We meet up, hang out, and if it's working, we move on to the physical stuff. Honestly, the word *date* makes me queasy. But what do I know?"

"Obviously nothing."

I neatly dodged his halfhearted punch and slung my guitar case over my shoulder.

"Have fun, sweetie. And bring him around sometime. Maybe he can show Terry some tricks."

I stopped in my tracks and shook my head. "Actually no. Don't say anything about him to Terry. Will doesn't like him any more than I do. Terry is temporary and—"

Tim closed his eyes and let out a long, exasperated sigh. "Rand, Terry isn't temporary. We need him."

"No, we don't. We only need him until the Brooklyn show, but that's it. He's bad energy. One minute I could almost be convinced he's trying, and the next, he purposely baits me. We have a glaring personnel issue here. Stop fooling yourself. I've asked Mike to be on the lookout for a possible replacement."

"God, you're infuriating!"

"Just keep quiet about Will for now. Got it?"

"Got it. Do you need any more pointers?" he teased.

"Nah. I think I'll be all right, Timmy." I gave him a cocky grin as I pulled on my gloves.

I was mindful of Tim's watchful gaze as I swaggered down the hallway toward the elevator with the supreme confidence of a man who didn't have a care in the world. But the second I stepped inside, I tore the gloves off and shook my clammy hands. Fuck. Who was I trying to kid?

WE DECIDED to meet at an art house near campus known for showcasing foreign, classic, and offbeat indie films. I was relieved when Will said they were screening animated shorts, aka cartoons, that night. I took for granted the word *short* meant I wouldn't be crawling out of my skin and checking my cell for the time every few minutes. Tim was right. I didn't have the attention span required to sit still for long stretches. I couldn't believe I'd suggested a movie in the first place, but the gesture was what counted. I should have just asked if he felt like grabbing something to eat. Dinner would have been a safe bet, but I was equally lost there. I knew a few pubs and pizza spots but nothing special. At least nothing I could afford. No wonder I never dated… men or women. It was too damn stressful.

And going to the movies was like being tortured in the dark. I held a tub of popcorn on my knee and pondered stupid things like the etiquette of sharing snacks. Was I supposed to hand it over every once in a while, or was I the official keeper of the popcorn? If the atmosphere lent itself to direct questioning, I would have just asked, but I was too self-conscious.

And that wasn't normal. I felt a heightened sense of awareness about the oddest things. Like the man sitting in front of me wearing his baseball cap at a sideways angle. The outline of his stupid hat was in my peripheral vision and was an inch shy of impinging my view of the screen. Not that I cared. The annoying baseball cap and the ten-pound tub of popcorn were minor irritations. If nothing else, they kept me from spinning about the guy sitting next to me.

Will had met me after filling in for another intern at the theater. He was flushed from racing downtown to make the showtime. His cheeks were red from the cold and something else I couldn't quite identify. Maybe rouge. Something was different about him, but I couldn't tell. I glanced sideways and tapped his knee, silently asking if he wanted popcorn. It gave me an excuse to stare at him for a moment without seeming creepy. He looked over at me with a smile and shook his head. No glasses. That was it. I wondered why he wasn't wearing them. There was something else too. I stared unseeing at the screen and waited what I thought was a decent amount of time before letting my gaze wander back to him.

"What?" he whispered, leaning over the armrest.

"Why aren't you wearing your glasses?"

"I'm wearing contacts."

"Oh. Want some popcorn?"

"No thanks. You just asked."

I turned forward again. Eyeliner. He was wearing makeup. And there was something in his hair. Maybe gel. Huh. My gaze darted left. I was desperate for more information. I had zero interest in the avant-garde animated film the audience found hilarious. I reached for my water bottle and took a small drink, then passed it to him.

"Want some?"

"No thanks."

"You sure?"

"Positive."

The guy with the baseball cap turned in his seat. "Shh!"

I scowled at the back of his head and maturely resisted the urge to kick his chair. Will gave me a sharp look and put a calming hand on my wrist. He probably wondered what the hell my problem was. I was so fidgety. All I wanted was a chance to figure my date out. Was the makeup a theater thing? Was he wearing cologne? He smelled good.

When I shifted in my seat again like a kid on a serious sugar high, he pulled my sleeve and twisted his hand to hold mine. I was taken aback by the sweetness of the gesture.

My heart swelled, making me feel light-headed but somehow grounded. Like I was a balloon and he was the string tethering me to earth. I took a deep breath and willed myself to remain in the moment. To not overthink or act on impulse. It worked. Until he caressed my palm with his thumb in a sweet, soothing motion. That simple touch sent my pulse skyrocketing.

I shifted in my chair to get closer, forgetting I was the purveyor of the popcorn. As I leaned into him, my left knee dislodged the box from its perch and popcorn exploded. Everywhere. Pieces flew in the air, showering us and a few unlucky bystanders. I lunged for the almost-empty tub and knocked my water bottle from the cup holder. It began a slow roll down the cement floor, picking up steam as it cascaded from the third-to-last row all the way to the front of the theater.

"Shit." I winced as the full, jumbo-sized plastic container hit the wall.

"Now might be a good time to make a phone call too," snarked the dude in the baseball cap.

I held my tongue, knowing I deserved his scorn. Will was the one I couldn't read. He sat motionless with his lips pursed in what was either irritation or amusement. I just couldn't tell in the dark. His shoulders convulsed as he nudged my elbow.

"Wanna get out of here?"

"Fuck yes." I sighed in relief, not bothering to whisper.

Perturbed moviegoers gave us dirty looks as we scrambled out of our middle-row seats and headed for the exit. I blinked in the lobby light and gave Will a sheepish, lopsided grin.

He busted up laughing and shook his head in disbelief. "Wow. You don't get out much, huh?"

I made a comical face and shrugged. "Sorry. I'm a little out of practice at—" I waved my hand around me as if encompassing the movie theater and, hell, life in general.

Will chuckled as he dug his hat and gloves from his coat pockets. "Come on. I know a place nearby that serves amazing pizza and cheap wine. Sound good?"

"Very."

WILL LED the way to a nondescript eatery off of Sixth Avenue in the heart of Greenwich Village. This part of town played up its bohemian-chic vibe, but the fact was, it was really expensive to live or even eat here. It was home to a number of world-renowned restaurants, many of which enjoyed regular glowing write-ups in foodie magazines. However, there were still a few family-owned bistros to be found nestled between the well-known posh establishments. Johnny's was one of those places. It was tiny. As in there were maybe twelve tables squished so close together you were sure to hear a good portion of your neighbors' conversations. Every table had a red-and-white checked tablecloth and an empty bottle of Chianti that had a second life as a candleholder. It was warm and inviting. But packed. There was no hope of being seated without waiting for a long time.

"Wait here. I'll be right back." Will squeezed through the cramped entry and waltzed with confidence toward the kitchen.

I watched as he hugged a small, thin, young man with jet-black hair wearing an apron. They engaged in a short conversation involving a lot of gesturing toward the tables. I was too far away to catch details, but I clearly heard his friend squeal before he was shushed by another employee. I shoved my hands farther into my coat pockets for something to do. That jumpy feeling was coming over me again. I hoped Will hurried it up before the desire to move overrode reason.

"Benny is clearing a table in the front for us. He said it will be five minutes or less," Will whispered as he shrugged off his coat and removed his gloves.

I nodded and leaned into him, snatching his beanie from his head. "Who's Benny again?"

Will held out his hand, wordlessly admonishing me with a look that said "Cut it out and hand it over." I started to but changed my mind at the last second and pocketed his hat with mine in my coat. I grinned at Will's exasperated huff. He'd opened his mouth to say something when he was jostled from behind. I caught his elbow to steady him and took advantage of the close quarters to wrap my arm around his waist. He looked up at me in surprise. Hell, I was surprised too, but I didn't release him. I stared at him, trying to figure out what it was that—

It was the makeup. Maybe. I couldn't be sure, but I knew he was wearing more than I'd realized at first glance. I studied the black eyeliner and the foundation covering his sweet freckles. His lips were pink and glossy. And there was a hint of glitter under his eyes. He held my gaze with a bold grin that made my heart skip. I wasn't sure if the mysterious show of new confidence was cosmetically enhanced, but it was sexy as hell. He still looked masculine but with an edge I really liked. I licked my upper lip and gulped when he reached for my hand. I felt connected and aware of him at that moment as we stood in an overcrowded restaurant with his fingers threaded through mine. When his friend called his name from the tiny table for two at the front of the restaurant, he dropped my hand and the moment was gone.

"Your timing was perfect, honey. I have to get back to the kitchen, but I'll tell Maria to be sweet to you. Introductions?" Will's friend batted his eyelashes as he held out his hand.

"I'm Rand. Nice to meet you," I said.

"I'm Benny. And I'm about to faint." He shook my hand and fanned himself with the other theatrically. "How could you leave out details like he's gorgeous? Oh my!"

I threw my head back and laughed at the outrageous flirtation. It was too over-the-top to be taken as anything other than funny. Benny peered at me speculatively with one brow raised. I didn't mind the scrutiny. It gave me a chance to size him up too. He was small and lean with light brown eyes and golden skin that offset his dark hair and the electric blue highlights in his bangs that I hadn't noticed from afar. His soft features gave him a feminine look he certainly played up with campy affections… and, yeah, lots of eyeliner.

"Benny!" Will narrowed his eyes at his friend meaningfully.

"Fine. I'm going, I'm going. I'll send over a bottle of Chianti and bread for you boys pronto. Enjoy!" Benny flashed a wide smile and turned with a graceful pivot.

I chuckled when Will covered his face with the menu. I tapped on the worn plastic cover until he lowered it. "Sorry. Benny's kind of… fabulous."

"I like him. He thinks I'm gorgeous." I waggled my eyebrows, then sat back when our waitress came by with water and a bottle of wine. We listened politely to the specials, nodding in faux interest until she left us alone.

I stared at Will over the rim of my wineglass and nudged his knee under the table. The cozy setup for two tucked in the corner next to the window gave the illusion of privacy and, yes, romance. Add Dean Martin singing "Volare" in the background over the din of conversation and the night had turned into something almost magical. A far cry from sharing popcorn and watching cartoons.

"Cheers."

I clinked my glass against his and took a sip, keeping my gaze on him. I hoped to be treated to more of this sexy, confident side of Will. The guy who yanked me from the movie theater, then commandeered a prime table at a popular restaurant on a Friday night reminded me of his alter ego in a pink dress, hailing a cab with attitude. I saw glimpses of him behind a guitar but never this strong.

Will took a small sip of wine and smiled as he set his glass down. "The chicken parmesan is great if you're tired of pizza and pasta."

"I'll keep it in mind. How did we get here?" I furrowed my brow and reached for the bread the waitress placed at my elbow. "One minute I'm throwing popcorn at everyone watching cartoons and the next, I'm sitting in an Italian bistro sipping Chianti. Life is weird."

Will chuckled appreciatively. "It is. This seemed like a better option. I'm just glad it worked out. I was with Benny at the theater, and he mentioned he was filling in for his cousin here tonight, so… I took a chance."

"I'm glad you did. How do you know him?"

"We've been friends since our freshman year, and now we intern together. Benny's in production and set design. He's very talented. He designs costumes and sews like a pro, but today they asked us to help the makeup artist's assistant." He gave a short laugh before continuing. "I can't complain. It's better than being sent to get coffee for the crew. Again. Anyway, it's why I was running late tonight. I didn't have a chance to go home and clean up first."

He twisted the stem of his glass between his fingers as he lowered his head slightly and contemplated me. I wasn't sure what he was looking for, but I decided not to guess. Will was throwing me off my game tonight. I was in danger of falling far behind if I didn't start asking questions.

"So that's why you're wearing makeup?"

He grinned. "Yeah. Benny did mine before they put us to work doing some of the chorus line. It was fun. A little stressful but fun."

"You look good." Will eyed me warily as he picked up his glass. "I mean it."

"Thanks."

"I can't see your freckles, which is a bummer. But your eyes look bigger. More golden. You look… interesting. Different."

Will smiled, then looked up with a start when our waitress came to take our orders. I was hungry but not in the mood to study the extensive menu. I ordered spaghetti and meatballs, thinking it was probably a safe bet.

"Spaghetti?" Will mocked.

"What's wrong with spaghetti?"

"Nothing at all. I figured you'd order something more… exciting."

"I get enough excitement. I don't need exciting food. You can give me a bite of yours if you feel sorry for me, though."

"Deal." Will flashed one of those crazy, radiant smiles that made me wonder what the hell we'd been talking about.

I coughed nervously and reached for my water. Fuck, I was being weird. I struggled to get my bearings and think of a topic that wouldn't make me blush like a teenage girl.

"So your friend works here too?" Lame.

Thankfully Will didn't seem to think so. He inclined his head and leaned forward, resting his elbows on the table. "His family owns Johnny's. Believe it or not, this place has been here for a hundred years. I think his great-uncle runs it now. He told me it's tradition for everyone in the family to work here in some capacity in their lifetime. He's only helping out tonight, but he's done everything from wash dishes to wait tables."

"The food business is good character-building work. At least that's what I tell myself when I drag my ass out of bed to get to the bagel shop by five thirty fucking a.m. After my first sip of George's crappy coffee, I think one day when I'm standing onstage accepting my tenth Grammy award, I'll look back on this time in my life and be grateful it taught me that hard work and discipline matter." I gave a half laugh. "One day I won't be cold all the fucking time, and I won't sweat the cost of taking a taxi when the thought of riding the subway sounds unappealing."

"You're gonna live the high life, eh?"

I grinned and raised my wineglass. "Yep! I don't really think about money or fame when I'm doing what I love. It's only when I'm doing tedious things that I'm reminded there is a method to my madness."

"So you aren't just crazy?"

"All artists are a little crazy, Will. Even you. Tell me something wild and crazy I'd never guess about you."

Will frowned and shook his head. "I'm not wild. At all."

"You're wearing makeup, babe. That makes you at least a little wild," I astutely observed.

He cocked his head thoughtfully and smiled ruefully. "I s'pose you're right. Maybe the craziest thing about me is that occasionally I like it."

"You like wearing makeup?"

"Yes... and other things."

Our salads were delivered before I could ask any more questions. Once we were alone again, I didn't know where to begin.

"Other things?"

"Yeah." He took a bite of his salad and glanced out the window as though he hadn't just casually dropped a kinky conversation grenade. I let my fork clatter noisily on my plate and stared at him until he looked my way. "What?"

"You can't tell me things like that and not...." I waved my hand in the air expressively before deciding to just speak plainly. "Tell me everything. Every little kink. Let's get this out in the open."

"It's not really kinky. Just... different."

"My imagination runs at full speed 24/7, Will. I'm having this flashback to you wearing fishnet stockings, and when I imagine seeing your bare ass through that mesh.... Fuck! I'm getting hard right now. Let's get the torture over with so I can process this rationally. In other words, I'd like my brain to do the thinking here. Not my dick."

Will burst into laughter. I scowled and resumed stabbing my lettuce, if only to give my hands something to do. He bumped my knee under the table and let his rest against mine as he observed me. He dabbed at the corner of his mouth with his napkin, then leaned forward with a sigh.

"When I was a kid, I used to sneak into my mom's closet and try on her high heels. She had an outstanding collection, and there was something about wearing them, even for a few minutes, that made me feel...."

"Pretty?" I ventured.

"Maybe, but more like... adventurous. Whimsical. Something I'd have a hard time explaining if I got caught. The combination of doing something relatively harmless that I knew would be considered mischievous was tantalizing. I started with her heels and ventured to her makeup. But makeup was trickier because it wasn't easy to remove quickly. I could only do it when my parents were out of town and my sister was preoccupied. She was always a tattletale."

"So you're saying wearing makeup and heels appealed to your sense of general mischief. Like a peaceful 'fuck you' to conformity?"

Will chuckled. "Maybe. My mom never caught me. I used to buy clothes and shoes from consignment shops a few towns away with money I made teaching guitar and piano when I was a teenager. Freaky, huh?"

I shook my head with a wry grin. "I wouldn't say freaky, just different. But not in a bad way. Did you wish you were a girl? Is that why—"

"No, that isn't it. I've probably known I was gay since I was eleven. I did my best to not say or do anything to give myself away, but denying it didn't seem to change the fact every crush I had was on a boy. My palms used to sweat like crazy when Felix Calder stood next to me on the drum line. He was tall, dark, and dreamy."

"Yeah, yeah. Keep going," I said irritably.

Will chuckled. "Well, there's nothing much to tell. The bottom line isn't that I wished I was female. It was more about wanting to be someone else for a while. Like an actor in a play. I didn't have to be William Sanders, the skinny geek with glasses. I could be someone special."

"Didn't you feel special for your talent?"

He pursed his lips thoughtfully. "No. Just different. As silly as it seems, being in a disguise, even a flimsy one like a little makeup, is freeing every once in a while. I like it."

"I do too. It's sexy. And now we better move on to other topics before I spontaneously combust over here."

Will gave me a mischievous smile just as the server arrived with our dinners. "So… how'd you like the movie?" he teased, picking up his fork.

"Low blow, Will."

"Okay. How about food preferences? Other than bagels… what's your favorite go-to snack or meal?"

"It used to be popcorn, but I ruined that tonight too," I said with a dramatic sigh. I waited for Will's laughter to subside before adding, "Now I think spaghetti is my favorite."

The silly remark was meant to be flippant, but as we stared at each other over the candlelight with Frank Sinatra singing New York's praises in the background, it didn't sound like the throwaway line I intended. It sounded like something an infatuated adolescent would say to his crush.

I had a flashback to Sunday morning at Will's when I'd told him to follow my lead, like my three extra years on the planet gave me greater wisdom. What a joke. I was no expert. We were equals. I'd never felt a rush of heat and longing from just holding hands with someone. I'd never been content to sit and talk for hours asking "get to know you" questions that weren't centered around music. As the spaghetti conversation morphed into other Italian foods and restaurants we'd tried in the city, I realized I was as inexperienced as Will. I felt as though I was fumbling in the dark with a map I couldn't see.

WE TOOK the subway back to the East Village after dinner. The temperature had dropped another few degrees, making even a short train ride feel like a nice break from the frigid air. We sat side by side on the plastic bench with our thighs glued as we traded stories about childhood pets. Well, I did most of the talking, but Will seemed amused, so I embellished the tale of Lucy the lazy Labrador who was a well-known sneak-attack food stealer.

"I always got blamed, but it was usually Lucy's fault," I grumbled, adjusting my beanie as a freezing wind hit us when we emerged onto Houston. "And I'm walking you home. No arguing."

"I'm sure it was."

"What?"

"Lucy's fault."

"Didn't you hear what I said?"

"You're walking me home."

"Yeah."

"You're coming inside too, right?"

When we stopped at the corner to wait for the light, I gave him a lopsided smile and kissed his cold lips. "Yeah."

THE THREE-BLOCK walk to Will's place seemed to take forever. By unspoken agreement we made sure some body part was in constant contact. Shoulders, arms, and gloved fingers brushed as we speed-walked in an effort to ward off the chill and finally reach our destination. The minute we stepped into the lobby of his building, I gave up all pretense of playing it cool. I was horny as hell and had been for hours. I pulled Will against me and crashed my mouth over his. I did my best to soften the connection so it was more like a kiss than an assault, but when he groaned and threw his arms around my neck, my tenuous hold slipped. I plunged my tongue in his mouth as I held his head steady. My cock throbbed in my jeans, begging for release. I wanted everything all at once. I kept a steady chant in my brain, reminding myself not to move too fast or take more than he was ready to give. But it was really fucking hard.

"Upstairs," Will whispered, pulling me toward the narrow staircase.

We climbed the stairs to the third floor hand in hand. When we reached the landing, I wrapped my arms around him from behind and molded my chest to his back. He turned his head sideways to meet my mouth as I alternately bit and kissed his neck, jaw, and finally his lips. He twisted in my hold and sealed his lips over mine. We made out like a couple of teenagers until we were both gasping for air.

"I'll um… open the door," he panted.

I adjusted my cock and nodded, hoping he'd hurry. I was desperate to be naked and horizontal. I caged him between my arms and tilted my hips against him, making sure he could feel how hard I was through the layers of clothing between us. My intent was to give him a glimpse of what we could be doing with no clothes and hopefully spur him into action. But when he spun to face me and hooked his right leg around my left and grabbed my ass, everything went a little blurry. I heard a pained-sounding growl and belatedly realized it was me. The need to consume and devour threatened to overtake reason. I had to fucking pull it together. I pushed away from the door and studied Will's swollen lips and beautiful eyes, looking for a trace of caution or maybe even fear. There was none. He was as strung out as me. I leaned forward and licked his bottom lip, then bit it.

"Inside," I said in a low, gravelly tone.

Will nodded and turned to give the sticky lock his full attention.

The second the door was closed behind us, he was on me like an octopus. His arms snaked around my neck, his chest was fused to mine, and one of his legs was hiked around my ass. I kissed his jaw and his neck and gently untangled us.

"Slow down, baby," I whispered, licking a corner of his mouth. "We have plenty of time."

Will blinked and nodded furiously. He turned on the overhead light, shrugged off his jacket, and threw his hat somewhere on the other side of the room. Then he started working on the buttons on his shirt. I was caught between amusement at his show of exuberance and sheer lust. I didn't want to start putting up roadblocks when it was easy to tell this was the first time he'd really felt free to do and be who he was… an extraordinary, sexy gay man eager to test his power. On the other hand, I also knew I had to do something to keep us from careening toward an early finish line. With every piece of clothing he tossed carelessly aside and every inch of skin he revealed, I was in serious danger of losing the ability to speak.

I gulped and held up my hand. He offered a shy smile before moving closer until I could feel his breath on my lips and see the blatant desire in his gaze. I'd opened my mouth to say fuck knows what when he leaned in and pressed a tender kiss on my chin.

"Are you having second thoughts?" he asked in a husky tone I'd never heard before.

"Hell no."

"I didn't think so." Will pushed my jacket off my shoulders and yanked my sweater over my head. "You have too many clothes on."

"I know, but we should slow down and—"

"Rand?"

I swallowed and inclined my head. Speech was no longer a feasible means of communication for me. He began the tedious chore of unbuttoning my shirt as he continued, "Slow is fine, but it's all right to turn it up a notch. I won't break. I promise."

I pulled him against me. We groaned in unison when our bare chests collided. I ran my hands along his spine, then bit his shoulder before reaching down to fumble with his belt buckle and zipper. I slid my hands under the elastic of his briefs and squeezed his sweet, bare ass. Just touching him made me light-headed and hungry for more.

"Take off your jeans and get in bed. It's freezing in here."

I toed off my shoes and quickly undressed. I was working on my socks when I noticed Will had stopped and was staring at me with his mouth wide open. Actually, he was looking at my junk, not at me. That immature, adolescent side of me I hadn't quite shaken resurfaced. I gave him a lascivious sideways glance as I held my thick cock for him to ogle. I didn't know why I did stupid shit like that. His wide eyes and the instant blush I knew wasn't from cosmetics made me feel guilty. I didn't want to tease. I wanted him to relax and enjoy how freaking amazing it felt to be with someone who wanted you as much as you wanted them.

"Sorry. I get a little goofy sometimes," I said with chagrin.

Will bit his bottom lip and gave a half laugh. "I noticed."

He didn't retreat or shy away from me. If anything, he seemed more determined. I reached for his left nipple and grazed my thumb over the sensitive flesh. He made a whimpering sound and leaned into my touch.

"Bed."

"Yeah." He turned toward the futon and pulled back the covers. I squeezed my dick and closed my eyes for a heartbeat when I saw the generous tent in his briefs. Exercising patience wasn't going to be easy.

I waited for him to crawl under the duvet and scoot toward the wall to make room for me. The futon was smallish. Maybe closer in size to a full rather than a queen-size mattress. On a cold winter night, it was the perfect size to share body heat. I lay down and immediately pulled him on top of me, loving the sensation of being burrowed in a cocoon with a sexy man in underwear. I snapped the elastic playfully as I buried my head under his chin, snuggling as close as possible.

"These need to come off."

"Hmm. I should probably turn off the light too."

"No. I need to see you. Light stays. Underwear goes." I bit his jaw, then licked it better as I hooked my fingers under the thin layer of cotton and lowered his briefs over his ass.

"Oh my God."

I didn't say a word but my breath caught when our naked cocks brushed. *Oh my God* was right. I pulled back far enough to grip us both with one hand.

"You feel so good," I said before biting his chin.

Will set his hand on our cocks and began stroking. Up and down. Slow but firm.

"Don't be too gentle. Harder. Like this." I moved my hand in time with my words, fluctuating between a tentative hold to something a hell of a lot rougher. The little grunting noises he made went straight to my dick. I tilted my hips upward, searching for friction.

"I want—"

"What do you want, baby? More?" I purred in his ear. I licked the shell before nibbling his earlobe.

He moaned as he rolled to his side and opened his legs wider. I nudged his inner thigh and fondled his balls.

"Yes. More."

My vision clouded when he closed his fist in a sure grip around my cock and stroked me rhythmically. I captured his mouth, then sucked at his tongue while I jacked him. I gathered precum dripping at his slit and rubbed it over the head, twisting my wrist and changing the tempo. Will arched his back and pulled at my hair with his free hand. His tongue glided over mine sensuously. He was on fire. Needy and frenetic. But I didn't want him to come from a hand job. Not when he was clearly telling me he wanted more.

I shoved my knee between his legs and rolled him onto his back. His eyes widened as I drew his hands over his head and ground my rigid length against him.

I licked his jaw as I rocked my hips. "I want to taste you."

"Yes."

I lifted myself over him and planted a firm kiss on his lips, then licked my way down his smooth torso. I stopped to trace his left nipple with the tip of my tongue, then sucked the pebbled flesh until he cried out. I gave the right side the same treatment, relishing the fevered sound of my name as my lover writhed under me and pulled my hair. I massaged his ribs, then splayed my hands over his flat stomach and licked a trail south. His leaking prick nudged at my chin, begging for attention, but I ignored it. I kissed the sensitive skin below his belly button, letting my stubbled cheek graze his shaft as I pushed his legs open wide. He lifted his hips, inviting me to do more, take more.

There was something really fucking sexy about being under the covers buried between Will's thighs. Every smell seemed more potent, every noise seemed to echo. It felt safe and warm and very close to perfect. I breathed in his scent and then flattened my tongue at the base of his cock and slowly licked my way up to the tip, then down again.

"Oh—fuck, that feels so good."

I stroked his heavy member and looked up at him, letting my tongue rest at his slit. "Watch me suck your cock, baby."

He gulped and leaned up on his elbows before pushing the covers over my shoulders. I smiled, knowing my crooked grin probably looked more dangerous than reassuring. I couldn't help it. I was in my element. There was only one thing I liked more than sucking cock—okay, two things. Having my own dick sucked or buried inside my lover was better, but I was in no hurry. This was heaven. Giving pleasure, making sure to apply the perfect amount of pressure as I licked, sucked, and stroked his beautiful dick was bliss. I was caught up in the sweet sounds he made as he alternately murmured my name or tugged on my hair. I changed the angle to take more of him and sucked even harder. Will pumped his hips upward and cried out.

"Rand... I'm gonna cum."

I glanced up at him with slick lips and sex-hazed eyes and tried to refocus.

"Do it. Cum in my mouth. I want to taste you. I want to lick you clean and—"

"Oh fuck!"

The first spurt of cum hit my chin as he convulsed under me. I didn't think twice. I swallowed him whole, sucking and licking furiously until the last spasm passed. When he went completely still, I released him with an exaggerated pop and rose over him. I tilted my head and observed him for a moment.

"C'mere," he said in a husky tone.

I lowered myself over him and kissed him softly. I felt his smile against my mouth and huffed in surprise when he pushed at my shoulder so I'd roll onto my back. He scrambled to climb on top of me and straddle my thighs, either unaware or oblivious of the enticing press of my cock against his ass. I sent up a quick prayer I could exercise some serious self-restraint before looking up at him. He had a postorgasmic, serene expression on his face.

"You liked?" I asked, doing my best to keep the smirk out of my voice.

Will threw his head back and laughed, a gorgeous, melodic sound I wished I could record. He was pure music. And sexier than hell. When he wriggled his ass, I had a feeling he knew he was torturing me, and he enjoyed it. I splayed my hands up his sides and over his abs. Will wasn't muscular by any means but he was toned. And this growing confidence gave him a lithe fluidity that made my mouth water when he undulated his hips and looked down at me with a cocky grin.

"I liked. My turn." He reached behind him and grabbed my shaft, then held it against his crack. The covers had fallen around his waist, leaving us exposed to the cooler air.

"Go for it." I smacked his ass once, then folded my arms behind my head with deceptive nonchalance.

Will cocked his head and licked his lips but didn't move. I was afraid he'd changed his mind until he shifted off my torso and knelt at my side. He palmed my dick gently as though studying its size, shape, and weight. Unbelievably I didn't utter a word. I let him explore at his leisure. He ran his fingers along my length and his thumb over the wide mushroom head, smearing precum in a lazy, circular motion. I gritted my teeth, willing myself to shut up and enjoy. When he lifted his thumb to his lips, I nearly came unglued. I watched in fascination as he darted his tongue to lick at the clear, sticky fluid.

"Holy fuck! Come here. Kiss me."

"What? Do you want to taste?"

"You're doing this on purpose, aren't you? I'm so hard it hurts, and you're licking at my dick like it's a fucking lollipop! Do it like you mean it," I growled.

"Okay, but which part should I do first? Do you want me to kiss you or do you want to taste this?" He swiped his thumb over my slit and set it on my bottom lip. "Or should I just suck your dick? I've never done it before, but I'll try to do what you did to me. That was amazing."

I grabbed his wrist and waited for him to look at me. "You never…?"

"No."

Thankfully I had the good sense to acknowledge his honesty with a short nod and keep my mouth shut. I sucked on his thumb before pulling him against me to thrust my tongue down his throat. He made a funny mewling sound as he melted against me with a sigh. I pushed at his shoulder a moment later and pointed south.

"I think we've covered everything except this," I said lasciviously.

Will chuckled. His eyes twinkled with humor and lust as he moved down my body and knelt between my thighs. I bent my knees and opened my legs wide to give him room to work. He smiled sweetly, then leaned forward to taste me. He licked one side of my shaft, then the other. He swirled his tongue over the head and along my slit, then repeated the motion a few more times before he opened his mouth and swallowed me whole. Finally. It was too much, too soon. He choked and coughed. I ran my fingers through his hair soothingly, though my heart was beating like a drum.

"You don't have to—"

"I want to." He glanced up at me, stroking my shaft in a rhythmic tempo before leaning over to try again.

This time he sucked only the tip into his mouth. He twirled his tongue experimentally, then went a little lower. He pulled back to gauge my reaction and must have been encouraged, because the next time he did it with a confidence that could make me believe sucking dick was his favorite new pastime. I licked my lips and did my best to keep my hands from guiding him or orchestrating his movement. This was his. I was only along for the ride. And fuck, it felt good.

He tightened his grip and stroked as he sucked. He was bold, fearless, and very fucking beautiful. I was mesmerized by this fiercely passionate side of Will. He threw everything he had into the act as though I were a new instrument he was determined to learn and play to perfection. As soon as the thought sprang to mind, I knew I wouldn't last. A telltale tingle at the base of my spine warned me I was approaching the point of no return. The urge to let my hips fly and fuck his mouth was overwhelming. I put a hand on his forehead and pushed him back. He didn't budge. Instead he flicked his tongue at the crown, then licked downward. When he reached my balls, I arched forward and nudged his shoulder with my knee.

"Baby, let go. I'm almost there." My voice sounded strangled, as though he had his hands around my throat while he sucked the life out of me.

Will looked up at me with wild eyes as he gently rolled my balls and bent to taste me one more time. The flash of confidence was my undoing. I came with a roar, clutching at his hair and the sheets as my orgasm hit me like a freight train. I trembled until the last aftershock gave way to a stunning sense of calm.

Will sat back on his knees and wiped at his mouth. I yanked him over me, then rolled him quickly to his back. I stared into his eyes for a moment and then licked the corner of his mouth. He flinched when he saw what I was doing but didn't pull away. I continued down his chin, then drove my tongue between his swollen lips to taste myself. He groaned and wrapped himself around me as I devoured him. When the need for oxygen became a reality, I kissed his nose and forehead and shifted over so we lay side by side with our feet tangled.

I reached for the covers just as he pushed them away. "I should clean up."

"I cleaned you. You're fine. Lie down and stay close. It's cold," I said, patting the spot next to me.

"You licked me. I don't think that counts." His smile told me he wasn't entirely grossed out.

We stared at each other, content to bask in the afterglow. But after a moment, I needed words to anchor me.

"Um, so…." I intended to say something witty or silly to downplay any potential weirdness, but my emotions were strangely close to the surface. I couldn't tell a joke without giving myself away.

"Yes."

"Yes what? You don't know what I was going to say," I commented, resting my hand on his hip.

"You were going to ask if I was okay or maybe if I liked what we just did. Right?" I made a funny face he took as agreement before continuing. "I loved it. Thank you."

I snorted. "Why are you thanking me?"

Will didn't answer right away. He held my gaze, then reached out to smooth a strand of hair behind my ear. "For being patient."

I didn't know how to respond. I let the silence stretch, and this time, was content to let it speak for me.

Chapter 7

THE COLD, harsh winter finally began a slow thaw in late March, giving way to the first hints of spring. Everything seemed to come alive. The city that never slept experienced a palpable revitalization in springtime. There was a surge of energy in the busier than normal streets and a sense that anything was possible. Creatively I'd never felt more inspired. I couldn't write fast enough. Errant melodies came to me at regular intervals. In the shower, on the subway, at the bagel store. I caught George giving me indulgent looks when he heard me singing under my breath as I rang up customers. Everyday life distracted me unless I could find a way to weave music into it. I was constantly humming into my phone to record hooks and refrains so I wouldn't forget them before I could get to the studio or to Will's. I knew I could rely on him to take even a simple few notes and not only remember them, but expand them into the beginnings of something special.

The guy was blessed with a deeper gift for music than I'd first realized. Hell, his first language *was* music. The more time I spent with him, I began to see that Will processed everything rhythmically. His brain seemed to turn words into notes and set a tempo according to his mood. A faraway look would come over him when he played piano or guitar. He could make himself skim the surface while he tried to explain the nuances of changing chords faster, but when he was allowed the freedom to drift creatively, he got lost in his work. I'd never been more in awe of anyone's natural talent. He was a genius.

As much as I admired his skill behind a guitar or a piano, it paled in comparison to what I felt just being with him. Our first "date" was the beginning of something new and a little bewildering. At least to me. I wasn't the type to become consumed with a guy. Or a girl, for that matter. Other than my high school years with Seth, I'd never really had one person I wanted to be with consistently. I'd had one-night stands or fuck buddies. Whatever was happening between Will and me was unprecedented. He was the first person I thought of when I woke up. And I was grateful most mornings I only had to glance over at the pillow next to me to find him. Don't get me wrong, we still had our separate lives. Mine revolved around my band with a few hours thrown in at the bagel shop, and his were at school or with his internship in the theater district. But when we weren't together we were in constant contact. We sent text or voice messages with mini recordings or bits of lyrics like we were lovesick students passing notes in class. It was a quirky way for two oddball artists to communicate.

I wasn't sure what we were doing, but I couldn't get enough. Crawling into his futon to spend hours exploring his body was all I wanted. I loved how his tentative touches gave way to ardent caresses, the way he moaned my name and clawed at my skin when he was about to fall apart. His fiery responsiveness was intoxicating. He looked at me with beguiling wonder when he floated to the surface as though I were a fucking god. And before I could say a word, he was on his knees sucking the life out of me. What he lacked in finesse, he made up in passion. Though truthfully he was a quick study. An incredibly sexy man with a voracious desire for sex. Will occasionally indicated he was ready to take the next step when our sweat-slick bodies moved as one and my dick inevitably nudged his hole. As tempting as it was to grab a condom and lube and bury myself inside him, a niggling fear in the back of my head held me back.

What would happen after he'd checked off every box on his list of firsts? Would we ride out this intense physical connection, part ways amicably, and possibly never see each other again? The thought made me uncharacteristically melancholy. I'd never been here before. And I didn't understand it. He wasn't my type. I usually went for guys, and girls for that matter, with an edgier side. Not sweet, vulnerable types with secrets. Yeah… I was catching on that there was definitely more to Will than he gave away.

So I chose not to worry and just enjoy. It was springtime in a magical city where anything could happen. Including Rand O'Malley falling for a cute, nerdy guy in glasses with an alter ego who wore eyeliner, lip gloss, and sometimes even fishnet hose upon request. Maybe I was acting out of character and maybe this wouldn't last, but for now… it felt good.

If only I felt the same way about my band.

THE MUSIC business moved in fits and starts. It wasn't easy to build momentum and maintain it. Some of the shows we hoped would give us leeway to a bigger break hadn't added up to much. I didn't blame Mike. I understood there was a good deal of luck involved. We'd met with a few record labels and had a couple of kickass shows that, if nothing else, proved we could hold an audience's attention. We expanded our online presence at Mike's suggestion and tried to come up with innovative ways to promote our brand. We were a good band with a great bluesy sound who put on an entertaining show. But I was beginning to wonder if we were truly special. There were so many good acts on the scene. We had to find a way to differentiate ourselves without compromising our sound.

The weak link was Terry. He'd definitely improved and there was no doubt he tried. But you can't fake natural ability, and the sorry fact was… he didn't have it. He was a serviceable guitarist without any flash or pizzazz. It wasn't his fault we hadn't catapulted to instant fame, but my instinct told me he was part of the problem. He should have fit in with Cory, Tim, and I seamlessly. He had the same general style of dress and attitude, but he was aloof. And he still rubbed me the wrong way. Constantly. My mouth was too fucking big not to call him on stupid mistakes. I would have welcomed him telling me to shut the hell up and fight to play what he thought worked better. I hated the insolent sneers or vague nods that said "fuck you" louder than if he shouted it at the top of his lungs. He was a problem I didn't have a ready solution for.

Spiral had an important gig at the beginning of April. The venue was slightly larger, and according to Mike, a bigwig from a Los Angeles-based label had committed to attend. Cory and Tim were excited. Terry gave a half grin to show his enthusiasm, and I walked out of the room to avoid raining on their parade and potentially launching for Terry's throat.

"Hey! Where you going?" Tim called after me as I made my way down the narrow studio hallway toward the elevator.

"I need air. I'll be back in a while."

Tim followed me to the elevator. He stuck his hands in his pockets and observed me intently. The worried frown juxtaposed with his inked, toned biceps and worn jeans made me smile. He looked part badass drummer, part concerned parent. He stepped in the elevator with me, ignoring my wordless glare warning him to leave me alone. In deference to the three other people sharing the ride, I kept quiet until we reached the lobby.

"Timmy, leave me alone."

"Not until you tell me why you aren't jumping for freaking joy. This is big, Rand. Why aren't you celebrating? If you tell me it's because Terry bugs you, I'm gonna fucking kick your ass."

I snorted and rolled my eyes for good measure as I moved toward the exit. "He definitely bugs me, but that isn't it. I've been thinking—something isn't working and I can't put my finger on it. I want to say it's Terry, but it's something else. Something the Hollywood exec is going to notice. I'm more worried than excited because he isn't going to give us pointers. He'll write us off, and Spiral will be marked as a nice little band with a small club following but not necessarily destined for prime time."

"Rand—"

"We need to think about how to create interest. A gimmick… or something. I know it's not in our budget, but I'm wondering if we should go for it and hire a PR guru to help us with our image." I sighed and leaned against the building's brick façade and watched the late-afternoon passersby hurry to catch subways or buses home.

"It's my turn to be brutally honest. Money is a major factor. I don't think it's wise to borrow, and we're strapped as it is."

"I know. I wish we knew someone who'd give us some advice we could trust. For free."

"Let's brainstorm. We can probably come up with something." He squinted and twitched his nose as though deep in thought, then smacked my shoulder and gave me a bright smile. "Maybe we could give away a door prize to the first hundred people. Like a keychain."

"A keychain?" I scoffed.

"What if we dressed differently or wore wigs or—"

"Hmm. Maybe…."

"Maybe wha—oh hi. How's it going?" Tim waved as Holly and Leah rounded the corner.

"Good. Are you guys still practicing? We were gonna hang out for an hour or so before I have to get to school and Leah has to get to work," Holly said, flipping her long, blonde hair over her shoulder.

I liked her. She was sweet, good-natured, and hopelessly infatuated with Cory. She was pleasant company, and I didn't mind her hanging around the studio. I only wished she was better friends with Will than Leah. Leah made me… itchy. I didn't get her. There's no way a girl like her was interested in Terry. She was too hip for him. She was sharp, witty, and had a body like a—whatever.

I knew to tread lightly with Leah. She was a music blogger with a growing readership who followed new music artists in the city. She'd written Spiral up a few times and was definitely one of our biggest champions, but I didn't trust her motivation. I think she liked Terry enough to have sex with him, but I sensed she was looking for something else. And when she gave me that lusty come-hither look, I knew exactly what she wanted.

This was definitely a first. Leah was hot. She was pretty with an edgy street style that combined a Goth look with something bohemian. I liked her long black hair and her gorgeous inked arms. She was the type of girl I usually ended up in bed with, even if it was for only one night. But her obvious flirtation hit a sour note with me, and not because I knew she was screwing my guitarist.

"We were just taking a quick break," I said as I stepped aside.

I was weighing whether or not I should just head to campus when Tim filled the girls in on our PR conversation. I gave him a perturbed glare he pointedly ignored as he warmed to the topic. "What do you think about glow-in-the-dark wristbands or a flashy keychain?"

"What's with you and the keychain? I'll buy you a fucking keychain if you need one so bad. I'll be back soon. See you guys."

"Wait! Where are you going?" It was Tim's turn to glower at me.

Leah set her hand on my elbow and tossed a bemused look between us. "Hang on a sec. The keychain idea isn't a great one, Tim. Sorry. Wristbands are better but the idea shouldn't be to give out souvenirs. It should be to get more people in the door. You need to spread the word. I can contact a few other bloggers I know and see about doing a series of stories about you guys before your Brooklyn show. That will help. One of my friends has done some freelance work for *Rolling Stone* too. Good contact to have."

"Wow. That would be awesome. Do you do PR too?" Tim asked.

"I'm trying to get more into it. I'm doing some basic social media content for a couple artists at a small label. It's fun."

"That's really cool. Maybe you could help us out," Tim gushed, giving me an enthusiastic look that clearly said all our problems were now solved. He was probably a little confused by my blank expression.

I wasn't so sure having Leah join us was a great idea. Even if it was for PR exposure.

"I'd love to. I actually mentioned it to Terry. I'm surprised he didn't say anything."

"Hmm. What would you need from us?" I asked.

"Human interest info. A couple of them may want to do interviews. Would you be okay with me e-mailing you questions?" She pulled her cell out of her gigantic black-fringed bag and shot a sexy sideways glance my way.

"Yeah, sure." I gave her my e-mail address and thanked her again. "I gotta run. I'll see you later."

"Wait. I'll come with you. I can ask a few questions while we walk and get the ball rolling, so to speak. Do you mind?"

"Uh... no, that's fine." Oh boy.

I braced myself for an uncomfortable twenty minutes or so. I was torn between wanting professional exposure and being wary of having her undivided attention. I wondered where I should head to shake her off. Ducking into a coffee shop might prolong the encounter rather than shorten it, so I walked toward Washington Square and hoped this wouldn't be a completely awkward chat.

"Everyone's going to want to know basics about Spiral. Where you're from, what your interests are outside of music, who you're dating, etcetera. Then they'll want to get into the nitty-gritty of your sound. Who your influences are, how long you've been playing.... So, where shall we start?" Her tone was professional with a hint of humor. For whatever reason, it set me at ease.

"All right, then. We're from Baltimore. Except for Terry. I don't remember where he's from—"

"Minneapolis."

"Ah. Right. I guess you can fill in the blanks for him."

She raised her eyebrows and gave me a look I couldn't read without a roadmap. "Hmm. Tell me about Baltimore."

By the time we reached the park, I'd talked my head off about myself, my interests, and the band's direction with little prodding from Leah. She listened and occasionally asked to stop to take notes in her phone. Our arms brushed as we walked, and when we stopped, she stood very close. But on crowded city streets, it wasn't a red flag. It was just New York.

As Washington Square came into view, I stopped at the corner and peered through the trees into the park.

"I need to stop here," I said.

"No problem. One last question."

"Shoot."

"Do you have a girlfriend?"

Leah's expression was carefully blank, like she was in reporter mode asking random questions that may be of interest to her readers, not necessarily her. My smile was slow, a lazy curve of the lips that morphed into a full grin. She was too obvious for her own good. Or mine, maybe.

"No, but I'm... seeing someone."

"Is it serious?"

I didn't know how to answer that one. And I suppose my hesitation spoke for me.

"I get it." She returned my grin with something a little saucier and laid her hand on my arm. "I'm in the same boat. Catch you later. Oh wait! I'm going to need your cell number for further questions. I won't have anyone call you directly. I can be the middle man, or girl, for you," she said with a wink.

"Sure." I gave her my number, distractedly wondering what I should do now that we'd reached the park. Will hadn't returned my earlier text. I debated heading back to practice when I saw a familiar figure standing near a slick new-model Range Rover.

"Bye, Rand." I looked down at Leah just as she leaned in to kiss the corner of my mouth. I was surprised by the gesture. But alarmed a second later when I glanced back at the Range Rover to see Will staring at me.

He was standing next to an elegantly dressed woman near the curb on Waverly Place. The late-afternoon sun hit the gigantic diamond on her left hand as she held open the SUV's door. I didn't know much about fashion, but having a friend who'd modeled with major couture houses in Europe gave me a basic knowledge. Enough to recognize that the Louis Vuitton bag, the huge dark sunglasses with the double *C*s on the sides, and the red-soled, fancy high heels were really expensive. Her dark brown, shoulder-length hair looked pretty against her bright pink sweater-coat. She looked sophisticated and worldly in a very New York way. And Will looked a lot like her. Was this his mom? She certainly didn't look like she was the average parent visiting her kid in college. I rubbed my tatted arm when a chilly spring breeze whipped along the street. I was proud of the colorful Celtic designs on my biceps, interlaced with tongues of fire and mystic symbols. As an Irish American, they were meaningful to me. But I could tell this lady wasn't going to be impressed. Nor was she going to like me, I mused. And at the moment, it didn't look like the guy next to her did, either.

I waved my hand over my head and yelled his name in greeting. "Hi there. How's it going?" My smile was wide and friendly.

"What are you doing here?" Will asked through his teeth.

He took a few steps away from the SUV and the watchful gaze of the lady in pink. He was perfectly pressed in a blue collared designer shirt and khakis. I wanted to run my fingers through his hair and mess it up, but his expression wasn't inviting. He looked highly irritated with me. And yeah, that kind of got me going… until he shook his head in warning and gave me a fierce stare. A series of tiny facial gestures played out between us in which he begged me to not say anything stupid, and I silently agreed to try my best.

"Sweetheart, who is your friend?" The woman gave me a thorough once-over before sauntering forward. She shot a look at Will, but she seemed more curious than concerned by my sudden presence.

"I'm Rand O'Malley. Nice to meet you," I said, offering her my hand.

She didn't take it right away, and when she did, she gave me one of those dreaded "fish" handshakes, the kind that does the talking for you. In her case, it said I wasn't one of her people, and she didn't particularly care for this encounter to last longer than necessary.

"Likewise. William, are you ready? I'm exhausted. I have a call in to Martin, but if he doesn't return it soon, we'll have to dine without him."

If there was one thing I hated, it was being dismissed or ignored. Not only had she not introduced herself, she'd turned her back to me after giving me that lameass handshake and immediately brought up Martin the Kink Master as though that wacko was more worthy of her time than me. Will gave me an apologetic look and started to speak, but it was too late. My mouth was already open.

"Oh. I thought we had plans tonight."

I was treated to a two-way stare. Both looked surprised, but one looked like he wanted to kick me in the nuts. Will cocked his head slightly and widened his eyes before addressing me in a low, careful tone.

"I'll call you later, okay?"

We held eye contact for a long moment. Everyone, including the icy woman standing nearby, faded away. I swallowed hard, making sure our fingers brushed before I stepped toward the curb.

"What did you say your name was?"

I turned back and lifted my hand distractedly to hail a cab. "Rand."

"I don't recall you mentioning a Rand. Are you a student here? Do you know one another from class?"

"No. I never went to college. High school was hard enough to finish. I'm in a band," I said with a sly grin. "And I work in a bagel shop in my spare time."

"Lovely." Her tone and her lingering stare at the swirling designs on my tatted arm clearly said she didn't think anything was "lovely" about me. "How do you know one another, then?"

I looked at Will. His mom, his story. When a taxi pulled up in front of the Range Rover, I decided that was my cue to leave.

Will stopped me with a hand on my elbow. "Mom, we're... we know each other from...."

I glanced from Will to his mother to the cab driver, who was busily honking at me to get my ass in gear, then back at Will again. I saw his intent but cautioned myself not to speak for him.

"We're kind of... seeing each other," he blurted.

"Seeing each other? Whatever does that mean?" His mother lowered her sunglasses halfway down her nose in true diva fashion.

Silence. Well, city silence. We stared at one another mutely as the cacophony of urban noise echoed around us. When the moment went on a beat too long, I decided it was up to me to end it. I looked from mother to son, willing myself not to unleash my irreverent self and give Mama a blow-by-blow, pun intended, of what he meant. Will wouldn't appreciate it. But he'd certainly given me the clear to say something.

"It means I'm his boyfriend. Pleased to meet you, Mom." I extended my hand but wasn't surprised when she left me hanging. I turned to Will and kissed his cheek before moving toward the waiting taxi. "Call me later."

THERE WAS a prevailing air of tension in the studio when I returned to practice. Terry skipped every other chord with a regularity that made me think he was under a chemical influence. Tim and Cory were irritated with my disappearance but were more concerned with keeping the peace once Terry began hacking away at the guitar strings. My plummeting patience exasperated everything. I was pissed at Terry for being a lazy shit, pissed at Tim and Cory for coddling the bastard, and I was pissed at myself for my own lack of concentration and orneriness. Everyone in the room welcomed the diversion when I stepped out of the studio to answer my phone.

"Hey."

"Who's the girl?"

I let out a half laugh and began to slowly pace the bland hallway with its industrial-style carpet, low ceilings, and fluorescent lighting.

"I was going to ask you the same thing."

"That was my mother, Rand. I cannot believe you did that."

"What did I do?" I infused my tone with levity, but I missed the mark.

"You know exactly what you did. God, that was the most awkward two hours of my life!"

"You mean she didn't like me?" No answer. "Hey, it wouldn't be the first time. I'll try not to let it hurt my feelings. But I will point out you didn't have to introduce me as your—how did you put it... 'someone you're seeing.' You could have said I was just some weirdo you're tutoring. I would have played along."

"I wouldn't do that, Rand. I'm not sure I would have told her you were my boyfriend exactly, but—"

"What am I, then?" I couldn't help asking. His words stung and I didn't know why. I wasn't sure I was ready to be someone's boyfriend. My intent had been to get a reaction from his mom. Not make a statement. My mood was off, and this wasn't a wise discussion to have on the phone.

"You're an infuriating ass, that's what you are! Who's the girl?"

"She's Terry's girlfriend. She thinks she can help us with PR stuff and—"

"Hmph. I'm sure."

"Look, I'm sorry." I let out a rush of air and let my head hit the wall as I slouched to a kneeling position in the deserted hallway.

"It's okay. It was uncomfortable, but then again... I expected it. My mom wasn't ready to hear that I really *am* gay. That's all."

"Are you saying she didn't believe it until I showed up?"

"I don't know what she believes. You know how it is when someone challenges your view of them? I think that's what happened when you said the *BF* word. She was so quiet at dinner that even Martin notic—"

"Martin? Fuck. I can't do this now."

"Rand, don't be ridiculous. You know he—"

An eerie red haze clouded my vision. I jumped to my feet and paced the hallway like a caged animal.

"Ridiculous? Are you fucking with me? That old married prick has seen your ass. He propositioned a scared college kid whose rich folks cut him off 'cause he's a fag. It's not the kink I care about, it's the fact he took advantage of you. Plain and simple. It's crazy that you can sit at a table with that guy while your prim and proper mom takes one look at me and decides *I'm* the dangerous one!"

"I didn't say—"

"You didn't have to! She said it for you. It's a fucked-up world, Will. As long as you dress up your sins real pretty, all is forgiven. The minute you start speaking the truth, *bam*! Watch out. Righteousness comes easiest to people who can afford fancy cars and designer clothes. If a fucking LV bag is all it takes to pass sound judgment, then I want me one of those." I pitched my voice to sound like a madman on a pulpit. I was mad. I was on the verge of the kind of crazy that lent itself to an amazing stage show. Or an embarrassing meltdown.

"What the fuck are you talking about? LV bag? Louis Vuitton?"

A sense of defeat washed over me. What the fuck indeed? I punched the wall and attempted to shake off my fury and indignation. I hated being judged and falling short. I hated defending myself knowing I'd already been tried and convicted. And I hated that Will didn't understand.

"Hey, I'm sorry I put you on the spot with your mom. I don't know if I meant to or not, 'cause Lord knows I hate ruining anyone's dinner but—"

"Will that girl be at the show Saturday?"

"Leah? Yeah, probably. She's with Terry and—"

"Benny can help you with PR too. I can bring him by on Saturday."

Huh? "I'd be happy to talk to Benny, but Leah does it for a living and—"

"Yeah, I bet she does."

"There's no reason to—"

"What time is the show?"

"Ten. Why?"

"I'll see you there. And Rand?"

"What?"

"You're right. Life isn't fair. But in this case, the problem isn't Martin. It's me. I don't know how to fix where I'm from. I'm trying, but… it isn't easy."

He hung up before I could question his cryptic words. I stared at my cell for a long moment, wondering what had just happened.

Chapter 8

EMOTIONS WERE high before we hit the stage Saturday night. It may have been nerves or it may have been a case of simply spending too much time together. Tim was frantic when he couldn't find his bag of drumsticks and pissed when he realized it was because Cory's jacket was lying on top of them. I ignored their bickering and tried to stay in a preshow mellow mood by practicing vocal exercises as I strummed my acoustic guitar. I was doing my best not to join their bitchfest, though I couldn't help checking my watch every few minutes, wondering what the fuck was keeping Terry. We'd left him bellied up to the bar with Leah, Holly, and a few of their friends forty-five minutes ago. Cory had gone to see what the holdup was but came back without him, though he assured me Terry would be back soon.

He wasn't. And the show was supposed to start in ten minutes. I was tempted to waltz out there and drag his ass back here like a caveman. I had a niggling feeling this was a power play. He'd been out to give me the proverbial finger earlier at the bar by draping himself over pretty girls in low-cut T-shirts and doing shots from glasses perched precariously between their breasts while I tapped my fingers on the bar and checked my cell for messages. I chatted with Leah while we watched her man make an idiot of himself. She didn't seem overly concerned, nor was she hanging on me the way she sometimes did. Good. Usually I'd participate in a little preshow good-natured silliness and mindless flirting, but tonight was an opportunity. I wanted to remain as clear-minded and focused as possible. Everyone got ready to perform their own way. If he needed a drink and to have his ego and maybe other body parts stroked by a few female fans to loosen up beforehand, I'd be the last to judge. However, if he walked onstage drunk tonight, I was going to fucking kill him.

"There's a guy out here who's insisting to see you, Rand. You have ten minutes 'til the lights go down. Should I send him away and tell him to catch you after the show?"

I glanced up at the harried-looking young woman with curly red hair wearing a headset. She'd introduced herself earlier as Michelle, the stage manager. She was a bit uptight and obviously took her job very seriously. If I wasn't distracted by our lack of a guitarist, I would have tried to make her laugh. Not tonight. I couldn't crack a smile myself at the moment. Her gaze was locked on me as she typed something into her iPad and furiously chomped on her gum.

"Did he give you a name?"

"Benny!"

Benny was jumping behind the stage assistant waving his arms like he was hailing a taxi at rush hour. I caught a flash of red at each hop but couldn't see his face until the woman stepped back. He might not be who I was hoping to see, but at least he was entertaining.

"I'll see him."

I gave a half laugh as Benny loudly huffed, "Golly, thanks, Mr. Rockstar."

"Would you do me a favor and track down our guitarist?" I asked Michelle. "He was last seen at the bar."

Her eyes widened in panic before she nodded briskly and hurried out of the room. Which left Benny standing in the doorway, looking curious and, yes… ultrafabulous. He wore a snug, bright red T-shirt with faded holey jeans rolled up to show off his short, hip black boots. His dark hair was slicked back at the sides and mussed on top. This time his highlights were an impossible shade of red. I didn't remember him wearing glasses the night I met him at the restaurant, but tonight he was wearing a pair of stylish lenses that amplified his heavily lined eyes.

"I have to cut out right after the show, but I'm here to talk PR."

"Now?"

"I know. We couldn't get in any earlier. It's wall-to-wall people out there!" He lowered his voice conspiratorially as he added, "I'm here at the request of 'you know who.'"

"Where is he?" I couldn't say why, but I felt myself relax knowing Will was nearby.

"In the audience," Benny said, moving his wrist in a flamboyant circular motion toward the door. "I'm sure you'll see him afterward. He mentioned something about you needing PR help and a stylist."

"I don't need a stylist."

"You don't?" he asked, giving me a dubious once-over.

"I appreciate it, Benny." I moved back to the door to escort him out. "But this isn't a good time. Our guitarist is MIA and—"

The backroom door banged open on cue. Terry stopped in the doorway and clung to the jamb as though he needed its support. He gave a peace sign and stumbled into the room. The stage manager looked at me in a combination of horror and accusation as though I were somehow responsible.

"Five minutes," she reminded us curtly before turning to leave.

Benny gave Terry a sharp look, then looked back at me and sighed theatrically. "You definitely need a stylist. We'll talk another time. Break a leg, boys." Benny waved and moved to the door but stopped in his tracks when Terry opened his mouth.

"Who's the fag?"

Maybe it was the drunken swagger or the insolent sneer or perhaps it was the offhand homophobic slur. I'd been more patient than Terry deserved for the band's sake, but it was over. I let out a feral growl and lunged for his throat. He gasped in surprise when his back hit the wall hard. The urge to curl my fingers around his neck until he choked for breath was strong. I waited until he grabbed at my hand desperately with a hint of fear in his eyes before I spoke in a low, menacing tone.

"Listen up, Guitar Hero. We didn't work this hard to have you fuck it up. I don't care what you drink, what you snort, or who you screw until it affects this band. You better hope you can stand on your own two feet and play without sucking as usual. Get your mind on the music and keep it there. Got it?" When he gave a short nod, I let go of his throat and stepped back, ignoring the shocked, open-mouthed stares of the others before turning back to add one more thing. "By the way... I'm the fucking fag, asshole."

Terry cocked his head and looked at me with the oddest expression before he stumbled back a step and collapsed in a heap on a metal chair next to a small table.

I watched as my friends scrambled around the slumped form in the chair, calling his name and lightly smacking his cheek.

"Jesus, is he dead?" Tim asked as Cory lifted his wrist to check his vitals.

"No, he's passed out cold."

We stared at each other helplessly for what felt like twenty minutes but was probably closer to twenty seconds. Typical club noise invaded the small backroom: clinking glass, pieces of conversations and laughter, and the incessant bass from what sounded like a Nine Inch Nails classic.

It was surreal. I could hardly process the calamity unfolding around us. I was all for the age old adage "the show must go on," but I wasn't sure how to bounce back from losing our lead guitarist minutes before the lights went down with hundreds of people in the club and... oh yeah, a fucking record exec from LA.

"I hope he wakes up with a bigass hangover." Benny shot Terry a disgusted look as he sashayed toward the door.

I barely heard Benny as panic warred with nausea. I had to take over. I hoped I could remember some of what Will taught—

"Benny, where's Will?"

Three sets of eyes turned to me with varying degrees of concern. "He's out there. Why?"

"We need him."

Benny stared at me, then shook his head mournfully. "He won't do it, Rand. He's shy and—"

"I know, I know." I shoved my hands through my hair in frustration. "What's he wearing?"

"Huh?"

"I know him. He didn't come here in his khakis."

Benny cocked his head curiously. The corner of his mouth lifted on one side, and his eyes lit up. "That doesn't mean he'll—let me see what I can do."

He flew out the door just as Michelle returned. She surveyed the room before pointing at Terry.

"What happened to him? Never mind. I don't want to know. You're on now."

"Uh, yeah. We're going to need a minute or two," Cory said.

"You don't have a minute. You have now. If you're not out there within five minutes, we're pulling your act. You are not Maroon fucking 5. Figure it out!"

The door slammed shut, leaving an echo of muted music and laughter. I chuckled without humor and gave my friends what I hoped passed for a smile. "Let's do this."

"How?" Tim picked up his sticks and joined me at the door.

"I've got no fucking clue. But we have to try."

We walked out together onto a darkened stage at Freddie's House of Music to the sound of thunderous applause, the likes of which we'd never heard before. This was a maximum-capacity crowd of fifteen hundred excited fans. Their cheering and wolf whistles had an anticipatory tone, as though they'd come specifically for Spiral. The idea alone was enough to lift my spirits. If the extra enthusiasm had anything to do with Leah's networking efforts, we owed her big-time.

I looked over at Cory with a cocky grin that actually felt sincere and gave him a short nod. I had no idea what to expect, but as the first familiar bass riff ripped through the air, I felt fire rush through my veins. This was where I belonged. I didn't need a script for this part. I knew how the music moved, and I was a master at riding the spaces between the notes. It was time to let go of what I couldn't control and do my thing.

"Hey Brooklyn," I called out with the flair of a seasoned leader who was accustomed to playing much larger venues with my band's name in bright lights. The audience's resounding cheer was the spark I needed. A burst of energy quaked through me as Tim joined in on his drums. The steady lively beat coupled with the quirky bass signaled the beginning of a song I'd written years ago, "Tonight." The song was three chords. The lyrics were catchy and playful. It was a fun, feel-good way to start the show. The real zinger would come from a superior guitarist who could bend the notes and take off with a crazy solo, but we'd work with what we had.

I hummed the opening bar as I made my way across the small stage with one arm raised like a crazed orchestra leader striking up the band. I took a deep breath and was about to sing the first line when an electric guitar reverberated behind me. I literally jumped in surprise, and I could tell by the raucous hoots from the first few rows, the audience assumed my reaction was an act. I turned to face the source of the music. And nearly dropped the microphone.

Holy shit.

It was Will. Except it wasn't. He'd morphed into the guitar god I'd always insisted he was. The spiked short blond wig, tight black jeans, and Doc Martens paired with a red sequined top, a ton of eyeliner, powder, and glittery lip gloss in no way diminished his vitality and presence. He looked like a cross between David Bowie's Ziggy Stardust and his own creation… Billie. His over-the-top appearance juxtaposed with the band's basic jeans, dark T-shirts, and copious ink looked interesting and sexy as fuck. I couldn't keep my smile from taking over my face as I signaled I was ready when he was. He nodded tentatively, then strummed the first few notes of the song, luring me in and inviting me to lead. To move, to sing, to do what I'd set out to when I landed in Manhattan months ago… take this fucking city by storm.

And so I did.

Song after song, Spiral built up a steady frenzy until every single person was on their feet dancing, singing along to Rolling Stones and Howlin' Wolf covers or swaying to original songs they didn't know the lyrics to yet. I'd been practicing with Will for a few months now. He knew our material, but better than that, he knew how to coax a superior sound from an instrument he'd mastered at a very young age. He was a maestro. I doubted anyone noticed his obvious panic or how stiffly he stood at the beginning, because by the end of that first song, he was gone, carried away by the music. The wacky getup that initially added interest became hard to see when he let go and lost himself. He played with a soulful beauty that could convince anyone he played for them alone. He brought an intimate layer to each song that challenged me to give my best. Together we were electric.

And so was the audience. Initial enthusiastic applause soon gave way to ardent cheering. The four of us fed off the crowd and each other with an infectious joy that comes from doing something you really love. It was evident to anyone paying attention we were in our element. I didn't stop once to think about important record execs or our drunken band member passed out in the back. This was all about living in the moment.

Near the end of our last set, I stopped with the microphone inches from my mouth and smiled. The crowd went wild. I was overcome with an impulse to thank Will somehow. He was brave and fearless and utterly amazing. He'd set aside his anxiety just to come here tonight. Jumping onstage defied expectation. I turned sideways and locked my gaze on his. My adrenaline level was already through the roof, but I swear my heart flipped in my chest when he smiled at me. I grinned and inexplicably sang the chorus to the first song that popped in my head. Michael Jackson's "Billie Jean." Will looked confused, and my bandmates no doubt wondered what had gotten into me, but the audience fucking loved it. The juxtaposition of singing along to an old pop song after rocking out to the blues was silly and fun. I switched to Pharrell's "Happy," and the crowd sang along without music and with only a little guidance from me. The jubilant, festive mood in the room was palpable. This was why I was in a band. Not for money, fame, or fortune. But for moments like this when music became a communal experience. Something never to be forgotten.

I turned sharply at the pealing sounds of an electric guitar. Will lifted his instrument like a rock superstar from an eighties music video and took over. I laughed outright and theatrically fell to the ground as though he'd slayed me. Just as I was about to spring to my feet, Will set his boot on my stomach and looked down at me with a confidence and charisma I'd never witnessed before. I felt dizzy with lust. The desire to pull him down and take him then and there was strong enough to let me know I was in trouble.

Maybe everyone noticed, maybe not. I only knew everything had changed. Again.

I WAS the last to leave the stage, right behind Will. When we were out of eyesight, I grasped his hand and pushed him against the wall. We stared at each other for a heated moment before coming together in a fierce, demanding kiss. I ground my pelvis against his as our tongues dueled frantically.

Tim coughed and smacked my shoulder. "Romeo, you're gonna need to find a more private spot than this to make out." He extended a hand to Will. "You must be Will. You were fucking incredible. I don't know how to thank you."

Will shook Tim's hand and nodded. I listened to them muddle through introductions without my help, but when I saw Cory turn back toward us, I wanted out. Holly, Leah, Mike, and a host of others, including Terry would be back soon. I didn't want to deal with introductions. Or try to explain things I couldn't quite get my head around. Like what had happened tonight.

"You ready?"

"Yeah. Let's go." Will's smile was incandescent. He looked young and carefree in a way he never had before.

"Hey! You can't go. What about Mike and the Hollywood guys?"

"You deal with them. We're outta here. And remember... quiet."

"Rand!"

I grabbed my jacket from the empty back room and noted there was no sign of Terry. I'd have to fire him in the morning, I thought as I led the way to the exit.

THE CITY lights blurred and blended from the taxi window as the Manhattan skyline came into view. I wanted to revel in the sight of the majestic skyscrapers and the lights dotting the many bridges over the East River. I wanted to bask in the glory of a job well done in a town that enjoyed chewing you up and spitting you out. But I could barely focus on my surroundings. Every sense was in tune to the man at my side. I watched his hands resting on his thigh and the way his chest moved as he breathed. His gaze wandered out the window, but instinctively I knew he was in the same condition as me. He caught my stare and offered a lopsided grin, then laced my fingers through his and squeezed.

A rush of emotion threatened to overtake me. I was always more impassioned after a gig, but this felt different. I wanted to give my turbulent thoughts a name and a label so I could put them aside to examine later. If I could assure myself I was experiencing a spiked high due to a successful live performance, I might be able to sink into the feeling and simply enjoy the ride. But I couldn't lie to myself. Everything felt different because of Will. More significant, more intense. I closed my eyes and willed myself to relax as I clung to his hand and felt the hum of the city move around us.

When the taxi turned onto Will's street, I'd never been so happy to reach a destination in my life. I paid the driver, then hurried to meet Will as he opened the lobby door of his building. Every step felt like shedding skin. Need and desire fueled my movement. I was dangerously close to doing something that might get us arrested. I had to hold it together.

Once we were safely inside, all bets were off.

We hurried up the stairs and burst into his studio, barely remembering to close the door and turn on a light before we launched at each other. Our mouths fused as we pushed away fabric to finally reach skin. Will slid my T-shirt up my chest and pinched my nipples hard. I winced and had started to back up when he bent over to lick the sensitive nub and suck it.

"Fuck, that's good." I soothed my hand over his head and tugged at his wig. "Take it off. Please."

He unbuckled and unzipped my jeans before glancing up at me with a funny smile. He sank to his knees, pushing the fabric over my ass and around my ankles so fast my head spun. He brushed his chin against my balls and sighed deeply as though he were lost in the moment. I watched him closely and willed myself not to guide him. His glittered eyelids closed as he breathed me in and licked the tip of my dick. I let out a sigh and reached for his head. His mouth was warm and inviting. He swirled his tongue lazily, then looked up at me with a beguiling expression. Will's eyes sparked with lust. He stroked my shaft slowly, then leaned forward to lick me from base to tip and back again.

"More."

"Take what you want," he commanded in a strong voice.

"Wha—what do you mean?"

"If you want me to suck you hard, show me how you want it."

I did my best to let the haze of desire clear before I answered. "You aren't ready for anything rough, baby. I like this. Just suck... don't lick. Okay?"

"Don't tell me I'm not ready. Don't tell me what I want. Show me."

"Fuck." I grasped his head and guided him back to my dick forcefully.

He shivered slightly, obviously turned on by the promise of something a bit raunchier. I tried not to move my hips, but it soon became obvious that his stubborn, repetitive licking was meant to push me to demand more of him. He wanted wild and naughty. Something he wouldn't dare ask for if he was dressed as himself. Tonight he wanted to let go.

"Look at me," I commanded in a husky tone. Will lifted his gaze but let his tongue rest on my slit as he waited for instruction. I gulped at the sight of the clear precum glistening on his bottom lip. "Open your mouth wide. Wider. Now suck."

When I swayed my hips to meet his hot mouth, he was ready. He sucked the wide head and twirled his tongue tentatively at the tip before hollowing his cheeks to take as much of me in as possible. He alternately stroked, licked, or sucked like a madman, raking his nails over my ass to spur me to move. My best intentions to set a moderate pace soon fell apart. My head fell back as I snapped my hips forward, fucking his mouth relentlessly. He hummed as he tilted his head. The deeper angle and added vibration sent a tingle up my spine.

"Stop. I don't wanna cum yet." I pushed at his forehead, marveling at his self-satisfied grin. The little fucker was killing me and he loved it. "Let me taste you."

"No, I want you to fuck me."

I asked for it, I thought as my heart went into overdrive. His eyes held the perfect balance of daring and hunger. He bit his bottom lip and knelt forward, stroking my impossibly hard flesh as he waited for my direction. What a joke. I was definitely not the guy in control here.

"Stand up."

He slowly obeyed in a funny act of defiance. I sensed a game in play, but I was too strung out to ask the rules, and a clarifying discussion would only be an erection killer. It was up to me to figure him out on my own. I kissed him hard and pulled back to study his face for clues. He smirked and batted my hand away, then stepped out of reach and yanked the sequined top over his head. I crouched to take off my shoes and step out of my jeans but kept my eyes locked on him as he pushed his jeans down his long legs and revealed a pair of fishnet hose.

"Oh. Wow."

Will hooked his thumbs under the elastic and made sure he had my full attention before moving them halfway over his ass.

"Stop!"

"Don't you want me to take them off?"

I stared mutely for a long moment. The wig, the makeup, the stockings. This ensemble was his armor. It was what made tonight possible. Stripping it all at once would be cruel. I had to proceed with care.

"Take the wig off." My tone was low and commanding. I stood up, completely naked with my hands on my dick.

He scowled. "But—"

I stepped toward him and poked my fingers through the mesh fabric. "Please. Wig off. Tights can stay. For now."

"I don't want to be me." He stopped, looking strangely defeated. Unbelievably I caught his meaning.

"Hey. Look at me, baby. I know who you are. Leave it if you want, but I only want you. You." I smiled and gently tugged at the blond wig. I grabbed my thick cock and held it meaningfully. "It's pretty fucking obvious, right?"

He cracked a smile and rolled his eyes before unpinning the wig. I moved next to him and tapped my flesh against his thigh while he worked.

"Not very exciting when the pieces start to fall away," he commented idly as he tossed it on the small table next to the futon.

I ran my fingers through his soft hair and pulled him against me. "I disagree. It's sexy as fuck."

Will chuckled as he snaked his arms around my neck. "What exactly does 'sexy as fuck' mean?"

"No more questions. Bend over the bed."

When he hesitated, I smacked his ass once, then steered him where I wanted him. On his knees. I gulped at the gorgeous view for a moment before moving behind him. The touch of skin through the mesh hose felt illicit somehow. I slid my throbbing cock along his crack, fascinated and frustrated by the barrier. He swayed his hips, silently begging me to stop staring and do something. I wondered if he'd freak if I did what I really wanted. What the hell? I might as well find out, I mused. I pulled the fabric over his ass, then licked my middle finger and rubbed the sensitive skin around his hole. He moaned loudly and arched his back. I gently pushed inside him, then began a steady in-and-out motion until he begged for a second one. I added the digit, then sank to my knees on the bed and licked the soft skin around his entrance.

"What are you do—oh fuck!" He buried his head in his pillow at the first probing touch of my tongue.

Fuck, he smelled and tasted divine. I hadn't done this in a long time. It was too intimate an act to do with just anyone. I didn't feel that way about blowjobs or, hell, even anal, but this was different. I loved the way he purred like a cat, moaning as he clutched at the sheets with one hand and jacked himself with the other. As crazed with desire as he was, I could feel him relaxing. I had a feeling he'd beg me to fuck him any second now. When I sat back and pushed the tip of a third finger inside him, I got my wish.

"Now. Please. I want you, Rand. Fuck me."

I couldn't talk. I reached for a condom and lube on the table next to the discarded wig and suited up as fast as possible. When he started to roll over I stopped him, swatting his left cheek hard.

"Stay on your knees." I shoved the fishnet fabric farther down his thighs and massaged his ass. He wiggled seductively and moaned when I lined my cock at his entrance and pushed. I ran a soothing hand over his back and along his sides, cooing to him softly until he moved backward and whimpered for more.

Heat consumed me. I felt light-headed as I slowly made my way inside him. It took every ounce of strength I possessed to keep my movement to a minimum and not slam into him. I held his hips and ran my hands over his back and along his sides. I was ultra-aware of his breathing and body language. When he pushed his ass back to take more of me on his own, I let out a huff of surprise and had to widen my stance to steady myself or fall over.

"Fuck, Will."

"Yes, that's what I want." He craned his head sideways and gave me a pointed look. "Fuck me."

"Baby, slow down."

I swallowed hard as I let my hands drift toward his shoulders. I slowly pulled out, then pushed back in. He didn't know what he was asking. He couldn't know how rough or out of control I could be. I kept a moderate pace with long, even strokes until he growled and bucked backward, impaling himself fully on me.

"More."

I gritted my teeth but obeyed as I reached around to grab his bouncing cock. He made a keening sound of pure pleasure and covered my hand, wordlessly asking for more pressure, more friction.

"Take it eas—"

"Rand, fuck me!"

When the stars cleared and the dizziness faded, I had no choice but to give him what he asked for. I leaned forward and pushed him flat on the mattress, covering his back as I drove inside him. I threaded my fingers through his and let my hips fly. Will met me thrust for thrust, crying a litany of nonsensical grunts peppered with "fuck me, fuck me."

I'd never seen him so wild and unfettered. He moved under me with purpose. Like a man who knew exactly what he wanted and was willing to try anything to get it. When I pulled him to his knees, he reached for his cock again.

"Not yet," I said, swatting his hand away. I licked the shell of his ear, then traced a path along his jaw to the corner of his mouth. "Get on top of me."

I gently pulled out and flopped gracelessly onto my back. I tucked my left arm behind my head and held my rigid cock as I watched him scramble to remove the tights still gathered around his knees. I chuckled softly and then a little harder when he gave me a dirty look.

"Not funny. I can't get these off," he scowled.

"Come here. Let me help."

When he came close, I rolled to my side and hooked my arm around his left knee. I pushed the fabric around his ankles but wouldn't let him back away from me. He peered down at me curiously, then let out a loud groan as I swallowed him whole. I bobbed my head, reveling in his musky scent as I sucked him hungrily. After a minute, I pulled away and gestured for him to straddle my thighs.

"Ride me." My voice was hoarse and low in the quiet room. Will licked his lips and nodded. He brushed his hair out of his eyes, lined my cock to his hole, and lowered himself on my shaft. "Oh fuck, that's good."

He laid his palm flat on my chest and began a rocking motion. Slow and steady at first, until he found his rhythm and took off. His hips snapped back and forth, and his cock bounced against my stomach, leaking copious amounts of precum. I swiped my fingers through the moisture, then grabbed hold of his dick and jacked him with a firm grip. I could tell he was close when his tempo faltered.

"Cum for me, baby."

He let out a guttural cry as he fell apart, spurting semen over my hands and across my chest. I pulled him into my arms and sealed our lips together. I rubbed his back and shoulders in an attempt to soothe him until the shaking stopped, but I couldn't stop moving. I was so close. Will propped himself up to gaze down at me. The look in his eyes was potent. The look of someone just learning how much power he possessed. And with his mussed hair, heavy makeup, and swollen lips, he was sexier to me than ever.

I held his hips steady, dug my heels into the futon, and fucked into him. There was no tenderness, no mercy in the act. It was lust and need and a fiery chase toward release. I pulled him against me, clutching him close as the first wave of orgasm hit me like a sledgehammer. I pumped my hips furiously, riding out the intense spasms, shuddering helplessly under my lover.

My heartbeat was, by far, the loudest sound in the room. I could hear a soft voice nearby, but I couldn't make out the words clearly over the rush of blood to my head. It was spoken so low I wasn't sure I was meant to hear. But as the buzzing faded and my pulse slowed, I caught it. *I love you.*

My eyes widened and a new sheen of sweat broke over my skin. Holy shit. Love? I didn't know what to say. I wasn't ready for this. Was

I? I'd never said those three words to a lover. Sure, I told my friends I loved them all the time, and sometimes I actually meant it. But this was different. I gulped and tried to formulate a plan, a speech, a... something, so when Will looked at me and said it again, I'd be prepared.

I was sure I was about to experience my first full-blown panic attack, when he sat up and kissed my nose before gently disengaging our bodies. I stared at the ceiling, wondering if this was where things got weird. Silence stretched between us. But it wasn't uncomfortable. It was... kind of perfect.

He sighed heavily and made a hand signal somewhere in my peripheral view.

"What are you doing?"

"It's messy here." His eyes were closed but his smile was smug. Not wistful or lovesick.

I rolled to my side to observe him, grateful my pulse was returning to normal. He lifted his hand again and made the same funny circular motion.

"Are you conjuring some kind of magic to get cleaned up, or is that a signal for me to get to it?" I asked with a mock scowl.

Will turned his head and grinned. "Get to it. It's the least you can do."

"You know, it's actually better if you let it dry and then—"

"Rand."

"I'm going, I'm going," I grumbled, scooting off the bed.

I returned with a wet washcloth and a couple water bottles. I handed over the water and was about to give him the washcloth, but at the last second I changed my mind. Instead, I scooped him into my arms and turned him onto his stomach. He grunted in surprise and threw an evil glance over his shoulder. When I slid the warm cloth between his cheeks, he set his hand on my wrist and sat up. We stared at each other for a moment. He obviously wanted me to stop without making a big deal about it. He should know me better by now, I mused.

"Let me help you out. It's the least I can do," I teased, throwing his words back at him playfully.

"Ha-ha. Hand it over."

I handed the cloth to him with a wicked grin. "Careful. Jizz side up."

"You are disgusting," he primly observed as I chuckled beside him. I uncapped my water bottle to keep my hands busy.

"Guilty."

He made a show of propping his pillow against the wall and leaning back before crossing his arms. He gave me a stern look. I didn't have the heart to tell him the smeared makeup across his eyelids lessened the fierce effect.

"You enjoy making me squirm."

"It's part of my charm," I replied glibly. The silly exchange was a weak cover. I had so many questions. I wanted to know everything going on inside his head. "Why'd you come tonight? I'm glad. Very glad... but I didn't expect it. It was a pleasant surprise."

He took a deep breath and focused on something beyond my head. "I've been wanting to but... I guess seeing you with the Goth glam girl the other day made me—"

"Leah? I told you—"

"I know."

"Well, you were amazing. Thank you."

His grin split his face in two. "You're welcome. It was so... cool to be up there. Liberating. I know I'm only as amazing as my disguise, 'cause the real me would never dare perform like that, but wow. It was intense. Magical. I'm sorry Terry passed out, but I had a blast."

I tilted my head and studied him with a smile. "I'm pretty sure that *was* the real you. You do know you aren't two people, right?"

"It helps if I think I am," he replied with a teasing gleam in his eyes as he took a swig from his water bottle. "Anxiety would get the better of me otherwise. It's better if I think of tonight like I was in a play. A one-night show. It was exhilarating and wild, but it wasn't real. It's not my life. Even now... lying here in bed with you feels like a dream."

"But it *is* real, Will. Underneath the glitter and eyeliner, you're still you."

We stared at each other for a long moment. The ability to compartmentalize aspects of our personality to function in polite society was perfectly normal, but I couldn't help thinking Will took his talent to an extreme.

He looked away and set his water bottle on the table next to him before turning to me with a small smile. "You're missing the point that the glitter and eyeliner is what got me here. It's why you're in my bed now, Rand. The part of me you like the most isn't the real me."

"Huh? Who was that yelling 'fuck me, fuck me' a little while ago? I need that guy's number," I joked as I leaned in to kiss his upper thigh. Fuck, he smelled good. Like sex and sin with a hint of innocence.

"Ha. Ha." He laid his hand over my head and gently stroked his fingers through my hair. "I'm hungry. Want to order pizza?"

"Wait up. I have one more thing to say."

"Of course you do."

I smiled up at him, loving the contrast of his sweet caress with his annoyed tone. "Here's the way I see things... the right way of seeing things." I waited for the eye roll I knew was coming before I continued. "I think you're like a caterpillar outgrowing his cocoon. You have these wings you know how to use, but you don't, because the bright colors make you nervous. You'll figure out on your own that you're the one who's kinda like magic."

We stared at each other, wearing matching, goofy grins for a long moment. "So I'm a butterfly? I guess it's better than cheese." Will chuckled and bent to kiss my forehead. "Pickup or delivery?"

"No one takes me seriously." I sighed in mock irritation. "Delivery. I'll take sausage, mushroom, peppers, olives... oh, and onions too."

"I don't like onions on pizza. And where are you going? You're supposed to call for pizza."

I hopped out of bed and headed for the bathroom. "I'm showering, you're calling. Put onions on half, and babe?"

"Hmm?"

"Make it an extra-large. I'm starving."

Chapter 9

A PERSISTENT buzzing roused me from a deep dream. The awesome kind you want to last as long as possible to see where it leads, though you know the minute you wake up you'll never remember the important details. I let out an unintelligible grunt as I stretched my hands over my head and blinked against the bright sunlight cascading through the blinds. I was alone in Will's bed. I allowed myself to revel in the silence.

I hadn't been truly alone in a very long time. It felt decadent. It was hard to imagine a time I might actually have a place of my own. Even a small one like this. I listened for the telltale sounds of him moving nearby, but other than the muted buzzing noise coming from the pile of discarded clothing on the floor, the room was quiet. I glanced at the empty space beside me as I reached for my jeans to pull out my cell. It immediately lit up like a Christmas tree.

There were at least ten missed calls, voice messages, and a slew of texts. I stopped at the one from Will sent an hour ago.

I'm meeting my mom for brunch. C u later, sleeping beauty

I stared at the message before typing my response.

I love brunch. Where should I meet u?

Tim, Cory, and Mike had each left multiple texts. And there was even one from Terry. I was reluctant to read any further without coffee. I was very aware that a performance high was often followed by a crash. In a band, that meant there were three other egos to soothe when the occasional bouts of self-doubt surfaced the next morning. The "we rocked it!" could easily spiral into "we sucked." I wasn't mentally prepared to deal with anyone else's highs or lows yet. Nor was I ready to deal with Terry. I set my phone aside and sat back on the futon to put my shoes and socks on.

Not happening. I'm near Central Park at the Plaza Hotel. Want 2 meet after?

I typed a series of immature emoticons but hesitated before sending my reply.

Sure

Will countered my devils, skulls, and horned, purple emojis with sunshine, bumblebees, and a ladybug. I chuckled and was about to respond when a call came through.

"Rand's phone," I said, pitching my voice in a woman's high falsetto designed to irritate the caller.

"Gee, is he there?"

"I'll check."

"Thanks, and while you're at it, let that fuckhead know I've been trying to reach him all freaking day!"

I dropped my vocal affectation and sighed wearily. "What's the matter, Timmy? You need me to pick up some toilet paper on my way home?"

"You're a riot. Have you listened to any of your messages by chance?"

"Nope. I just woke up. I can't deal with the real world until I'm properly caffeinated. You know the rules."

"Well, since I finally have your attention and time is of the essence, I'll give you a breakdown."

"Did you really just say 'time is of the essence'? I can't do this without java. Bye, Tim."

"Don't hang up! There were three record execs in the audience last night, Rand. Not one but three. And they fucking loved us. Mike's over the moon, but he's freaking out because they all want to meet you." He waited a beat before adding, "And Will."

"Will? You didn't tell them his name or—"

"No. But we have a complication named Terry."

"No, we don't. He's fired."

"I'm not sure it's that simple. Trust me, we'd all rather have Will. You said he was talented, but I think you undersold him. The guy's a prodigy. We all think so. Mike's worried there may be contractual issues with Terry but—"

"There are no contractual issues. We never signed anything and we don't owe him shit. He's out. Period. End of story. And as manager, that's Mike's job. If he can't handle it, have him call me. But none of that means Will is going to want to take Terry's place."

A piece of black mesh next to the bed caught my attention. I bent to pick up the fishnet stockings and fingered the delicate fabric before lifting it to my nose, breathing in Will's scent. God, that was hot.

"Either way we need to talk. This is finally looking real, Rand. I think we're almost there."

This was usually when I'd insert some smartass comment to defuse the enormity of those three simple words, *we're almost there*. My speech about counting chickens before they hatched wouldn't come, because I had a crazy feeling Tim might just be right.

I TOOK the subway to Fifty-Ninth and Fifth Avenue. I paused at the corner in front of the entrance to Central Park, across the street from the Plaza Hotel. I wasn't going to meet Will at first. Last night was intense and unexpected from start to finish. I figured it was best to retreat for a day or two. I had to keep my head in the game and stop spinning over a guy. But Will wasn't just a guy. He was special. And I was having a hard time trying to figure him out.

We'd arranged to meet at one of the benches on the park side of Fifth. I started to turn down the pathway, but I was a little early, so I decided to wait for him in front of the hotel. I made my way to the corner and glanced across the street. The Plaza Hotel was a stately building with a grand entrance, complete with red-carpeted stairs. It was nice as far as landmarks were concerned, but I'd never pay money to stay there. Too ritzy for my taste, I mused. I pushed the crosswalk button and looked up again when a familiar figure caught my eye.

A balding man in a dark sports coat descended the stairs. He stopped halfway and stood with his arm outstretched. A moment later, a woman appeared. Will's mom. And Marty. He took her hand and guided her down the stairs to a waiting black Escalade. It was all very gallant—and nauseating. Maybe it was a bad character trait to judge others without knowing them, but I didn't like Marty or Mom. I glanced toward the main entrance looking for Will, then back at them when he didn't appear. They were standing close and talking. Then Marty lifted his hand to caress her face and kissed her lips before moving to the driver side.

I stared at them for a moment in shock. Whoa. They were lovers.

She laughed at something he said, then glanced aimlessly in my direction. I was far enough away she might not have recognized me, but when she hesitated before getting into the SUV, I was fairly certain she had.

I watched until the Escalade pulled away. The traffic was heavy in this area. Taxis dodged Citi Bikes and horse-drawn buggies. The sounds of many languages being spoken amid the honking and ubiquitous construction echoed in my head. All I could think was there's no way Will knew. I took a deep breath before turning back toward the benches to wait for him, wondering what, if anything, this meant.

CENTRAL PARK was stunning in the springtime. Daffodils and tulips dotted the wide paths under lush green canopies. There were more people milling about than usual, and who could blame them? After a harsh winter, it was hard to resist the lure of sunshine and a cloudless sky. I adjusted my sunglasses to block the early-afternoon glare as Will pointed out places of interest like a seasoned tour guide.

"This field is called Sheep Meadow because it was once home to a flock of purebred sheep. I think it was from the mid-1800s to the 1930s. The Tavern on the Green restaurant was where the sheep and shepherd lived. Crazy, huh?"

"Which part? The sheep in Central Park or the fact you know this stuff?"

Will lowered his Ray-Bans to give me an irritated scowl. I chuckled and pulled him against me, slinging my arm over his shoulder to kiss his cheek but licked it instead.

"Ew! Rand!"

I laughed as he swiped at his cheek and glared at me. His hair had grown out, so the tousled, sun-streaked locks fell into his eyes when he turned quickly.

"Sorry. The sheep story was really interesting. Tell me more."

"You aren't sorry. You're just annoying. I'm done talking to you."

"Hmph. Well, tell me about your visit with Mommy, then. I'm crushed I wasn't invited to brunch."

"I bet."

"Can I just say she's nothing like I expected?"

Will went quiet and gave me a chagrined sideways glance. "I'm sorry she offended you the other day. Sometimes I think she tries, but then I think she doesn't know how. I can't decide if that's terrible or if it's something I have to let go."

"I wanted to rattle her. I hate being ignored."

"Well, you succeeded. She asked about you again this morning."

"I thought she was only here for a night."

"Me too. She wanted to spend more time shopping in the city. She's gone now. I'm just glad I remembered to set an alarm this morning to meet her. I would have had a hard time explaining why I missed brunch."

"You're a twenty-two-year-old college student. I'm sure she'd understand."

"She wouldn't. And she wouldn't understand anything about last night, either." He turned a bright shade of red before continuing. "I mean, about the show."

"Gotcha," I said with a mischievous grin. I wrapped my arm around him again. "So where did you tell her you were last night?"

"A school function. I started to tell her I had to work at the theater until I heard she was going to a play with Martin and—"

I dropped my arm and stopped in my tracks. "Marty again?"

Will bit the inside of his lip and looked away. "Let's not go there. They're friends. I can't do anything about it."

"Do you think they'd still be friends if she knew about him?"

"Maybe," he said with a shrug. "I suppose it depends on how they rank our sins. All he did was offer a proposition. I didn't have to accept. Even if it didn't last beyond a couple dates, I'm guilty too. Besides, Martin is a successful, married man. I'm gay."

"That makes no sense. You're a lot of things besides gay." When he shrugged absently, I decided to ask another question. "Do you think there's anything special between your mom and Marty?"

Will's brow furrowed. He inclined his head thoughtfully. I could practically see the wheels in his head turning. When he didn't answer immediately, I was sorry I brought it up. "Why do you ask?"

"I don't know. I'm just being a jerk."

"As far as I know they're just friends. They seemed normal at breakfast. They both asked a lot of annoying questions about my post-graduation plans. No one likes the idea of me staying in the city for grad school. Especially if my degree is in music and theater. It's too gay."

"And you told them where to shove it, eh?"

Will chuckled. "Not exactly, but I wish I had. It's a particular talent of my mom's to make the word *gay* sound like an insult. A disease. I grew up thinking there was something wrong with me. My *parents* fed me that line. Not about me specifically, but in the years before I could say what it was that was different about me, the one thing I hoped it wasn't was gay. No one had anything good to say about homosexuality.

"I have this very vivid memory of coming to the city when I was about twelve. We'd been here before, so it wasn't the everyday sightseeing stuff I cared about. It was the theater. We had tickets to see *Spring Awakening*, and I couldn't wait. My dad's not-so-subtle eye roll didn't ruin anything for me. This was a big deal. I wasn't disappointed. It was so... amazing. I was blown away by the storyline, the music... everything. I think that's when I knew I wanted to do something in theater. I was moved to tears, and I couldn't hold them back. Dad was mortified. He looked over at my mom and snapped at her to deal with me before everyone got the idea I was gay."

"Your dad sounds like a dick."

"Well, he was right. I am gay." Will huffed humorlessly. "I'm not the son he thought he'd have. His strategy is to punish me by cutting me off emotionally and financially, like that will make me want to be who he expects. And my mom... sometimes I think she's in my corner, but then I'm not so sure. I think she puts on a show because she doesn't want anyone to know she has a gay son and a difficult husband. If she plays the role of doting wife and mother, no one will know we have skeletons in our closet. Like my gayness. Families are so... hard. There is so much pretense and old games that no one remembers the rules to anymore. Dysfunction at its finest."

"Every family is like that to some degree. The trick is not letting your folks or anyone else dictate how you find happiness. I like your 'gayness.' Be proud of it."

Will smiled. "I'm starting to feel like I can get there. If it's a sin to feel so good, I want to be a sinner. Like you."

I threw my head back and laughed, then slung my arm back over his shoulder. "That's the spirit!"

We stopped to make room for a gaggle of screaming kids chasing each other out to the open field behind us. I watched their progress, thinking it would be so nice to have no bigger worries than making sure you weren't "it" in a game of tag. Finding out Will's father was a homophobic jerk and his mother was possibly having an affair with the guy who propositioned him to be his cross-dressing escort felt heavy.

The people he should be able to count on for support weren't there for him. He really was alone. I was almost grateful when my phone buzzed loudly in my pocket, diverting my attention.

"You should answer. I'm curious to hear what the word is on last night."

"The word, eh?" I teased. A straggling kid darted in front of me to join his friends. I sidestepped him and almost dropped my cell. I juggled it at the last second and answered quickly without looking at the caller ID.

"Hi, Rand. It's Leah."

"Oh hi. What's up?"

"Great show last night. Your new guitarist is incredible!"

"Thanks. He was pretty awesome. We needed someone to cover for Terry at the last—"

"I couldn't believe he'd fuck up an opportunity like that."

"Yeah. Hey, can I call you back? I'm—"

"Of course. I just want you to know I'm in your corner, Rand. I want Spiral to succeed." Her voice dropped to a low, sexy note that instantly made me wary. She switched gears a second later, sounding infinitely professional. "I have some PR ideas I want to discuss with you. Can you meet tomorrow?"

"Um… sure."

"Good. I'll touch base with you in the morning."

I turned my phone off and stuffed it in my back pocket. A prickly heat covered my skin. I couldn't figure out the source without thinking it through, but I sensed a shift that required I move cautiously.

"Who was that?" Will asked nonchalantly.

"Leah."

"Oh."

"She has PR ideas and—whatever. I'm hungry. Let's get ice cream. I'll buy."

I pulled at his arm and yanked him up the path before he could ask any questions. Like why was Leah always around? Why did she want to meet? Are you really buying the PR bullshit? The last forty-eight hours or so confused me. I was trying to straddle some invisible line to keep my goals moving forward. I knew what I wanted, but it didn't seem so simple anymore. And I had a queasy feeling it was about to get a hell of a lot more complicated.

LEAH CALLED me the following morning as promised to set a time to meet later in the day. I assumed she wanted to come by the studio in the afternoon to talk to the band, but she had something else in mind.

"I know a great restaurant near the studio. I'll request a quiet table for two so we'll be able to talk. I'll text you the address. How does seven sound?"

"Uh. Good. I—I'll see you later."

It didn't sound good. It sounded like trouble.

I looked over at Cory standing next to the sink in our tiny kitchen. "Help."

"What happened?" he asked, methodically peeling a banana.

"She's after me." I gave Cory the short version of my recent interactions with Leah. "Has Holly said anything about what happened with her and Terry?"

"She didn't say much, but I know she dumped him. I get the impression they were never serious." He paused and cocked his head meaningfully. "You want to know what I really think?"

"I'm not sure."

"I'll tell you anyway. I think she was using him to get to you. Maybe make you jealous. Now you're playing hard to get and she's gotta have you."

I snorted. "I'm not playing hard to get. I'm just not interested."

"Since when are you not interested in someone like Leah? Whatever. I knew Terry wasn't gonna last. She constantly egged him on. I haven't been around a couple who does that much groping without alcohol being involved since high school. She wanted you to know what you were missing. If you ask me... she's the reason Terry didn't work out. She sabotaged this."

"That's a stretch."

"Maybe. Maybe not. But I'd be careful, man. She's sexy as hell, but she wants a man in a band. Lead guitarist is cool but lead singer? Even better. Looks like you're next."

THE CASUAL text she sent later with instructions to meet her at the bar made me think I'd overreacted and Cory was reading too much into things. So Leah was a flirt. So what? I was too. Generally it was a matter of no harm, no foul. But I had to question her motivations. I didn't really think it was all about sex or dating a guy in a band. I had a feeling she was looking to jumpstart her career. I didn't have a problem with hiring her on to do PR work if she was willing to do it for peanuts for a while. However, I was obviously going to have to make it clear this was a professional arrangement only. Which was why I ultimately felt like meeting her alone was probably appropriate versus meeting with the band in tow. I needed to get the uncomfortable part of setting boundaries over with now.

I was on high alert when I stepped inside the Orange Tree Bistro later that evening. It was fancy. As in not my kind of place at all. There were potted plants I supposed provided a rustic element, but the crystal chandeliers and ornate mirrors made me glad I'd thought to wear a black-collared shirt with my jeans.

"Hi there!"

Leah stood to greet me when the hostess escorted me to our table. Like me, she was dressed entirely in black as usual, but the slinky, formfitting material and plunging neckline weren't the norm. Nor was her effusive hello. She leaned in as though she were going to peck my cheek and at the last second aimed for my lips. I pulled back and gave her a curious look. The one she gave me in return said she'd happily skip dinner and move on to dessert.

"Nice place," I commented idly as I reached for the wine list.

"I ordered a bottle. I hope you don't mind. It should be here soon. In the meantime, tell me about your day."

A sommelier was at our table before I could respond. While he described the fruity blend of the wine he was about to pour, I nodded attentively and tried to figure out how to deal with this unexpected date. Because that's what it felt like. She was crafty, but I was on to her. It was up to me to keep us on track.

"I like the PR ideas you mentioned last week. We're strapped for cash, which is why we haven't hired a firm. I've been the one in charge of a social media presence. Mike helps now but we're bare bones." I snorted and took a sip of wine. "We may be for a while. We need a guitarist again now that Terry—"

"I broke up with him." She gave a short self-deprecating huff and swirled the burgundy liquid in her glass lazily. "I didn't mean to blurt that out, but I think I should be clear about our relationship. It wasn't ever serious, but it's definitely over now. It was easy to say good-bye to him after what he did to you guys. I'm sorry to be associated with him. I don't mean to come on too strong, but I want to work with the band. I've seen what you're capable of over the last couple months, and I want to help. That's all."

She was saying all the right things, and her expression was perfectly sincere.

"All right, then. Cool."

We shared a smile that seemed to convey mutual understanding and got down to business. We talked about markets, social media, and branding over dinner. It was refreshing to discuss strategies with someone who knew our music and had a feel for our general vibe.

"The guy who took over for Terry was genius. Who is he?"

"A friend who was thankfully in the right place at the right time. He's not going to take the vacancy, unfortunately. I'll have to find a replacement. Mike said he's got a couple possible candidates." I kept my tone carefully neutral.

"Too bad. I liked his aesthetic. It was fearless. I think the visual contrast he provided made an impact the other night. You might want to consider carrying it on. It's a flash of glam. Audiences love it."

"I agree." Will had given me the pop of interest I was looking for without realizing. It might be tricky finding someone willing to dress the part, but I liked the concept. "I know a potential stylist."

"Excellent. I have a couple of big projects I'm working on now, but I can start revamping your site and contacting bloggers now if you're interested."

"I am. I need to talk to Mike and the guys, but I have to ask... why do you want to help us? We're a long shot. We don't have a record deal yet and—"

"You will."

I liked the certainty in her gaze. I met her Cheshire cat grin with one of my own, suddenly very glad I'd braved this "date." Until she spoke again.

"You mentioned you were seeing someone. How serious is it?" The flirtatious note was unmistakably layered with sex.

"Serious. I think."

Leah chuckled softly and leaned forward with her arms on the table. "Good to know."

TWO CONTRACTS came through later the following week, and a dreamlike state fell over all of us. Nothing seemed real. How could anyone be offered that much money to do something they loved? It was crazy. The numbers were mind-boggling. There was a lot to consider in deciding which deal best worked for Spiral. Both were lucrative, but the one from the big-name record company seemed more like a standard-issue contract for first-time acts. The loopholes designed to protect the firm could pose a possible detriment to us creatively. The second offer seemed like a better fit. It was from a smaller label called Suite Dog Records, founded by alternative recording artists. After meeting with their representatives, I instinctively felt they were our best option for protecting the integrity of our sound. The last thing I wanted was to have an idiot engineer layer our music with synthesized tracks and gospel-inspired background vocals against our wishes. I wanted to maintain as much control as possible. The money was fantastic to sign and astronomical later on. More than I ever could have imagined. And if our first album did well, the sky was the limit. However, we had a couple problems to iron out. Fast.

"We need Will's name off the contract."

Cory, Tim, and I were sitting around the small conference table in Mike's office going through the contract line by line before we had a lawyer do it again, but it was a good exercise for us to formulate a plan of attack. Mike was having a harder time than usual sitting still. He'd never been involved in a deal potentially as big as this one. I could tell he was prepared to agree to everything I said until I finally shut up and signed the damn contract.

"We won't know unless we run it by him. If he says no, we'll counter, find a replacement pronto, and sign." Mike sat back with a huge grin, only to fidget in his chair, bouncing his knees like a three-year-old as a strained silence ensued. "You liked Isaac. We can offer him the job if Will doesn't want it. Maybe we counter for him to take over until Isaac learns the material. There are more than one or two ways to lock this in, but we need to know if he'd be willing."

All eyes were on me.

"Ask him, Rand. This is it. If he says no, we'll counter like Mike said," Tim advised. "This is big for him too. The money is outrageous. The signing contract alone catapults all of us into the black. He's a college student. They're always broke. Even if he only agrees to a short-term option, it's a win-win."

"I don't know if he'll see it that way, but I'll talk to him. Just make sure the lawyer knows about Terry. I don't want any problems to pop up with him after the fact."

"Terry isn't going to be a problem. He knows he's out," Mike said confidently. "He's the one who fucked up. He gets it."

"And he wasn't bitter at all? Yeah, right. I don't buy it, Mikey. I don't care if the little fella has hurt feelings. What I don't want is for him to create problems later."

"Everything will be fine. Just talk to Will."

Chapter 10

THERE WASN'T time to orchestrate an optimal time and place to let Will know the contents of the contract. I had to move quickly and choose my words carefully. I ran through the script in my head as I set a plain bagel in the toaster and untied the ribbon on my apron. I glanced up at George, hoping to get his attention without having to interrupt his heated debate with one of his regular customers about the Yankees' prospects without Derek Jeter.

"It's dismal, I tell ya. Dismal! I can't stand to see those San Francisco assholes win the Series again. It just ain't right."

Mr. G bowed his head in sorrowful agreement. I wanted to roll my eyes and razz them about the Orioles kicking ass this year, but for all I knew they sucked too. I hadn't watched any baseball this season, and I didn't have the patience to google their stats. I barely had patience to wait for a freaking bagel to toast.

"Randall, do you mind if I ask a nosy question?" George whispered in my ear. I jumped, surprised to find him so close when he'd been in an intense discussion on the other side of the counter a moment ago.

"Sure. Go ahead," I said distractedly as I slathered cream cheese over the plain bagel.

"Are you in trouble, son?"

"Huh? No. Why do you ask?" My confusion must have been obvious. The older man let out a relieved rush of air and patted my shoulder affectionately.

"Oh good. You've been so happy that I thought maybe you found a girl, but this past week you've seemed out of sorts. I know your family isn't nearby, but if you feel like talking… well, I'm happy to listen."

I was dumbfounded. I stared at him like an idiot, thinking I should have looked up the baseball stats after all.

"Uh… I'm fine. Thanks for asking. I'm just preoccupied."

"With a girl?" he asked with a wink.

"Not exactly." I wrapped the bagel in foil and pulled out a paper bag before looking George in the eye. "There's a guy I like who says he's out of the closet but is going back in soon. I'm kinda crazy about him and it freaks me out. And I've got a girl after me who looks, sounds, and acts like my type, but I can't fake interest 'cause I can't get the guy out of my head. It's confusing as hell. All I wanted was to come to New York and make music. I've done a great job avoiding complications, and now I don't know what I'm doing. So yeah… I've got things on my mind. That's all."

It was George's turn to look astonished. I wanted to laugh but I had to get going.

"Oh. I didn't know. I would have introduced you to my son, Ezekiel. You should have told me."

"Mr. G, like it or not, Zeke has a boyfriend. And I've obviously got more on my plate than I can handle. I gotta run. See ya next week!"

"Wait!"

I grabbed my jacket and darted toward the open glass door, yelling a brief good-bye. I didn't want to waste time explaining my sexuality when my gayness or bi-ness was the last thing on my mind at the moment.

I made it to Washington Square Park in record time. Will was sitting at a bench facing the fountain, checking messages on his phone. His head was tilted in concentration. He looked thoughtful but serene. Just the sight of him made me smile. I felt a surge of affection so strong my heart skipped a beat. I didn't know where it came from, but the intensity alarmed me.

"Here you go. Spicy jalapeño cream cheese on a cheddar-and-onion bagel." I snuck up on him from behind and wagged the paper bag near his ear.

"My favorite," he snarked. He grabbed the bag without turning around, much to my chagrin.

"I thought so," I observed, skirting around the bench to take a seat beside him. "You have glitter under your eye."

Will lifted his glasses slightly and touched his left cheek. "Oops. Benny needed a guinea pig last night. He was pretty excited you called him about being the band's stylist. Does this mean you've heard from a label?"

I nodded distractedly. It was crowded for a midweek morning. I had a strong feeling of déjà vu of the first time we'd come here together when it was freezing outside and we'd had the place to ourselves. We'd talked then about what we wanted to be, where we wanted to go. What a difference a couple months made.

"You okay?"

I looked down at his hand on my arm and felt myself relax. He pulled out a water bottle, uncapped it, and handed it to me. I gave him a weak grin and took the bottle from him, watching as he painstakingly unwrapped his bagel. He took a bite and wiped his fingers on the corner of a napkin before offering me a piece. I shook my head and reached for the paperwork hidden in the folds of my jacket.

"Is that the contract?"

I nodded solemnly but busted up laughing when he squealed. Who was I kidding? It was pretty fucking amazing.

"There are a lot of details to iron out, which means lawyers and bureaucratic bullshit but… voilà!"

Will wasn't fooled. His eyes lit with excitement as he set the bagel on top of his bag and wiped his hands again before taking the papers from me.

"Help yourself. It's better than usual," he teased, adjusting his glasses.

"I'll have you know, I've become an MBT. That's short for master bagel toaster. And when it comes to cream cheese application… I'm the man."

Will chuckled, though he didn't look up from the contract. "You're very talented. It's toasted to perf—why is my name on this?" His brow furrowed as he read on.

I leaned back on the bench with my legs stretched out in front of me. No doubt I looked like I didn't have a care in the world. With my face turned toward the sun and my arms draped casually over the bench, I may as well have been on a lounge chair in the sand. Damn, I was a fucking amazing actor.

I pursed my lips and slowly turned. Will's intense no-bullshit expression demanded an explanation without an addendum to my list of worries.

"They want you too." I sat up tall and bent my knee to fully face him. "There were two offers. This is the better one because of the way it's tiered. We can do some initial recording and play a few gigs here and in LA before things get serious."

"Meaning what exactly?"

"It means we've been offered a deal to record our first album with a real label backing us. We won't be a five-man show anymore—four musicians with a manager. We'll have a real live staff managing tours and general logistics. It's the beginning. Don't get me wrong, we'll have to work our asses off and there are no guarantees but… it means we've been given a shot."

"I'm happy for you but—"

"I know. Look—" I closed my eyes and let out a breath before continuing. "I know you didn't intend to join a band when you got onstage, but you made an impression, Will. They loved you. You were a big part of why we were amazing."

"How did they know my full name? Did you tell them?"

"No. Tim told Cory, who told Mike when he started getting calls about them wanting to meet you. Cory asked Holly and—"

"Rand, I—"

"There's a signing bonus. It's enough money to help you to pay off some of your student debt, or at least the money you owe Marty. And you'd still have cash on hand to help with grad school. There's no pressure for you to join us. We'll counter without your name if you don't want anything to do with it. But if you played through summer and helped train Isaac, the guy we're thinking of hiring, well then…." I shrugged, unsure how to continue.

Silence.

He set the contract aside and rewrapped his bagel. I cocked my head, mindful of his deliberate movement.

"Aren't you gonna eat?"

"I lost my appetite." He stared into the distance. Maybe the students filming near the fountain had his attention or perhaps he recognized the guy playing the baby grand piano nearby. Wishful thinking. I listened to the strains of a Beethoven sonata, thinking idly the piano was slightly out of tune.

"I'm going to class. I'll see you later." He stood abruptly, upending his water bottle in his haste to get away. It fell to the ground, splattering our shoes. I grabbed his arm when he bent to retrieve it.

"We need to talk, Will."

"I can't talk to you right now. I'm too pissed and I don't even know why. I'm happy for you, but this is your dream, Rand. Not mine. I didn't want anyone to know my name. That night was a one-time deal for me. My family would freak out and—"

"Leave your family out of this." I pulled his hand when he stepped away. "Maybe this isn't what you planned, but it isn't a bad thing. The reason you were so good that night was because you were doing something you loved. Something you're good at. You played to over a thousand people like you'd done it every night of your life in a wig, makeup, and a weirdass getup you wouldn't be caught dead in anywhere else in a city where no one gives a shit what you wear. Nothing mattered but the music."

The look he gave me was scathing. I was taken aback by his anger. I expected him to be confused maybe, but not pissed.

"Sometimes there's more at stake than just the music. This isn't about what I like or don't like. It's bigger than me. Or you. You're so…." He growled and spun away from me, then turned back and stabbed his finger into my chest. "Frustrating and egotistical. You think you know what's right for everyone, but you don't know this time! You don't know me."

"Hey!" I yanked him against me. "I do know you, and I see things in you that you can't. Or won't. I'm not begging you to join us. I'm not trying to convince you this is *your* chance of a lifetime. But I will point out… this will help you get out from under the mountain of debt that made you put on a wig and a pair of heels in the first place. You took a chance and you're being given an opportunity in return. That's all. Your choice. Read the contract and think about it."

I picked up the water bottle, set his book bag over his shoulder, and handed him the paper bag with his cold bagel. He took the bag but he wouldn't look at me. When I tilted his chin gently with my thumb and lifted his sunglasses, I was alarmed to see his eyes were wet with unshed tears.

"Will? Baby, what is it?"

He shook his head violently and brushed his hand across his nose. He looked anxious and upset. None of these reactions seemed to fit. I felt like we were talking about two different things and I had no idea what the second topic was about. I was baffled.

"It's nothing. I'll talk to you later."

"You know me better than that. You'll know I'll follow you and—"

"Yes, I know. You're relentless. You never stop 'til you get your way. Even though every once in a while, it would be nice if you… just left things alone." His quivering tone took the sting out of his words. Maybe I was tenacious when I shouldn't be, but I sensed I wasn't the real problem this time.

"Tell me what's wrong."

Will bit his lip and let out a heavy sigh before walking back to the bench we'd vacated. He crossed his arms and legs and looked toward some unknown object in the distance, though I knew he was very aware of my presence. I sat facing him with my knee resting on the bench and studied him for clues. He let the silence stretch uncomfortably before finally looking at me.

"I'm not who you think I am."

Huh? "Who are you?"

"I'm me, but—" He licked his lips nervously before continuing. "—I'm not the kind of person you like."

I cocked my head and waited. "What does that mean?"

"My parents, my world. I only told you part of it."

I wanted to say, "Yeah, I know. I can practically see your demons following you," but I waited for him to continue.

"I was cut off for belligerence. Going to NYU was not what my dad wanted. My petty defiance was an experiment that was supposed to last one year tops before I came crawling home. We're at year four now and I'm about to graduate."

"You told me that already."

"Well, my mom's recent visit was to make sure I remembered it was time to grow up, take back my words, and renounce my homosexuality. She said Dad had offered to pay my student loans in full and she'd quietly cover the amount I owe Martin. She wasn't happy when you showed up because this... my silence means a lot to them."

"Why? Nobody here cares if you're gay."

"Some people care, Rand." He heaved a weary-sounding sigh and crossed his arms. "My dad is running for governor in next year's election. Charles Sanders. Have you heard of him?"

Holy fuck. Yeah, I'd heard of him. Charles Sanders was a well-known sanctimonious asshole. The sort who supported "old-fashioned" family values and religious freedom to take radical aim against immorality and liberal agendas. If you weren't white, straight, well employed and a steady churchgoer, you were bound for hell—and a dose of persecution from people like him who used fear to dictate their own version of the laws of human decency. He'd been on the news recently, voicing his strong opinions about gay marriage. There had been talk about him running for governor, but I must have missed the latest reports that he'd actually put his name in the hat. Poor Indiana.

I stared at him incredulously. Poor Will.

"You're kidding, right?" I asked hopefully.

"No. I should have told you from the start, but I didn't think I'd—I figured I'd graduate, step back in the closet during my dad's campaign, and then… maybe eventually make my way out again. Someday. I didn't think I had a choice."

I held my breath for a moment and let it out in a rush before asking my next question. "When were you going to tell me about your dad?"

"I hadn't thought that far ahead. I'm sorry. Since I met you, I've been living one day at a time. I've been sucking up memories and experiences I never thought I'd have. I was pretty sure you wouldn't want anything to do with me if you found out where I'm from. I figured our time would expire before it came up."

I ran my hand over my stubbled jaw. I'd barely come to grips with the contract in my hands, and now I was reeling from Will's revelation. You don't find out the guy you've been sleeping with is the son of a religious fruit loop with political aspirations every day. It was crazy and unexpected, but it wasn't what had my heart skidding to a halt.

"Are you telling me we've expired now? Like a carton of milk or something?"

"No. I don't want this to be over. I know this thing between us is new, but… it's more than that. I'm just not ready to say good-bye."

"Then don't." The weight on my chest was heavy. I wasn't sure what I was up against, but I was willing to fight if he was. "Can I ask you something?"

"Sure."

"Maybe your dad's dream comes true and he's elected governor—but what about you and your dreams?"

Will leaned forward, bracing his forearms on his knees. "What do you me—?"

"Give me the summer."

"What?" Will straightened and lowered his glasses as though it might help him understand what the hell I was saying.

"Give me a chance to show you a different way."

"What do you mean?"

"Play with us. You can dress up. Play a part. Be someone else. Wear a wig, makeup, whatever you need. Make some money and then decide what you want to be when you grow up. Give yourself an experience of a lifetime. Something to remember before you have to make big decisions. Pretend it's a summer job that pays really fucking well. We can keep us on the DL. The record label basically asked that I do that anyway."

"You told them about us?" His eyes widened with fresh worry.

"No, relax. But they wanted to do a cavity search on my personal life. I didn't name you, but when I told them I was bi and seeing a guy, they said they'd prefer I didn't shout it from the rooftops. At least not right away. I was planning on telling them to fuck off, but… I can keep quiet. For you. If it helps. Just—don't give up, Will. Not yet. Please."

"I want to say yes, but what do I tell my parents? My mom stayed in the city longer to make sure I remembered my family duty, which didn't include disreputable men with tattoos. How will I explain—?"

"You don't. Tell them you have a summer job. One that may require some travel. Tell them whatever you need to, but think about it. Would anyone recognize you in disguise? Even if they knew your real name, it's a fairly common one. They wouldn't associate you with some dude running for governor in another state. You can trust Tim, Cory, and Mike and… no one else will know so—"

"It's not your band or the people listening to your music my dad cares about. It's his voters. He's spinning over anyone finding out I'm gay as it is. Throw in makeup, a band of left-leaning, tatted punks… one who told my mom he's my boyfriend, and it's going to raise some pretty major red flags. He'll go nuts."

"He won't know. It's only a few months, and other than a couple stage shows, you'd be practically invisible. You'd spend most of the time training the new guy. Look… I'm being a jerk and I know it. A nicer guy would let you go and leave you to decide what you want. But I'm a selfish fucker, Will. I want it all. And I want you." I stood and picked up his messenger bag. I waited for him to join me before setting it over his shoulder. "The contract is in your bag. Read it and let me know what you decide."

"Okay."

We stared at each other for a moment in silent understanding.

"So what's for dinner later?"

"Really?" Will gave me another one of those incredulous looks like he couldn't believe he was stuck with me.

"Yeah. The world is upside down and backward, but we still have to eat, baby. How about Thai?"

Will bumped my arm playfully and chuckled. His smile wasn't overly radiant but it was hopeful. And at that moment, it was what I needed.

I was dangerously close to sensory overload. I could barely process Will's revelation and all it entailed. Nor could I forget the image of Mrs. Sanders with Marty and what it implied. Was his mother having an affair with her good "friend" while demanding her son pretend he was straight? The hypocrisy of their skewed so-called family values was outrageous.

And in the middle of all this, I'd finally been given my first real opportunity to make my dream a reality. Nothing was certain, but if timing was everything, I had to wonder what this all meant for Spiral's future... and mine.

WHEN WILL agreed to play with us for the summer, I was over the moon. Sure, it was temporary, but it was a great solution to a few problems. One of which was to get Isaac, our new guitarist, up to speed before we went into Suite Dog's recording studios in the fall. Isaac was a thin, good-looking, African American man in his late twenties with high cheekbones and vaguely feminine features. He was the perfect substitute for Will from a style perspective. He was nowhere near as talented, but he was good. Certainly better than Terry had been and better natured. He had a sharp sense of humor and was quick with a joke. If he could learn our songs and perform them well, he might just be the perfect replacement after Will started grad school in August.

A few weeks after we'd signed the contract, it was apparent to the entire band that we'd officially entered a new phase. We spent long hours practicing and more time than I cared to talking about promotion. Our contact at Suite Dog Records was a savvy visionary. I'd liked Ed Espinosa right away. He was a thirtysomething Puerto Rican New Yorker with a thick Bronx accent and a penchant for wearing fedoras with designer jeans and artsy T-shirts with wacky script or borderline offensive verbiage on them. And he loved Spiral. He was a great advocate with a nimble mind for business. He seemed to know his stuff. PR was a big deal, and he assured us we were in great hands with Leah. Ed hired her on the spot. He assured us her style would work well with a fledgling band.

Leah's job initially was to create a slow-burning buzz before our first track was released commercially. She seemed to be as well connected as she claimed. There was more traffic on our website than ever. Whatever she was doing was working. Leah was very professional in her new capacity, particularly around Ed. But when it was just the band, she vacillated from cool and laid-back to downright brazen. Tim and Cory would exchange amused looks while I tried to fend her off without alienating her and at the same time somehow not piss Will off.

He never said a word, but I noticed him watching her red fingernails rake over my forearm as she went on about a funny tweet she posted about the band. Flirting was harmless as long as everyone knew the score. But everyone was a little confused. Including me. I was stuck in a weird triangle I could have easily defused if I had the okay to reveal who Will was to me. I didn't. So for now, I was quiet. And it was starting to eat at me.

My MIND was all over the place as I pushed open the door of the bagel shop and headed west on Fourth. Thoughts of Leah's latest idea to do an intimate interview with only me warred with the instrumentation I had in my head for a new song. I had a feeling "intimate" meant her and me, and fuck I didn't want to have *that* conversation, the one I thought we'd had at the restaurant. I'd never had to tell a girl to back off because I was with a guy.

I was going to have to do or say something soon. It was driving me crazy. I quickened my pace just as someone yelled my name. I turned, but when I didn't see anyone I recognized, I moved on.

"Rand!"

I stopped again and immediately wished I hadn't.

"Terry. How's it going?" I gave him a brief once-over and uncharitably thought he looked like hell. His shaggy brown hair and beard were long and unruly, giving him an air of someone who'd crossed the line from hip and edgy to borderline sane.

"All right. I got my job back at Starbucks, so it's cool. Not as cool as a record contract but hey." He barked a short laugh and shrugged convulsively in a way that made me think he was unhinged.

"Right. Well, good luck. See ya." I turned away and started up the street only to be stopped again by his hand on my arm. I shook him off with a scowl. "What do you want, Terry?"

"I want my fair share. That's what I want."

I narrowed my eyes and made sure to skewer him with every last ounce of contempt I had.

"You got your fair share. And then you passed out. It's over, Terry. Your affiliation with Spiral officially ended at the bar that night."

"Oh yeah, the night your boy took over for me. I was starting to think you were a goddamn fag, but then I heard you're with my girl now. Jesus. You've got no fuckin' class, O'Malley."

"Excuse me?"

"You heard me. Stay away from Leah. She's mine."

I should have rolled my eyes and walked away, but I felt like setting the little fucker straight.

"I'm *not* with her, but that shouldn't matter to you. According to her, you're done. She's not your business, just like Spiral is no longer your business. Good luck, man."

When I took a step back, he grabbed my elbow.

"She's not the kind of chick who's gonna want a guy who's into dick too. Neither are your so-called fans. Most people think your kind is disgusting. Trust me. You don't want them to know, do you?"

I stared at him until he flinched and looked away. I took perverse satisfaction in knowing I made the little shit nervous.

"Are you threatening me?" I held up a hand when he sputtered like a fish out of water. "I wouldn't do that if I were you. You're exposed. You're a mediocre, lazy piece of shit. I've got no time for you."

"You owe me—"

I stepped into his space, so close I could smell his fear. The urge to wring his neck was strong, but he wasn't worth the hassle of dealing with the police. My tone was low and menacing.

"I owe you nothing. Not a fucking thing. You mess with me, you'll regret it."

I shoved him away and turned up the street. It took everything I had not to go back and knock him to his knees. I dialed Ed's number and left a quick message. For once I was grateful to pass the bullshit on to someone else so I could concentrate on what mattered.

I ARRANGED to meet Will later that day after he cleaned his things from the classroom he'd used to tutor. The area around NYU seemed a little quieter now that school was out. It was late May, so there were plenty of tourists, but then, they were all over the city at this time of year. I checked the time and glanced toward the heavy glass doors of the Performing Arts Center just as Will emerged carrying a guitar case. I greeted him with a smile and then immediately stuck my hand out to hail a cab. He gave me a curious look but didn't say a word. Taxis were reserved for odd hours or special occasions. It was a shared joke that I traveled primarily by foot or subway. And until the first big checks came in, I'd assured him that was how it would stay. I gave the driver a Tribeca address and sat back.

"Where are we going?"

"You'll see."

I glanced out the window while Will pretended to watch the snippet from *The Today Show* on the Prius's tiny television screen mounted in the backseat. The ride was relatively short. I paid the fare, then led the way into the modern luxury condo. Will followed me with a funny expression that made it very clear he wondered what the hell I was up to. I greeted the doorman, who smiled warmly and handed me a card key and an envelope.

"Karen left instructions. She said you'd be by about now. Take your time. She'll be here as soon as she makes it through midtown traffic."

"Thanks, Keith." I picked up the guitar case with my free hand and moved toward the elevator.

The building was brand-new and ultra-hip. The elevator barely made a sound as it jetted from the lobby to the fifteenth floor. I kept my gaze forward, grateful Will had yet to ask any questions, such as "what the fuck?" I stopped in front of 1505 and slid the card key in the lock before opening the door with a flourish.

Will stepped into the large, airy, unfurnished condominium and looked around. The two-bedroom flat boasted state-of-the-art amenities ranging from high ceilings to top-of-the-line appliances, pale wide-planked wood flooring, and upscale finishings. He walked toward the bank of windows and peeked out at the impressive view of the Hudson River and the Jersey skyline.

"It's nice, huh?" I set his guitar case down and went to stand by his side.

"Very nice. Why are we here?"

I took a deep breath and moved toward the black granite island separating the kitchen from the great room. "I'm going to lease this place. I mean, I'm considering it. What do you think?"

"Can you really afford this?"

"Yeah. I can. I'm only signing a short-term lease in case things don't go well during phase one, but I've been hoarding money like a miser for years to fund Spiral, and now that the contract has finally come in, I can relax a little."

"How short is your short-term lease?"

"Through August. If we tank, I can move back into a shared hovel on the Lower East Side. Or maybe move to Queens. So… what do you think?"

"Hmm. It's beautiful."

"Well, happy graduation, then. We move in on the First."

It would be hard to say which one of us was more surprised. I couldn't believe I'd said that out loud. But since I had, I decided to own it. I gave him an overly bright smile that clearly said the ball was in his court.

"I knew you were up to something. What are you talking about?" He adjusted his glasses and moved to lean his hip against the island so we stood a couple feet apart.

"I'm talking about living in style for a couple months. What do ya say?"

"I say you're crazy. Living together isn't keeping us on the DL."

"We'll say we're roommates," I suggested with a shrug.

"Roommates."

Will turned toward the window so I couldn't see his face, but something told me I was hitting the wrong note. I tried again.

"Logistically it's a great idea. This place is close to Suite Dog Studios, as in it's walkable. No taxis or subway necessary. Plus, it's really fucking nice. A swanky, convenient address… *and* there's a king-sized bed. Not a futon."

"Rand… think about it. It's a PR disaster."

"No, it's genius. We aren't under surveillance. No one will care if we're roommates."

"Leah will."

I stopped in my tracks.

This was the first time he'd brought her name up in this context. It wasn't so much her name as it was his tone.

"Maybe, but she'll think we're sleeping in separate beds."

"She'll be relieved to know," he said sarcastically.

I stepped in front of him and cradled his chin between my thumb and forefinger. "Hey. You know I'm not interested in Leah. I'm—"

"Why not?"

"Huh?"

"She makes it pretty clear she's interested in you." He bit his bottom lip and looked away. "Whatever. I'm sorry I said anything."

"Do you trust me?"

Our gazes locked for a long moment before he nodded. "Yes."

"Good. I'm with you. I've never been in a monogamous… arrangement, but I want to try it. With you. This is only about us. Not the band. Not Leah."

Will stared at me intently as though he wasn't sure he heard me correctly. "You're sure?"

"Yeah." I backed him against the island and held his face before kissing his mouth softly. "Come on, let me show you where your toothbrush goes, roomie."

"I'm not moving in with you."

"You know I'm gonna talk you into it," I said, tickling his sides.

Will's bubbly laughter echoed in the empty space. It turned into a groan when I slid my hand over his crotch and palmed his cock through his jeans. I expected him to push me away, but he wound his arms around my neck instead and sealed his mouth over mine. I moaned into the kiss, licking his lips as his fingers combed through my hair. And then my cell rang. Loudly. I rested my forehead against his for a moment until he kissed my mouth and stepped aside for me to answer it.

"Hi, Karen. Yeah. I'm here now. That's all right. Yeah—I'll see you soon. Thanks."

I put my phone away and slid my hand in Will's. "Come this way. We've got fifteen minutes and I need your help."

He let out a half laugh as I led him down the short hallway toward the master suite. "I'm still not moving in with you. What do you need my help with?"

"I have to buy stuff. That king-sized bed I was talking about and linens and… oh shit, I'll need towels too. Check this out."

The bathroom was gorgeous. A rough-hewn light-colored stone lined the mirror wall, giving way to a slick pane of glass separating the large walk-in shower. The fixtures, tile, and lighting were simple, modern, and tasteful. And after sharing a 1960s bathroom half this size with two buddies, it was downright luxurious.

"Wow. This is really nice." Will's eyes widened appreciatively.

"This is where your toothbrush goes. And there's plenty of room for makeup and stuff in here—" I said, pointing at the drawer space in the cabinetry between the sleek dual sinks.

He smiled as he caught my gaze in the long, rectangular mirror. I folded my arms around his chest, then slipped my fingers under his T-shirt to tweak his nipples. He let his head fall back on my shoulder, exposing his neck. I nibbled his throat as I moved my right hand south to unbuckle his belt and unzip his jeans.

"But we better test things out first."

He craned his neck and gave me a reproving look. His hands moving over mine were a good indication he didn't mind, though. "Rand, it's not your place yet. We can't—"

"We have to. If the sex is no good in this room, we'll have to try another. Don't say no, baby. We have twelve minutes." I freed myself from the confines of my jeans and lowered his to expose his beautiful ass. I set my palm over his mouth. "Lick it."

He obeyed, then leaned forward with one hand on the marble countertop and one on his dick. My mouth went dry. I couldn't believe he was giving in this easily. This was the guy who rarely consented to holding hands in public. The fact he was wantonly arching his back and presenting his ass like a fucking gift was a crazy turn-on. I reached around and wrapped my fingers around his shaft. He was already hard and leaking precum. He looked at me in the mirror's reflection and bit his bottom lip.

"You better get to it. You have eleven minutes."

"Oh. My. God." I blinked to clear my lust-hazed vision and felt inside my back pocket for a condom. I could only hope it was lubed. I hurriedly opened the packet and rolled the latex over my rigid cock.

"Do it." He pushed back so the head of my dick rode his crack.

I spit on my fingers, then eased one inside him. I watched him carefully in the mirror to gauge his reaction. He didn't move until I curled the digit and stroked his sweet spot. His eyes took on a hedonistic look of pure ecstasy. I added a second finger and more saliva, still amazed he didn't comment. He moaned as he stroked himself. Then he reached for my cock, lined it against his hole, and pushed.

"Fuck, Will." I set my hands on his hips and held him steady for a moment until he nodded and pushed backward.

The motion was a slow in and out, give and take. Inch by inch I made my way inside him. When I was buried balls-deep, I leaned forward and kissed the back of his neck, surging forward, then pulling halfway out. The movement was gentle but insistent. An easy rhythm and a steady pace. He let go of his cock and met my harder thrusts with his hips tilted. His unfettered movement fed the fire inside me. The urge to plunge into him and fuck him senseless was strong, but he was running the show now. I held myself still and let him fuck himself on me until he lost his rhythm and gave me a curious look in the mirror.

"Keep going, baby."

Will's nostrils flared. The tentative slide soon gave way to a furious bucking motion. I stroked him as he rode me hard. It took every extra ounce of energy I had to stand upright. The sight of our jeans trapped around our ankles, the feel of his thick member pumping in my firm grasp as his muscles clutched me in a vise grip was intense. But it was the reflection in the mirror of his beautiful face with his glasses slightly askew on his freckled nose that was my undoing.

I wrapped my arms tightly around his chest and lost my last thread of control. My hips snapped as my orgasm threatened. I wanted him to cum first. I was desperate to hold on. I tilted his head and bit his jaw as I strained to find his mouth. When our tongues met, that was it. I couldn't hold back. Wave after wave pulled me under. I felt Will's release coat my fingers and tried to keep moving, but it took every bit of strength I had left to stand upright. The violent shaking nearly brought me to my knees.

Will's soft laugh rang out in the stone-and-marble bathroom. I looked up at his reflection with a smile, intending to join in because really… what the fuck were we doing? But my breath caught in my lungs. I swallowed hard and closed my eyes in an effort to get my balance back. He was perfect. Sweet, lovely, and so fucking beautiful. I wanted him.

And not just until August.

Chapter 11

IRONING OUT loose ends made it difficult to be productive creatively at first. It was as though I'd been operating a small business with a couple partners for a few years and we'd been bought by a big firm. The only thing we were responsible for now was churning out quality product. It was hard to let go of controlling the details at first. I'd been working behind the scenes dealing with logistics, as well as trying to write and perform, from the start. I fretted over basic changes, like working in a newer, nicer recording studio and having a bunch of new faces hanging around. It took some getting used to in the beginning.

On the positive side, having the freedom to give 100 percent of my time and effort to the music was electric. And sharing it with Will made it even better. Going from a couple of hours practicing a day with someone as good as Will, to playing full-time was a rush. He was by far the most superior musician we'd ever worked with. He made us better. Professionally we'd turned a corner thanks to the tall, skinny grad student with glasses who played guitar like a dream. But it was the personal side that had me in knots. He only had to look up at me after playing a complicated solo, with his sweet smile in place, and something inside me melted. It was torture not to touch him. By the end of the day, I was consumed by a hunger that left me edgy and anxious to get him alone.

I was grateful I'd splurged on my new place in Tribeca. The location was great. We could walk from the Hudson Street studios versus taking a subway to the East Village late at night, which was a huge bonus when we were both desperate for skin. And so was the luxury of leaving clothes where they dropped, drinking OJ straight from the container, and walking around naked at midnight. I'd never had a place of my own, and I loved it. Though most of the time, I wasn't alone. Will stayed over almost every night. If anyone asked, we could claim it was a matter of convenience and lie about him staying in the extra bedroom. I doubted anyone cared, and the only ones who knew we were more than friends were Tim and Benny. Cory may have suspected, but we hadn't discussed it. We were all caught up in the music and the moment. It was easy for us to slip into living a secret life. There was an idyllic quality to it I could liken to childhood summertime memories, like staying up late to catch fireflies and count stars.

Sure, it was hot and humid and the city was crowded. But it was invigorating. I hardly noticed pesky inconveniences, such as having no furniture. Actually, I did notice. I just didn't necessarily want to buy any. Buying stuff felt… permanent. It felt like a statement. I wasn't ready for statements.

"Why does the idea of buying a sofa make you sweat?" Will asked as he dodged a pedestrian walking a French poodle.

We were navigating Broadway on a Saturday morning in mid-June on a quest for inexpensive… stuff.

"Is it really necessary? I don't want to own things I won't need for long. There's a difference, young man, between want and need."

"Oh brother. Are you sure you're qualified to preach, O'Malley?"

"Probably not, but I—is this it?"

Will pointed at the home-goods store and grasped my arm when I kept walking down the street. "Come on. You can do this. I'll be here for support if you need me. What's the budget?"

"Ugh. I don't like that word." I sighed heavily as we entered the air-conditioned store. According to Will, I should be able to find a couple of decent pieces without emptying my wallet any more than I already had.

"You should love it. Give me a number and I'll point you in the right direction."

"Fifty bucks."

"Cheapskate. Try again." He walked with purpose toward a vignette featuring a bright orange modern-style sofa with a clear acrylic coffee table. "What do you think of this? It says it's a sleeper too. If you really want to convince everyone I'm your roomie, this might work."

"It's very… orange."

"Sit on it."

I gave him a dubious look but did as instructed. A good-looking young man with short, dark blond hair, chiseled cheekbones, and a cheery smile immediately descended.

"Hi there! Can I help you find anything?"

When I didn't answer right away, Will took over. "Yes, we're looking for furniture. A sofa and a coffee table to start. This guy is a little tight with a buck, so if you can keep this reasonable and somewhat painless, you may be able to make a quick sale."

The sales guy chuckled merrily and shot a curious glance between us. "I'd be happy to help! I'm Ryan, by the way. Are you furnishing a new home or—?"

"Yes. There's a bed, but that's about it," Will said.

I sat back on the orange sofa and crossed my legs while Will gave a rundown of what he thought would look best in the living room. He tried to draw me into the discussion, but when I pulled out my cell and told him I trusted his taste, he didn't seem bothered.

"Fantastic! Let me show you a couple pieces upstairs," Ryan gushed.

"I'll be here, honey. I've got a couple e-mails I need to respond to." I held up my cell as though it were proof of my sincerity.

Will scowled before turning to follow the enthusiastic salesman. "Okay, hon."

His syrupy tone should have been a warning, but I was slow on the uptake sometimes. And frankly, I was thrilled to get out of a shopping venture. Yes, I needed furniture. As much as I loved my new king-sized bed, I was getting tired of standing in the kitchen to eat. A picnic or two in the middle of the great room was fun initially, but the hardwood floors were a killer. I just didn't want to shop. Or part with money. I supposed I should have thought about that when I'd decided moving into an unfurnished luxury condo was a good idea. Typical O'Malley, I thought with a shrug.

Fifteen minutes or so later, I'd returned an e-mail, sent a few texts, and played a game on my phone. I was officially bored and ready to move on. I stood and looked at my surroundings for the first time since we'd walked in. This was an enormous warehouse-style building with exposed ducts and high ceilings. There were at least two floors, maybe three. But I couldn't tell without exploring, and I didn't want to. My feet felt stuck to the floor. I glanced toward a generous staircase with steel railings, hoping Will would magically appear. If I were really lucky, he'd tell me he bought a couple things and managed to keep the bill under a hundred bucks.

I sighed heavily when a full minute passed and it was clear my wish might not be granted. I meandered the downstairs area, looking for the cute, nerdy guy with glasses wearing a *Harry Potter* T-shirt. No luck. I trudged upstairs and did a brief survey of the area before I found Will and Ryan chatting away. As I approached I heard bits of their conversation about textile durability and how much sun the living room gets. Yawn. I considered sneaking downstairs and texting him from the Starbucks on the corner, but something about the way the two men had their heads bent over the swatches stopped me. They were laughing as they perused the large ring of colorful fabrics. I couldn't tell what the joke was until I closed the distance, but from a purely observational point of view… they looked good together. Like they fit. They were both clean-cut, well-dressed, and even looked to be about the same age. I felt a surge of emotion I didn't have a name for, but I didn't like the feeling. At all.

"…he always wanted it that way. You get used to not doing it all the time, but when it's gone, it's all you can think about," Ryan said in a soft voice. I missed the next line, but whatever it was made them both chuckle. Wait. Weren't they talking about sofas?

"I can't imagine not doing it. I'm obsessed!"

Doing what? It? Was this a sex conversation? No way. That wasn't Will's style. He was too private and straitlaced to joke about sex with a random salesman.

"You have good hands for it. I bet…."

Whoa. He was flirting with Will. Not okay. I cleared my throat loudly, announcing my presence. Will turned with a gigantic grin that nearly swept me off my feet.

"Hi, honey. I think we're almost done," he said, putting a little extra emphasis into the term of endearment.

"Good. I'm ready when—"

"Your husband was just telling me the orange might be a bit too much for your taste so…."

I think he was still talking, but after the "*H*-word" was dropped, it was hard for me to hear. A panicky sensation overcame me. I blinked a few times and licked my dry lips before finally looking at said husband. Will's mischievous expression and twinkling eyes were priceless. I was completely thrown off my game. In a weird way, it was like the night I recognized him in the bar wearing a dress. Sure, I'd been surprised by the dress, but it was his attitude that really got me. He possessed an underlying steely note of determination with a dose of "don't fuck with me" that was evidence of true strength of character. No boasting or posturing necessary. There were so many facets to the seemingly reserved, uptight musician. He had the uncanny ability to make me stop and think about what the hell I was doing. And put me in my place in the most unexpected ways.

Right now, for instance, I was standing in a furniture store sweating bullets because I'd been called someone's husband. It may have been his response to being the one stuck doing the shopping while I hung out playing *NBA Jam* on my iPhone, but there was no mistaking he had my attention now.

"Uh, yeah. It's a little bright, but—"

"I understand. I have another book of swatches. Let me grab it real quick!"

I was ultra-aware of Will's scrutiny, but I waited a beat before making eye contact. "Husband?"

Will busted up laughing. "You should see your face! Your coloring is a little off, sweetheart."

"Sweetheart? Husband? Honey? What am I missing?"

"Your brain, idiot! You're the one who rented an unfurnished condo. Not me! If you think I'm going to do your shopping while you sit around and—"

"Okay, okay. Calm down, hothead. Geesh!" I wrapped my arms around him and squeezed him tight.

"Can't breathe," he hissed.

I pulled back slightly and kissed his forehead with a chuckle. "Sorry. I wasn't trying to take advantage. I'm just—"

"Lazy."

I winced. "Only about stuff I don't care about... like a sofa. But, husband? That's so…."

Will grinned. "Permanent? I knew *boyfriend* wouldn't catch your attention, so I went for the big gun. Makes you sweat almost as much as parting with a few dollars, huh? Well, think before you act next time. Don't rent a place without furniture. Don't drag me to—"

I shut him up with a kiss. It was meant to distract him but quickly became something more. The sound of a book hitting a desk nearby jolted us back to the real world. What were we doing making out in a public store in SoHo? This was the antithesis of keeping things on the DL. I swallowed hard and stepped back to find Ryan standing a few feet away with his hands pressed together in a prayer-like gesture. He sighed theatrically and fluttered his eyelashes.

"I hope you don't mind me saying this, but you guys make the most adorable couple! How long have you been married?"

Will smirked and glanced at me.

"Feels like just yesterday… or six minutes ago, right, babe?"

LATER THAT night, I lay on top of Will gasping for breath. His legs were wrapped around my ass, and his fingers were tangled in my hair. I gingerly rose on my elbow and stared down at him. We shared a smile… one that wordlessly asked how the hell we wound up here again. I kissed his swollen lips and slowly moved off him. He rolled to his side. His eyes were half-closed as he traced the artwork on my bicep, seemingly lost in thought.

"What's on your mind?"

He smiled at me. The gesture was tinged with a hint of sadness that instantly alarmed me. I wanted to squelch his melancholy before it took over. I wanted him to smile like he had all afternoon as we strolled through shops. We had sampled gelato and let an ardent salesgirl on Prince Street wash our hands with French soap, then moisturize them with cocoa butter. We'd laughed about nothing in particular and found endless entertainment in silly things, like trying on hats at J.Crew and checking out headphones at the Apple Store. Days like today made me grateful I wrote lyrics. I'd typed phrases into my cell to remind me of how I might capture the way I felt just being with him.

"I love this. Being with you."

"Me too. Why do you look sad, then?"

"I'm not. I—my mom's coming mid-August. I don't know the exact date yet, but she mentioned something about making a family appearance at a rally in September. I think she wants to make sure I'll cooperate. She asked me for my student loan statements. Told me to send them over for Dad to take care of immediately." His tone was almost bored, but his words sounded like a grenade going off in my brain.

My heart thudded in my ears. "What did you tell her?"

"Nothing. I told her I took a summer job and wouldn't be home to visit. She said she was disappointed, but honestly I think she was relieved. She kept talking about where I'd live when I come home in September. It was weird."

"Don't they know you're going to grad school?"

"I told her. I just think she assumes I'll change my mind or that they'll change it for me."

"Don't these people know you? They've obviously never gone furniture shopping with you."

Will chuckled. "No complaining, O'Malley. I finagled a deal *and* got you same-day delivery."

"And I was suitably impressed." I brushed his hair out of his eyes and leaned in to kiss his brow. "They aren't going to talk you into moving to Indiana, are they?"

"No. I'm sorry. I know you don't want to talk about it, but I figured you should know and—"

"Did she say anything more about Marty erasing your debt?" I fought the urge to yell or scream that his parents had no right to him. To his time or his consideration. Why was Will the one expected to make sacrifices?

"Yeah. It came up. She talks about him a lot. It made me wonder if you were right about there being something between them." I raised my brow curiously. "And she brings that thirty grand up like it's more pressing a worry than the two hundred thousand I owe in student loans. I don't get it."

"Maybe she's trying to keep him quiet and happy so your dad doesn't find out."

"It seems like too much trouble. Would she really get into bed with him to keep him quiet about the money he lent me?"

"Maybe it didn't start out as a money issue. Maybe it's the fact she helped you in the first place. At one point, it sounds like she tried to give you what you needed to stay in college. Maybe it was for altruistic reasons or maybe she wanted you out of the house. Who knows? Now your dad's running for office and she has to cover her tracks. One lie feeds the next until you aren't really sure what the truth was in the first place."

"It just seems like a lot of work."

"I agree. It's hardly worth it."

"It is if you're trying to project a squeaky-clean family image with no hint of gayness."

"I know this is all speculation, but I think she asked the wrong guy for help. Marty sounds like a real creep. And I can't help but wonder about your mom. Why would homosexuality register as an issue if extramarital affairs and bribery were in your closet?"

"Hmm. Like I told you before… everyone likes to rank their sins. Sometimes it's their so-called version of morality, and other times it's according to the effect it has on their bank account."

I bumped his arm playfully. "You're a wise young man. But this is a downer. Let's talk—" A buzzing noise interrupted me, and for once I didn't mind. "I'll be back."

I kissed his nose, then made my way to the great room naked to answer the intercom. If I were to move in for a long-term stint, I'd have to have the speaker system wired for access all over the condo.

"Hey, Keith, what's up?"

"There are a few guys here to see you. Your bandmates, they said. And a couple of ladies too."

I squinted at the speaker in confusion, then at my watch. It was nine p.m. on a Saturday, which meant the night was just getting started for my friends. Usually for me too, I thought absently. But ladies? Fuck. "Uh. Okay."

My skin prickled with panic. This was the kind of moment I'd lived for before I met Will. If my friends showed up unexpectedly when I was "entertaining," I would have thought it was hilarious to see everyone's reactions to interrupting a booty call. Not now. Will would freak out. We had to get dressed, get our stories straight, and hope like hell the place didn't smell like sex.

I ran back to the bedroom to find Will sitting naked in bed cradling his guitar. He gave me a quizzical look as I hopped into the jeans I'd left lying on the floor next to the bed.

"We have company. Get dressed pronto."

"What?" He set the instrument down and scrambled out of bed.

"You heard me. Hurry. What did I do with that condom and—what are you laughing at?"

"You're wearing my T-shirt. Inside out. Who is it?" he asked with his hand outstretched.

I threw his *Big Bang Theory* tee at him, thinking I ought to get myself one of those when I realized he was still waiting for my response.

"The guys. And the girls. Just hurry and"—I grabbed his guitar and moved toward the door—"gimme this. We can't tell them we've been making music in the bedroom. It's too fucking corny."

The sound of his laughter dispelled my anxiety… until someone pounded on my front door a minute later. I gave Will a thumbs-up sign when he moved into the bathroom and waited for him to close the door before I let the gate-crashers in.

"To what do I owe the honor?" I asked sarcastically as I stepped back to let everyone inside.

"We brought you food," Cory said, holding up a pizza box. "I thought you said you were heading to Johnny's. We decided to join you, but Benny told us he hadn't seen you so… we brought a couple slices of tonight's special."

"And some Pinot," Leah said with a sexy grin as she pulled a bottle of wine from a paper bag, moving toward me like a cat. "Show me where you keep your wineglasses."

"Uh… right. Kitchen. I'll be right there."

I gave Tim a death glare and turned to head to the kitchen when Benny stopped me with a hand on my arm.

"I'm sorry. I tried to stop them, but they're wasted. When they decided to surprise you, I figured I should come along for William's sake. The girl with the pretty ink is a shark. If you weren't fucking my friend, I might say she's perfect for you."

"You think I'm a shark?"

"I'm not sure about you, but I know she is. And she is gorgeous in a Stevie Nicks meets Kat Von D way."

"This is professional only." I scoffed.

"Oh please. She can practically smell the money."

"I don't have money."

"It's coming and she knows it. Look out, Rand. But more important… don't fuck with William."

"What's that supp—?"

"Enough about you. Tell me about the dreamy new music man," Benny said as he averted his gaze to Isaac, who was busy tuning a guitar he'd picked up from one of the stands at the far end of the living area.

"Back off, little guy. He's straight."

"That's what they all say. Including you."

"I never said I was straight."

"No, you didn't say anything at all. But that's because you know you don't have to." Benny chuckled at my irate expression. "Oh relax.

I'm not blowing anyone's cover, and I won't throw myself at the new 'straight' boy, but I might not have to anyway. I think he likes me."

"Don't scare him away, Ben. We need him. And as far as she's concerned—" I said, surreptitiously watching Leah make herself at home in my kitchen. "She's working for the label now. It's complicated."

"The best things in life are simple. Maybe you're making it more complicated than it has to be."

I started to ask how the hell I was supposed to keep anything simple with all this distraction when Leah called my name. Her tone was playful and sexy, but it made my blood boil in all the wrong ways.

"Hmm. She sounds real professional. You better go see to her. Where's Will?"

"Bathroom. I—"

"Rand!"

"Go on… before she starts reorganizing your shelves. If I know Will, he spent a lot of time deciding which glasses went where."

I rounded the island just as Leah was opening the fifth cabinet. I only knew that because she'd left them all open. Benny hadn't been joking about Will's organizational technique. He might have insisted he didn't live here, but he was the one who'd decided what went where… from the forks and spoons to the cutlery and wineglasses.

"Here they are! I was beginning to think I should give you wineglasses for a housewarming gift," she purred. "Bottle opener?"

I pointed to the drawer she was leaning against and crossed my arms in a deceptively casual manner. "I haven't seen you much lately." *It's been nice*, I mused.

"Miss me? I've been traveling for work. Did Ed mention we're trying to pull together some preliminary meet and greets for you guys in LA next month?"

"He said something about visiting the Hollywood offices, but I didn't get details."

"They're in the works. Should be fun. I'd love to show you around."

She moved into my space so we stood a foot apart. Her sultry expression and blatant overture set off a big alarm in my head. She was obviously drunk and didn't care about client boundaries or the fact there were at least five other people in the next room. Though the one I was most concerned about had yet to make an appearance.

"That sounds cool," I said, setting my hand on her forearm and stepping to my right.

She moved closer with her eyes locked on mine before hooking her fingers in one of my belt loops. She tugged at the fabric and slipped an arm around my waist. "I actually think 'hot' works better. Don't you?"

"Leah…." She swayed into me and molded her body against mine. I pushed her back gently, then turned to grab a beer from the refrigerator.

"Want one?" I offered.

"No thanks. I'll stick to wine. Did I tell you I talked to Terry recently?" She asked in a low voice, like she was telling a secret.

I popped the top off the beer bottle and took a swig before answering her. "Nope."

"He's a mess. I wasn't sure if he was strung out and high or just really bitter. He said something strange about you."

"Surprise, surprise."

"He said you're gay."

"I'm not."

"That's what I told him. I could tell when we kissed at the bar that nigh—"

"I'm bi," I added. "And I'm hungry. I'm going to grab a piece of pizza. See ya."

"Wait!" I halted midstride and took a deep breath before turning around. When Leah closed the distance I could tell she'd put on her PR hat. She no longer seemed drunk and out of control. She was calculating and cool. "That's sexy actually."

"Huh?"

"Sexual fluidity is the rage. People are captivated by the idea but…."

"But what?" I took a swig from my beer bottle, making sure to keep my expression carefully bored.

"It can be a PR nightmare unless… you're with a woman first."

"People keep telling me that, but I'm beginning to wonder if anyone really gives a shit."

"They do. Think about it. The majority of the population is heterosexual. They expect guy-girl, not guy-guy. They might not have a problem with it per se, but as an unknown, new artist, bi works as long as you've been associated with someone of the opposite sex first." She dropped the professional tone for a blatantly seductive one. "I kind of wish I was bi. Women are sexy. They just don't do it for me in bed. I've tried."

"I'm not sure how to respond to any of that," I said with a half laugh.

"You don't have to." And like a switch, her tone was all business again. "From a purely professional point of view, I'm glad I brought it up. I have the perfect solution."

I took another long drink. My gaze darted longingly toward my friends. Where the hell was Will? "I don't think—"

"I'll be your beard."

I gulped. Oh fuck. "Leah."

"Listen. It's a good plan. You told me you're seeing someone, and since that someone is never around and you're super secretive about it, I'm going to assume your someone is a guy. I'll be your girl." She chuckled a little evilly at my obvious dismay. Damn, this chick had some balls. "Don't freak out. It's the best plan to make sure Spiral doesn't get derailed over something silly. We'll take couple-y photos, and I'll make sure to distribute them for the personal-interest angle to prominent blogs and websites. I'm not going to be around much before our LA trip. I'm traveling for work… but that's okay. It's better not to saturate social media with—"

"Leah, stop. You're getting carried away. I don't want to begin my career lying." She didn't need to know I'd made plans to do exactly that when I first arrived in New York.

"Trust me, this is the right kind of lie." She pulled out her cell and came to stand at my side like she wanted to show me something. My brow furrowed.

"What are you doing?"

"Smile," she instructed, standing on her toes so she was closer to my height. When I turned to give her a puzzled stare, she sealed her lips over mine and snapped a picture with her phone. "We'll start with this."

I put my hands on her shoulders, intending to gently push her away, but she was all about forward momentum. She took advantage of our proximity and slipped her arms around my neck.

"And maybe I can persuade you to make it something closer to the truth." Her tone dripped with sexual innuendo.

And because timing is everything, that was exactly when Will walked into the kitchen.

"Hi, Leah. How's it going?" he asked, banging a cabinet door closed.

Leah started and jumped back a step, leaving me enough room to maneuver to the other side of the island. "Oh, hi, Will. I didn't realize you were here."

Will filled a glass of water, then turned with an inscrutable expression. "Yeah, we were just going over some instrumentation."

"Ah." Leah leaned against the counter and shot a shrewd look between us. "Sounds important. I didn't realize that was the kind of thing you worked on at home. Alone."

Will raised his glass in a mock toast. "Not alone. We do it together. It's the kind of thing you work on everywhere. In the shower, in bed or... right here in the kitchen."

My mouth opened and closed at least twice. Did he realize what he was doing? This wasn't the same as announcing we were married to a random salesman selling us a sofa. This was Leah. He was pissed and obviously feeling territorial. I watched as he moved around the room, methodically closing every cabinet Leah had opened. He came toward me and wrapped an arm around my waist before leaning in to kiss me. It wasn't an affectionate or sexy kiss. It was a statement.

"Right, babe?"

I nodded and felt my smile morph into a Cheshire cat grin. The kid with the glasses had done it again. He'd knocked me off my feet with his quiet daring. I reached to pull him close, but he stepped away with a cocky smile before heading to join our friends.

"Hmph. Looks like you need help more than you think," Leah snidely remarked as she picked up her wineglass and sauntered after him into the living area.

I stood at the island, observing the activity in the adjoining room. It looked like a friendly, warm gathering of friends and coworkers. There was music, laughter, and the gentle hum of soft chatter that would have made anyone looking in the window wish they'd been invited to the impromptu party. On the inside, it felt slightly dangerous. I could almost feel the silky thread of a web of lies. Lies of omission or lies told to protect others. It made me wish for something simpler. However, that wasn't what I'd come to New York for. I wanted superstardom. The loftiest platform where my voice could be heard the loudest. I didn't know how to keep it simple and reach that goal.

Chapter 12

SPIRAL PLAYED a series of shows to sellout crowds at small clubs in June and July. Every week the pace seemed to accelerate. It was exhilarating. We fed off each other's energy. A lively studio session often inspired unplanned onstage magic in the form of a song we'd played around with that didn't make the playlist but seemed perfect in the moment. Or a comedic reminder of something silly we'd done that would make one of us laugh in between songs. We were young and unjaded enough to be able to find humor in our mistakes. And we were beginning to understand it was important to let the audience in on the joke. If they felt part of our onstage nonsense, they connected with us as well as our music.

I still spent a couple mornings a week at Bowery Bagels, but the rest of my time was dedicated to practice and shows. And Will. I was worried my place might become an impromptu hangout spot for the band after the first time they'd descended unexpectedly, but our intense schedule didn't leave us much extra time. We were all exhausted after practice and wary of becoming sick of each other's company. Which meant Will and I had plenty of opportunity to be alone. No one questioned us. After Will kissed me in front of Leah that night, it was really a moot point. Our friends didn't care. And the only person who potentially did was out of town. A lot.

Leah had been too busy with other projects to spend as much time hanging around Spiral. I talked to her occasionally when she contacted me about promotional ideas or a blog post featuring the band. It was generally professional. The only time I felt uneasy was when she posted the picture she'd taken of us in my kitchen on our official website. It was captioned "at home with Rand." A simple enough statement anyone might easily interpret as an intimate moment. Will didn't say a word, though he had to have overheard the guys giving me a hard time about it. We seemed to have an unspoken truce when it came to talking about things that bugged us. Neither of us wanted to discuss his family or what he'd do at the end of summer. And we never brought up Leah. I'd decided not to tell Will about her idea to play the part of my beard. It would only upset him. I didn't see a point in bringing up a topic that would snowball into the greater one of "what are we doing?"

Time felt too precious to waste worrying about the future. It was better to live in the moment and concentrate on the perks of being signed with a legit record company. Like an all-expenses-paid trip to Hollywood to meet with the label's offices. Our calendar for our five days in LA with the band was jam-packed with a very official itinerary of nonstop schmoozing.

Visiting California was like a dream to me. I felt like a kid who'd just found out he was going to Disneyland for the first time. I could barely sit still. Of course, that may have had something to do with my seatmate. Leah insisted on sitting next to me on the five and a half hour flight to give me a rundown of events. I listened and nodded in all the right places. I even cooperated when she insisted on taking a series of in-flight selfies with me when making a scene would have drawn more attention than I wanted. It made me fidgety as hell. It looked like my reprieve from her ardent attention had ended. This was business, I reminded myself for the umpteenth time.

"Is this your first time in LA?" Leah asked with a devilish grin. When I confirmed it was, she launched into an extensive list of must-sees while we were in town. "I'll take you to one of my favorite restaurants on Melrose. It's very intimate and—"

"Small and intimate doesn't sound like the best venue for a band," I commented as I craned my neck for a glimpse of Will. He was sitting next to Isaac near the back of the plane.

"Just you and me," she purred. I turned back to find she'd invaded my space. She was wearing a tight V-neck tee that barely held her tits. She took advantage of the confined area to rub them against my bicep.

I gulped and looked away. Then immediately turned back and gave a short laugh. This was ridiculous.

"Leah…. This is business."

She sat back in her seat and studied me carefully. "That's right. It's business. So leave the boyfriend out of it. Fucking this up now by getting caught in an indelicate situation with Will would be a disaster."

"Excuse me?" I gave her a withering glance as a surge of protectiveness raged through me.

"You heard me. Don't be obvious. You'll only fuck up Spiral's chances, and let's get real... he's temporary. The son of an ultraconservative gubernatorial candidate is a bad bet."

"How do you know—?"

"Rand, that's almost cute. It's my job to know this stuff."

My gaze and tone of voice were steely. "Do not say a word about him."

"Relax. I won't. He's temporary background noise until the real party starts. Have fun with him if you want. Just remember what you're here for."

"I know exactly why I'm here," I said in a low, menacing tone.

"I think you're letting your dick do the thinking for you. For the next few days... you're mine."

I had to get away from her before I did anything stupid. I unbuckled my seat belt and made my way toward the back of the plane. I tapped Isaac's shoulder when I got to their row. "Do you mind switching with me for a while, man? I've got an aisle seat next to Leah."

"Leah the man-eater. Hmm. I think you owe me one. I'll give you thirty minutes," Isaac huffed.

Will looked up at me curiously with his head cocked. "Is she eating you up?"

"Yeah. I needed a break."

"Want a magazine?" He pulled out a *People* magazine and a bag of M&M's.

I picked up the candy and pointed to the magazine. "You read this stuff?"

"I always buy them for plane rides. What's she up to?"

"I don't want to talk about her. It's nothing new. Let's talk about fun things, like what we're gonna do first." Will listened patiently as he thumbed through his magazine, nodding every once in a while to let me know he was listening. "When we're done with the official schmooze-fest on Wednesday, I say we go to the beach. We can check out Malibu and the Santa Monica Pier. Do you want to go to Disneyland or Universal on Thursday? Maybe we can do them both that day."

"They're at least an hour away from each other, and they're all-day kind of places. You'll have to make a choice. It's one or the other. Not both."

He shoved his magazine into the bag near his feet and plucked the bag of M&M's from my hand. I grabbed them back with a scowl and poured a generous amount on the cocktail napkin on the seat tray in front of me and set to work separating the green ones.

"I bet we could do one in the morning and the other in the afternoon. We have to maximize our time, babe. We only have three days alone," I complained, popping a brown M&M in my mouth.

"Does she know about that?"

I'd booked an extra three days on a whim, thinking it was wise to take advantage of the opportunity to relax and not worry about business. I gave him a perturbed look and shook my head.

"No. But I'm nearing the end of official fucks to give."

Will snorted. "I don't blame you. What color are you eating next?"

"Red," I replied with my hand out.

"Let me guess… you're saving the green ones for last." He pushed the armrest out of the way and leaned into me.

"Correct. They have magical powers, so it's best not to dilute them with the other colors. If possible, I try to eat the yellow and blue ones together too."

"Because yellow and blue make green? You're ridiculous." Will laughed. His eyes were creased with humor as he set his left hand on my knee and scooted closer still. I squeezed his hand and twisted my wrist to hold it. His smile widened, and I swear my heart flipped in my chest.

"Hmm. Let's see if this works. I have six green M&M's. Three for you. Three for me. Go on, eat 'em," I said, pushing the napkin to the edge of the tray.

Will rolled his eyes but took the candy and ate one. "What's supposed to happen?"

"Not one at a time! Who does that? All of them." I waited for him to obey before I explained my reasoning. "Good. You, my friend, are about to get very horny. Can you feel it?"

"Yes. Definitely." He gave an exaggerated nod. "Not good, though. We aren't landing for another two hours."

"Tricky business at thirty-five thousand feet, I agree, but we can—"

"Don't even suggest it," he warned, pulling his hand away to reach for his discarded magazine.

"What?"

"We are not having mile-high sex. Behave," he whispered sternly.

"What do I do with these green M&M's? If I eat them, I'll go mad with lust. I won't be able to—" I gasped in horror when he scooped them off the napkin and ate them all in one swoop. "I can't believe you did that."

"Someone had to save you from sitting on a plane for two hours with a boner. Especially when you have to go back and sit next to Leah." He chuckled at my groan and shoved my elbow when I poked his side. "Stop reading over my shoulder."

"What am I supposed to do for two more hours? I can't go back to my seat, and I'm going stir-crazy. C'mon, baby."

"Shh! Geez!" He batted my roving hand from his inner thigh and cast a sideways glance at the older woman snoring in the window seat next to him.

"She can't hear. I'm bored. Entertain me."

"Is this the longest flight you've ever been on?"

"Yep. I feel boxed in. I've already paced the aisle a few times to get a break from Leah. The flight attendant is getting irritated with me."

"Next time things will be different. Your personal secretary will book your seat in first class with an unlimited supply of M&M's and champagne waiting for you."

"You think?" I asked with a lopsided grin.

"Sure. Eventually you'll be riding in a tricked-out bus or flying on private jets. You'll choose your own prime seat, have all the candy your heart desires, and best of all… you can have sex in the bathroom and not think twice about the other hundred people on the plane who might need to use the facilities."

"I like the sound of this."

"The life of a rock god," he singsonged. "You were born to do this, Rand. You're going to be amazing. Anything can happen. I'll be able to say 'I knew him when….'"

"You won't have to say that. You'll be with me," I said with a frown.

He nodded slightly, one of those noncommittal gestures passive-aggressive people mastered early and used often. It made me angry. I tweaked his earlobe, desperate to move back to neutral, fun topics, like getting lost in theme parks and checking out hunky guys at the beach.

"I don't need private jets, champagne, or caviar. I'm good with M&M's in coach class sitting next to a cute guy in glasses."

Will held my gaze with a sweet smile, then reached for the bag of M&M's. "Want more?"

"Sure, but hold the green ones."

"Good idea. We'll save those for later," he said, raising his brows lasciviously.

The gesture was unexpected. I burst out laughing and startled the woman next to Will, who woke with a loud snort. We both went still, then snickered quietly when the snoring resumed a moment later. As I divided the chocolates by color, pretending not to notice when Will put the green ones back in the bag, I knew with absolute certainty I'd give up the so-called perks of an elite lifestyle to always have this in my life.

LOS ANGELES was magic. Eighty degrees, blue skies, palm trees, and home to some of the most beautiful people I'd ever seen. I was sure a surgeon was to thank in many cases, but who cared? I loved every minute of the time we spent in the real world's land of make-believe. It was fresh and vibrant with a unique energy that may have been due to the perpetual sunshine. Whatever the cause, I found it invigorating. I jotted poems and phrases into my phone I hoped to turn into song lyrics later. I wanted to remember everything from the gorgeous mountain background to the funny-accented "surfer-dude speak" and the insane traffic on the endless ribbons of highway. The people were either extraordinarily nice or vapid and egotistical. The ones I didn't trust were somewhere in between.

Thankfully the execs at the Suite Dog Hollywood offices were smart and seemed to share the same vision for Spiral as the East Coast team. We toured the recording studios and met with a few radio contacts regarding guest appearances in the fall. We were all jazzed by the positive reception. It gave us hope we'd hit the ground running after our first single was released. Success, failure, or interminable mediocrity weighed on my mind after my bandmates left for home. I was cognizant of impending change with sharpened clarity. Visiting the recording headquarters and playing to an alternative-music-savvy audience was eye-opening. As was dodging Leah's overtures and gritting my teeth when she posted every selfie she took of the two of us on the band's website.

I looked forward to the few days alone with Will. It would be good to be with someone without an agenda. Though in a way, it frightened me too. I couldn't help turning Will's words over in my head. *"Anything can happen."* It was true. Anything *could* happen. I had to find a way to protect the part of me that was not up for sale and rewrite my own personal definition of success. One that had nothing to do with Spiral. A few days away from the nonstop grind was what I needed.

After a day at Universal Studios and another sightseeing in and around Hollywood, we spent our last day cruising the beaches along Pacific Coast Highway. Marina del Rey, Venice, Santa Monica, and Malibu. We walked in the sand or stopped for a quick bite to eat and checked out the touristy shops. It was a carefree day with no particular destination in mind. We laughed about nothing at all and made up silly stories to entertain ourselves about the tourists wearing Hawaiian shirts and black socks. We knew we looked equally ridiculous taking endless photos with anything from a palm tree to the guys dressed as superheroes in front of Grauman's Chinese Theatre. By some unspoken agreement we never once mentioned the band. This time was for us. The real world, with all its complications and uncertainties, was not welcome.

On our last evening in LA, we lay tangled in crisp, white sheets, wearing our briefs. A catnap before dinner quickly became another excuse to explore one another. We licked and sucked on lips, jaws, and throats. Our hands were in each other's hair as fingernails raked along sun-drenched skin. Slow kisses quickly turned passionate, and the press of our swollen flesh became an urgent humping motion.

"Which do you prefer, New York or LA?"

"Huh?" I tore my mouth from his to suck in a breath of air and propped myself on my elbow. I stared into his eyes as I brushed his hair from his forehead. "That was a really awkward segue."

Will's grin morphed into a slow chuckle, then a full belly laugh. He hooked his leg over mine and switched positions so he was on top of me. "That was bad. I apologize. What's your answer?"

He splayed his hands over my chest and traced the circular designs around my left pec before bending to flatten his tongue over my nipple. I moaned and pulled his briefs over his sweet ass. He looked down at me with a naughty spark in his eyes that went straight to my dick.

"Uh… you really want to talk now?"

"It's a simple question," he said, moving his hand between us to palm my rigid dick.

"New York."

He stroked me through the thin fabric as he bent over to reach for the lube and condom on the dresser next to the bed. His smile was sure and cocky. "Me too."

"Or maybe LA. I don't know. I haven't spent enough time here. Why New York?"

"Theater. You asked me once… but I wasn't clear or maybe I didn't know the answer yet. I want to write an amazing score. Or twenty. I want people to sing to my music. Kind of like you, but in another genre. That's when I'll feel like I've made a difference. What about you?"

"I don't—know, but let's—" Will knelt between my thighs and pushed my briefs aside before licking my cock from base to tip, then swallowed me whole. "—Jesus, Will!"

"Answer."

"I want to hear my songs on the radio," I admitted with a blush. "I want to know that people sing along in their cars or in the shower. I want—"

"You want it all."

"Hmm. Now I want you."

"So good but so bad for me," he whispered in an almost catatonic tone.

"I'm good for you," I insisted as I tilted my hips toward his mouth and ran my fingers through his hair.

He sucked me fiercely and stroked my flesh with a fluid twist of his wrist. I panted as I tugged at his hair, silently begging for more. He released me suddenly but moved his hand steadily over my aching flesh. I groaned at the heady sensation and struggled to listen when I heard him murmur softly. My heart was beating too loudly, and the rush of blood to my cock made it difficult to concentrate on anything but the sound of a condom being unwrapped. I licked my lips and ran my hands along his thighs as he straddled my chest. He uncapped the lube, then leaned forward to finger his hole.

"Do you want to help?"

I nodded. This confident, take-charge side of Will always turned me on. I licked his stomach as I pulled his cheeks apart and ran my finger over his opening. He groaned and leaned into my touch until he was riding the single digit. He moved over me, leaking precum wildly as he begged for another finger. His lusty gaze and gyrating hips were evidence he was in another zone. He whispered nonsensical words that ran together with the cadence of another language. If I listened to the tone, I might catch some meaning. But not now. My body demanded I pay attention to the primal senses. I was ready to move, to possess. No more playing.

The second my sheathed cock breached his entrance, my vision blurred. He was so tight. So amazing. He went completely still and then tentatively swayed his hips. I was completely under his spell. Will set the pace, swaying and rocking, then changing the tempo on a whim like he was playing an instrument. And when he threw his head back and closed his eyes, I had the feeling I was witnessing a metamorphosis. As though this sexual dance was tantamount to some kind of internal feeling I was connected to but didn't necessarily understand.

It wasn't my nature to watch anything from the sidelines for long. I grabbed his ass and rolled him over quickly. He started to protest, and strangely the trancelike state was broken. He looked up at me in surprise, like he hadn't realized how he got on his back so fast. I gave him a feral grin, then plunged my tongue in his mouth as I drove deep inside him. I fucked him relentlessly. My hips pistoned wildly as I lost myself in him. The bed creaked and the headboard thumped against the wall. We scratched and clawed at one another as a fevered passion built around us. I was consumed with a desire to be as physically close to him as possible. My heart tripped, and my pulse sped ominously as my orgasm approached. I wanted to slow down but it was too late. I was drenched in his sweat and mine. And fuck, it felt good.

I bucked and shook with the force of my release, gasping for air as I held Will close. He came a second behind me. He clung to me tightly, whispering in that low, strange tone over and over again. "I love you, I love you." If I hadn't recognized the cadence from our first night together months ago, I would have missed it.

I stared into Will's lovely face and kissed his freckled nose, wondering if he knew he'd spoken aloud. He opened his eyes and smiled. And just like then, I was speechless. There was more love, friendship, and affection in that look than I'd ever known. It was pure and perfect... and meant for me. And it scared the hell out of me.

WHEN WE returned to New York City, we hit the ground running. We practiced nonstop in preparation for our final shows. The temperature had spiked in these last few weeks of summer. The August heat was cloying, even at night. Add a new moon and a raucous audience of a few thousand people and anything could happen. Our final show before we were due to start the next phase of our musical journey was pure magic. It was one of those rare occasions when everything came together as planned and, if possible, surpassed expectation. The crowd was wild. They swayed and sang along to nearly every song. Their exuberance spurred me on. I danced like a fool and recited impromptu bits of lyrics I made up as I went along. They ate up every bit of silliness, laughed at every joke, and rooted for each band member.

We'd decided beforehand to have Isaac play with Will as a sort of changing of the guard. The stage was too small to have them play at the same time, so Will started the show, then Isaac took over, and Will came back for the encore to play the final two songs. By that time I was dripping with sweat and every nerve ending hummed. I was accustomed to this adrenaline rush now. I could gauge its intensity and ride it to the very end without relying on drugs or alcohol to avoid crashing later. That night it was off the charts, and by the time Will walked back out with his guitar slung over his shoulder and a wicked grin on his face, I was blindsided by emotion.

He was more beautiful to me in that moment than ever. He was dressed in skintight, ripped, black jeans and a matching mesh top with his blond wig, heavy eyeliner, and lots of glitter. I couldn't keep my eyes off him as he leaned into his instrument and blew everyone away with his genius. I stood next to him clutching the microphone, wondering if we'd do this again or if it was the beginning of good-byes.

As the harmony built, and the audience began to sing the background vocals, the moment took on a surreal quality. It felt like an unforgettable blip in time. I was driven to acknowledge it, commemorate it somehow. I didn't think, I acted. I closed the distance between us and wrapped my hand around the back of Will's neck and pulled him forward to seal my mouth over his.

The kiss was brief. It was fairly tame by anyone's standards, but when I pulled away, I was relieved the one person who might take exception to the unrehearsed display had a huge grin on his face. I laughed aloud as the crowd went crazy and my bandmates looked on, shaking their heads at my idiocy. As we transitioned to the final song on our set list, I gave him one last, longing look and a smile meant for him alone. He acknowledged it with a lopsided grin, and the wave crashed over me, leaving me clearheaded and sure. This wasn't an adrenaline-induced high. This was love.

As we made our way offstage, the guys gave me a hard time for moving off script and shamelessly pandering to the audience for attention. Will, on the other hand, just laughed as I shrugged good-naturedly. Let them think it was a publicity ploy. The truth was no one else's business. Will got it. That was what mattered. I could easily forget the reasons I couldn't pull him back into my arms when we walked offstage.

Until I saw Leah.

Her grin was savage. A take-no-prisoners sort of look that went well with her ensemble. She was dressed entirely in black leather, like a dominatrix. Her only concession to color was her inked skin and her bloodred nail polish. I stopped in front of her, wiping the sweat from my brow as I eyed her with a mischievous grin.

"Come on now, Leah. It was a good show. Don't tell me you didn't like it," I taunted.

"Being your beard just became a full-time job. You like living on the edge, don't you?"

"It has its upside." I huffed humorlessly and leaned into her space. "By the way, I don't need a beard. Thanks anyway."

She snaked her arms around my neck before I could pull away and yanked my head down so our noses brushed.

"Play smart, Rand… or you'll be finished before you even get started. You aren't the only hot new band out there. Consider this a friendly warning. Some secrets are harder to hide than they're worth. Thanks to Terry, I literally have the power to end this ride before you're out of the gate. Think about it."

I watched her walk away, thinking it was strange that no one else in the room noticed the sudden dip in temperature. They were too busy celebrating. Someone broke out a bottle of tequila, and over the wolf-whistles, Tim lifted a glass in toast to Will before singing a purposefully pitchy rendition of "For He's a Jolly Good Fellow." It was just as well. No one deserved to have the night spoiled by a crazy PR lady who'd decided she wanted a piece of my soul as well as in on the ground floor. We'd deal with the fallout later if necessary.

Chapter 13

MY PHONE vibrated on the nightstand at an ungodly hour the following weekend. I probably would have slept through it, but the poke in the ribs and the bright sunlight streaking across the white duvet were harder to ignore. I grunted and buried my head under my pillow in an attempt to escape. No such luck.

"Rand, make it stop," Will grumbled.

"Ugh." I reached for my cell and was about to chuck it across the room when I saw the time and the caller ID on the display. 7:04. "'Lo?"

"Rand, we've got a problem." Tim's voice sounded shaky and upset. I was more alarmed by his tone than his words.

"What is it?" I asked. My forehead was creased with concern as I sat up in bed, letting my feet fall off the mattress.

"Go online and read the news. You've been outed." I blinked a couple times in an attempt to clear the cobwebs, when he added, "Why didn't you tell us Will was Creepy Sanders's son? Jesus! Did you even know? Check your messages, by the way. Ed wants us at the studio immediately. As in get your ass in gear and be there within the hour."

"Uh…." I glanced over at Will, who was peering up at me curiously from his side of the bed. The white sheets and duvet rode low on his hip, partially exposing his ass. He looked sleep-mussed and sexy… and now worried. I turned my back to him when Tim spoke again. "Okay. I'll see you there."

I stared at my cell, willing my heartbeat to slow so I could deal with whatever shitstorm was coming with a modicum of levelheadedness.

"Who was that?" I felt Will's hand on my lower back and leaned into his touch for a second before reaching for my discarded shorts next to the bed.

"Tim. I'll be right back."

I gave him a wan smile and hurried into the living room to find my computer. My hand was trembling as I swiped it over my stubbled jaw and then rested my elbows on my knees. I stared at the laptop on the coffee table and counted to five before finally flipping it open.

I didn't see anything out of the ordinary at first. There was a supposed newsworthy story about ten fast food items you should avoid and another about fall fashion trends. I saw another about cool tree houses and travel destinations before I glanced at the headings. *Health Lifestyle*. Oh.

I scrolled down and found the heading titled *Politics*. And froze.

Family Values, Lipstick, and a Rock-and-Roll Kiss, read the headline. *Charles Sanders has been vocal on his view that homosexuality is abhorrent and detrimental to society as a whole. But it appears the über-conservative gubernatorial candidate has a gay son. In an interesting twist....*

Holy fuck. The accompanying photo was the kiss from last weekend's show. It was a good, clear shot, but I couldn't help thinking one stupid picture certainly wasn't evidence of sexual orientation. It could be a fluke or an attempt to get the audience's attention by doing something some idiots still thought was outlandish, like a man kissing another man. A relatively tame display in the world of music. But it could cause havoc for an intolerant politician's campaign. If it hadn't been for Will, I would have whooped with childlike glee at the idea of pissing off a stodgy, hypocritical asshole. However, I knew this wasn't a matter of "good guy versus bad guys." Real life was much more complicated.

I closed my laptop when I heard Will moving behind me.

"Want coffee? What did Tim want? Seven on a Sunday is way too early. I wouldn't usually bother going to school, but I have a ton to do today, so it's just as well...."

I tuned out his words and observed him as he moved around the kitchen. He was dressed in navy pajama bottoms and one of my old concert T-shirts. I loved the homey feel of watching him putter around, opening drawers, then measuring coffee for the state-of-the-art industrial machine I promised to buy with my first check. It was the kind that made it hard to fuck up a superior cup of java. No doubt he was waiting for me to poke fun at his interest in the new toy the way I did most mornings. We were a couple of twentysomethings who acted like newlyweds. Husbands. The realization should have frightened me, but it didn't. I never thought I'd want this. I wasn't looking for it, but I loved what we had together. I was overcome with a feeling of protectiveness for it. For us. I didn't want to lose this life. And I didn't want anyone or anything to harm him or make him unhappy.

He was talking about how long he'd be at school and something about making dinner later. I nodded as I moved to sit at one of the barstools. He was chattier than normal. I wanted to play with him, say something off-color to make him laugh or roll his eyes. I wanted to tease him, throw my arms around him, and see how long it would take to get him back in bed. I wanted him to smile at me and assure me I was worth whatever was coming his way.

"Well?" Will stood on the other side of the island with two coffee mugs and glanced at the coffeemaker, then back at me. "What did he want?"

I tried a smile I knew fell short of the mark. I opened my mouth but nothing came out. Sweat beaded on my forehead and my palms felt slick. Not good.

"Are you okay?" He moved around the island and ran a soothing hand over my brow. "Maybe you should go back to bed."

I swallowed hard and backed away from his touch. "I'm all right. I mean, I'm not but—fuck, I…."

I felt his worried stare as I turned to grab my computer from the living area. The walk to the adjoining room and back again was like moving through quicksand. I moved slowly and with dread. I set the laptop on the island between us.

"Tim called to tell me what was in the morning paper. And online. We've been outed."

"What do you—?"

"Just read it."

He gave me a funny look, then adjusted his glasses and looked at the screen. It took less than ten seconds for the color to drain from his face. He went so still I wondered if he was breathing.

"Will?"

He shook his head, then went eerily still again. I wasn't sure what to expect, but it wasn't this macabre silence. He stepped away from the island and headed for the bathroom. I went after him, grateful he didn't lock the door. I pushed it open and stopped in my tracks. He was standing at the sink splashing water over his face repeatedly. Water was everywhere. It ran down the mirror, over the marble counter, and onto the floor. There was something alarming in the violence behind his action. It was manic and a little crazy. I was paralyzed for a moment. To say I had limited experience in offering comfort would be an understatement. I had no bedside manner to speak of. When things got tense, I tried humor.

I could rarely think of a solution or worthwhile advice to give when it mattered most. It wasn't my forte. But the guy splashing water all over the fucking bathroom with his glasses strewn carelessly on the counter wasn't just anyone. He was mine.

I picked up a towel and handed it to him. He didn't look up and he didn't take it. I winced when he made a strained retching sound, like he wanted to vomit but wouldn't let himself. He looked like hell. I stared at my reflection to give him a moment to pull himself together. I didn't look so hot, either. My coloring was off. My hands shook and my heartbeat seemed unsteady. Fast then slow then fast again.

"Will, take the towel. I—"

"Leave me alone for a minute. Please."

"Baby, we need to talk."

He straightened slowly, then hunched over the counter again. I studied his body language as I watched him brush his teeth. He leaned heavily on the marble and kept his gaze down. I could practically see a wall forming around him, blocking me out. He reminded me of the perfectly pressed and distant Will I'd met at the beginning of the year. The one who communicated best through music, not words. Will finally took the towel from me, swiped carelessly at his face, set his glasses back on his nose, and walked out of the room.

"Will." I followed him back into the kitchen. "We'll figure this out. We can—"

"There's nothing to figure out." His eyes welled ominously. He pursed his lips as though it might check the flow of unshed tears.

"Hey, we're in this together. We can spin it however we want. Blame it on me. It was my fault, and you were an innocent bystander. We'll say I was egging the crowd on. No one will take it seriously."

"Right. Except you're forgetting the part about me being onstage in a wig, makeup, and—how did this happen? Who told them? I can't believe I got fucking outed on CNN.com! It had to be Leah."

"Yeah. I think that's a safe bet. She promised she wouldn't say anything, but I shouldn't have trust—"

Will held up his right hand, then picked up his coffee mug and set it back on the granite countertop hard. The sound ricocheted in the room ominously.

"What do you mean? Did you know about this? Did you know she knew about me?"

My heart beat a little faster as I moved to his side. The rigid set of his shoulders wasn't inviting, but I needed to be closer. I turned his words over in my head, wondering how to answer. I could claim anyone in the band could have googled and found out his dad was Charles Sanders, but I'd tried that myself and found that if you weren't actively searching for clues and missing links, the connection would be easy to miss. Sure, it was there, but it wasn't obvious. I could tell him I didn't know, but... I couldn't lie.

"Yes."

Silence.

His breath hitched slightly, but his gaze didn't falter. "Why didn't you tell me?"

"I didn't want to worry you. She said she wouldn't say anything and—"

"You believed her? She's a viper. She's out for number one only. She wants in on the ground floor, and I'm in her way. Did you honestly not think she'd use whatever she could against me? Or were you too concerned about your own ride to the top you didn't think twice about who got fucked over on the way?"

"You know that's not—"

"It turns out, I don't know anything! I trusted you and now...."

"Will, let's be rational. Does it matter who knew or how long?"

"Good question. When did you know that Leah knew who my father is?"

I gulped as the ground beneath me shifted. When I didn't answer right away, he scoffed and gave me a contemptuous glare.

"The flight to LA."

"A few weeks, then."

"Look, if you think about it, you got caught being yourself and so did I. Our cover was blown, but is that really so bad? Being honest is better. Your parents have known that you're gay for years. They're the ones who chose not to be truthful. You're just having a fucking life. A life you like. How can that be bad?"

Will gave me an incredulous look and let out a decidedly humorless half laugh. "You're unbelievable."

"I'm just saying we should think and not overreact—"

"You think I'm overreacting? You think I should just relax? No big deal, right? Fuck you! Fuck you and your incredible ego. This was a mistake!" A sudden fiery wall of frustration poured from him.

"This is not a mistake. It's a… predicament. We'll figure it out."

Will picked up the empty mug and crashed it against the granite island. Shards of porcelain went flying everywhere. I stared at him with my mouth wide open. Gone was the mild-mannered, sweet guy I thought I knew. His eyes blazed. I felt his anger like a physical storm moving in the air around us.

"There is nothing to figure out," he screamed. "Don't you get it? I'm about to lose everything. Everything! You, my family…. Why couldn't you fucking tell me the truth?"

His voice echoed as a heavy silence fell. I was momentarily paralyzed with shock. Will never yelled. I was the hothead. He was the voice of reason. But certainly not now. He wasn't making any sense.

"There was nothing to tell. You aren't going to lose me, baby. Nothing has to change. Nothing."

"You're wrong. I knew this couldn't last but—God, I can't believe it's ending like this."

He let out a long sigh that morphed into a pained, choking noise. He was scaring me more than I wanted to admit. I searched for something calming to say to restore balance, but I was a novice here. I stepped around the broken pieces of coffee mug to close the distance between us.

"Nothing is ending, Will. We'll work this out."

Something in his rigid stance caved a little. The armor was slipping. I was fascinated and a little afraid of his rawness. It was like seeing someone stripped bare against their will and unsure of how to react. Will went perfectly still for a long moment, then slumped in defeat. He shook his head unhappily, then shoved his fingers through his hair and bit his lip.

"Will, I'm sorry."

"Right." He took a deep, ragged breath and closed his eyes. "Well, I asked for it. I acted like a jealous idiot. I shouldn't have kissed you in front of her. I shouldn't have let her know I was the one standing in the way. I knew putting myself out there, even in disguise, might backfire. I should have known better. There's no winning. If you tell the truth, it gets used against you. If you lie and get caught, you better come up with a good reason or a better story to trump the last one. I'm out of lies, and nobody likes the truth. I don't know what to tell my parents. I'm not moving back home but—"

"You aren't going anywhere. Just... hang tight. When I get back from this meeting, we'll discuss this and—"

"It's over, Rand."

"It's not over, but we'll get through it. We have—"

"No. You aren't listening to me. This was always temporary."

My heart thundered in my chest. "We don't have an expiration, Will. We aren't temporary. If we—"

"Stop it!" We stared at each other until the sound wave gave way to a heated silence. "There is nothing to get through. We're over. I'm not standing in your way. I won't be your liability and I won't be your fucking afterthought on your way to the top."

"You aren't my aft—"

"You don't know what I am to you, Rand. You aren't ready for me. You want one thing and you're willing to overlook some unpleasant truths to get it."

"What unpleasant truths? What are you saying?"

Will barked a short, humorless laugh. "This was never just a summer job for me. You were never just the guy I was tutoring. God, Rand, you're an overgrown kid one minute and a fierce crusader the next! I love your big mouth and your ridiculous sense of righteousness. I love that for as impatient as you are, you always wait for me to catch up. But the problem is I lied to you months ago when I said I wouldn't fall for you. I knew all along I would."

My mouth went dry. I felt like I was sitting at the very top of a roller coaster waiting for the drop. "What's the unpleasant part?"

"The truth. I love you."

That sounded promising. I tried a smile but something told me I wasn't out of the woods. "Then why—?"

"We won't work. You'll never be able to put me first. I can't trust that you feel the same way about me, and honestly... I'm not sure I trust *you*. Nobody gets everything they want without sacrificing something."

I grasped his shoulder with one hand and lifted his chin so he'd look me in the eye. "Stop this. You *can* trust me. You're being crazy. We'll figure this out. One thing at a time. Just hang tight. We'll—" He closed his eyes as if in pain and pulled away from me before turning toward the bedroom. "Where are you going?"

"I'm going to take a shower and then... I have to call my parents."

"Okay, that's good." I nodded in agreement. Action was good. I willfully ignored his stiff posture and barreled through with a list of plans. "I have to go to the studio. You call your folks and go to school. I'll pick up whatever you want for dinner, and we'll talk over a bottle of something amazing. Do you want me to meet you on campus or—?"

"No, I need to pack some things and—"

"Whoa! What things? What are you saying?" I rounded the island and grabbed his elbow before he reached the hallway.

Alarms were ringing. Great, red, flashing lights warning me the roller coaster was on a steep and treacherous descent. Will yanked his arm away but he wouldn't look at me. I leapt after him, pinning his back to the wall and caging his head between my arms. I wanted to scream at him for walking away. For having the temerity to leave me. The tears welling in his eyes stopped me. I inched away and gently traced his cheekbone, nudging my thumb under his glasses to wipe at the moisture on his eyelashes.

"I told you. I'm leaving."

"You can't go, Will."

"Please don't do this, Rand. Please don't pretend it's okay. Be honest. You want too much."

"Baby, I want you. I can't lose you. This isn't about anyone else. Your parents, Leah, or the band… it's about us. You and me."

Will gasped. A tear trickled unchecked down his cheek. My heart was in my throat. I never felt more vulnerable in my life. I pulled him into my arms and held him tightly. His body trembled and shook with a heart-wrenching misery as he gave in to tears. He pushed me aside after a minute and wiped his hand over his nose absently.

"Go on, Rand. Go to your meeting."

"Will you be here when I get back?"

He smiled weakly and turned away.

I stared at the empty space in a kind of trance. Every nerve ending in my body was buzzing. I didn't know how to proceed. I was torn between an almost-mesmerizing paralysis and the need to do something. Fix something. But as I stood with my fists clenched and my heart in my throat, I was overwhelmed with fear. Maybe I did want too much. Maybe I was the hypocrite who asked for more than he was willing to give. I didn't want to be that man. The idea alone was enough to stop me cold.

Everyone had their own agenda. Everyone had their own truth. Mine was my music. For the first time in my life, I had a feeling it wasn't enough.

BY THE time I pushed open the glass door to the conference room in Suite Dog's deserted office, I was a certified wreck. I knew I had to give Will space to deal with his parents, but it took everything I had to walk away and attend this "damage control" impromptu meeting. I could only hope it was a short one. Unfortunately the second I stepped into the room and saw the serious expressions of the men gathered around the table, I knew my crappy morning was about to get worse.

"Did you read the *Times*?" Cory asked, leaning forward on his elbows. In deference to the August weather, we were all dressed in T-shirts and shorts. No doubt we were wearing matching anxious expressions.

"CNN. Where's Ed?" I asked, flopping gracelessly into the nearest chair.

Tim pointed to the doorway just as the man in question materialized. Ed set a few water bottles on the table, then slapped my shoulder in a companionable gesture I read as reassurance before taking the seat next to me. He sat at the edge of his chair and cast a look at everyone gathered before he spoke.

"We have a situation. It's not a big deal, but it needs to be addressed and we need to be on the same page, which is why I asked you all here."

I didn't miss that every eye was on me, but I was a beat or two behind and not interested in playing guessing games. I raised my brow and uncapped a water bottle while I waited for Ed to get to the fucking point. Ed met my gaze and let out a rush of air.

"Leah quit. She left a cryptic message about political bullshit I couldn't decipher until I saw today's headlines."

"Leah did this, didn't she?" The question was rhetorical. Like Will said, it had to be someone from the inside. No one else outside the band would have known who he was without being told.

"Maybe it was her. Maybe it was that Terry guy. He left a message after Will's last show that sounded like a ransom note. Leah said she'd handle him and—well, here we are. We'll assign you a new PR person immediately. We can spin this, man. I'm not worried. The bi angle obviously is the best way to explain it, but the relationship part is trickier. The other pictures of you and Will aren't going to be so easy—"

"What other pictures?"

Tim, Cory, and Mike looked at me with something akin to sorrow as Ed opened a manila folder and pulled out a sheath of grainy photos. They were all recent pictures of Will and me. Some were of us in LA. Hanging out on a towel at the beach with our feet entwined. Or leaning across a table for two at the exclusive restaurant in West Hollywood we found on our last night. There were a few taken in the past couple of days of us doing everyday, boring things like walking in the park. But in every photo, the way we looked at each other gave us away. We were completely oblivious to anyone around us.

I willed the wave of nausea aside as I reached for the water bottle again. My mouth was cottony and I felt warm all over, like I was sitting outside under the blistering sun instead of in an air-conditioned office building.

"Who took these?" I don't know why I asked. I knew Leah was responsible.

Ed shrugged. "My guess is Leah hired someone, but I don't know. The solution is you come out as bi and make it sound like a short-term fling. We can fix this. I'll set you up with a hot chick and we'll make sure to take pictures of you—"

"Hang on. Do you think they're going to sell these to the media too?"

"If they're out for the money and a little revenge… yeah. The media or Mr. Sanders directly. Whoever will pay more. As far as Spiral is concerned, it's free publicity we need to manage well. The object in the music business is to build an audience. Finding out a temporary band member's megaconservative dad is running for governor will take a little finessing, but as the saying goes… there's no such thing as bad publicity. Well, not for us anyway."

I took another sip and waited for him to fill the heavy pause. I could tell he had more to say, and I knew I wouldn't like it.

"The thing is… you'll need to distance yourself from Will. At least until this dies down. It should be easier now that he's not playing with the band and—hang on, man. Where are you going? We need to discuss—"

Fuck that. I was out the door and down the hallway in seconds flat. I heard Cory calling after me as I stabbed at the elevator button. They could spend the day brainstorming about branding the band's image based on fucked-up publicity while I figured out how to damage control my personal life.

I SHIELDED my eyes from the morning sun before realizing my sunglasses were perched on my head. I dialed Will's number as I raised my arm to hail a taxi. Details, like what I'd say or how I'd fix things hadn't come to me yet. I was an expert at getting myself out of difficult situations. Charm and a dose of humor usually worked wonders. However, my confidence was shaken by my conscience. As much as I wanted to blame Terry and Leah for being lowlife assholes, I knew I was equally to blame. I should have been watching out for him. I should have warned him that she knew who he was. I'd thought at the time I'd kept it from him so it wouldn't upset him. Maybe the truth was that I knew it might lead to the calamity unfolding around me now. Will was right. I was a selfish prick.

"Babe, are you home? I'm done at the studio. I'm on my way back. We're gonna be okay. We just need to talk, okay? Call me."

I hopped in the taxi and stared at my cell, willing it to light up. My screen lit up almost immediately with a text from Tim, followed by one from Cory. I sighed and flipped it over. I couldn't deal with everything at once. Will came first.

I PAID the driver and raced inside my building, nearly knocking over a jogger in my haste. The elevator ride was quick, which was good and bad. Good because I was in a hurry. Bad because I still didn't know how to handle this. I let myself in my condo and immediately knew something was wrong.

I took a brief look around. The sparsely furnished living room looked like it had before we'd gone out last night. Sheet music was stacked neatly on a corner of the coffee table. I glanced across the great room to the kitchen. My laptop was still on the island, but the broken pieces of the coffee mug he'd shattered in a rage had been picked up.

"Will?" I made my way to the master suite.

The room was so damn white. Blindingly so. The walls were white. The sheets and comforter were white. Sunlight flooded the area, making everything seem stark, cold, and empty. There was no one here. I pushed the closet door open. His clothes were gone. His shoes were gone. I moved into the bathroom. His toothbrush was gone. I opened the drawers, hoping to find lipstick, glitter… anything he might come back for.

There was nothing. He was gone.

A BUZZING noise roused me from my thoughts later that night. I set my guitar aside to answer the doorman's cheerful voice telling me I had a delightful visitor named Benny. I sighed heavily, resting my forehead against the wall for a long moment.

"Okay."

Maybe Benny could tell me how to get ahold of Will. I'd left multiple text and voice messages, but he'd ignored them all. I'd gone by his apartment, the university, and loitered around Washington Square Park for a while. When I started to feel like a stalker, I came home, picked up my guitar, and dodged every call from people desperate to get ahold of me in an effort not to miss the one I hoped to get from the guy who wasn't returning his messages.

I held the front door open for Benny.

"Hi. You look like hell. Pale, pasty. I might have a little powder in my bag if you—"

"Benny. I've been calling you. Is he with you?"

He gave me a head-to-toe once-over, then moved into the living room. He sat on the sofa and nodded. "Yes. I'm here to give you the key. I was supposed to leave it with Keith downstairs but—here." He set it on the coffee table, then fixed me with a sad expression.

I shook my head and slumped on the opposite end of the sofa. "Is he okay?"

Benny shrugged. "No, but he will be. He's stronger than he seems, but you know him. He does things his own way. Give him time to think things through. His conversation with his folks didn't go well. They're blaming him. Told him not to fool himself… you were using him all along to further your career—"

"That's bullshit!"

"I know. So does he, but you know how it goes… people twist the truth all the time. Turn on the news when you think you can stomach it. It must be a slow day because it's all over the place. 'Governor hopeful's son comes out as a gay cross-dresser.'"

"Fuck."

"Well said. How about you? Are you okay?"

"No. And I don't know what to do to make things right. I hate feeling so helpless. I need to talk to him."

"Be patient. But don't give up." He patted my knee and stood.

"Wait." I jumped to my feet and handed him the key. "Take this. Tell him the doorman wasn't there. Make up something. Just don't… leave it."

Benny nodded solemnly and gave me a hug. "You're a good guy, Rand. Make something good happen."

He was gone before I could respond. I picked up my computer and said a quick prayer the most recent headlines weren't as bad as Benny claimed.

They were worse.

Political bullshit about agendas and campaign platforms based on family values. Will's name was thrown about carelessly with adjectives like "queer cross-dresser" as though those were the only adjectives to describe someone as amazingly talented and vibrant as him. It was grossly unfair. I felt like the punkass teenager I once was, raging against the system. But I wasn't a kid anymore. I was smarter now than I was then. I had power. I just had to figure out how to use it.

Chapter 14

TWO DAYS later, I was still at a loss. How could I do anything if he wouldn't talk to me? I had to know what he was up against before things got out of hand. The story was buried under bigger headlines when a hurricane ripped through the Southeast. I asked Ed about making a statement, but he was adamant we keep things quiet on our end. Spiral wasn't a household name. We hadn't even recorded our first single yet. We were small fish in a big pond. All we had was promise. Ed's strategy was for the band to lie low until we were due in the studio to record. I had a headful of worry and way too much time on my hands.

Thank God for bagels.

"GOOD MORNING, Randall. How are you this beautiful Tuesday?" George greeted me at the back door with his customary welcoming smile. He held out his arm with a flourish as though he were inviting me inside the most wondrous place on earth. I held back my eye roll and admitted to myself that I was grateful for this silly familiar tradition. What had begun as a means to remain focused and clear-minded had become an unlikely refuge. It was like being on a treadmill for me. It gave me a break from my thoughts and a place to interact with people whose main focus wasn't music. They were there for bagels and pleasant conversation.

I followed George into the storefront and listened to his newest gripe about Zeke's boyfriend. Something about him not attending a family birthday party, which George found extremely offensive.

"I wish Ezekiel would see that man is using him! Do you know anyone nice? Maybe if he met someone unexpected and charming, he'd come to his senses."

"I don't know anyone appropriate, George. I'm the kind of guy you don't bring home to Mom and Dad. Same goes for most of my friends."

"That's ridiculous. You're a good man, Randall. You have a good soul. I know these things."

I kept my head down as I tied my apron strings. It probably wasn't polite to tell George he didn't know shit. "What do you need me to do first?"

"You can—" He furrowed his heavy brow and set his hand on my forehead like a worried parent. "You don't look so good. What's wrong? Is it William?"

Maybe it was the kindness in his eyes or his concerned tone, but I cracked. I literally wanted to break down and fucking cry like a kid because I was frustrated as hell that I didn't know how to fix the mess I felt horribly responsible for.

I bit the inside of my cheek and nodded. "Yeah."

"Did you break up? Is he ill? What happened?"

I didn't stand a chance with George. He was too real and his worry was too genuine. It had been less than forty-eight hours since my world began to collapse. I could use a friend. I told him everything. I told him about Terry, guitar lessons with Will, and even about discovering Will dressed in drag. I told him about his cold, conservative parents who were focused on him keeping his sexuality a secret for the sake of political aspirations. I lamented their lack of appreciation for his talent as I paced the store impatiently.

"He's a prodigy, Mr. G. A once-in-a-lifetime type of musician. I've never been around anyone so gifted and so... good."

"You're in love with the boy, aren't you?"

I gave a funny half laugh that wouldn't fool anyone, but I couldn't say the words out loud. Not when my throat was choked with tears that wouldn't fall.

"If you love him, Randall, you better make sure he knows."

"Love isn't the thing. It's his dad, the record deal.... I should probably tell you I'll need to quit at some point. I'm not ready now but... eventually."

"What does that mean? Love isn't the thing. Love is the only thing that counts. Nothing is impossible if you love him. His parents may have a perfectly valid reason for what they believe and how they want to conduct their lives, but so do you. So does William. You may not agree with their philosophy and vice versa, but that's not important. What matters is doing what is right for you. Are you going to let someone else dictate who or what can make you happy?"

"Of course not, but—"

"Listen…. Love is like a bagel."

I couldn't help it. I rolled my eyes. "George, you had me for a minute but—"

"It's a never-ending circle. No two are exactly alike, and best of all they come in many flavors."

"That really makes no sense." I sighed.

"It doesn't have to. I'm an old man. I've earned the right to talk crazy because I've learned a few lessons in life. Some that took longer than they should have. I've learned not to judge how others find happiness or love. I have a gay son I love deeply, but there was a time I tried to change what I didn't understand. I thought it was my job to teach him my version of how to be a man. Being a parent doesn't make you smarter. Perfect idiots procreate every day. A good parent learns from their children as much as they learn from us. Perhaps William's parents will understand one day—"

"Not likely."

"Then he's lucky he has you."

George patted my shoulder sympathetically before waving to the first customer of the morning. "Good morning, Mr. Katzmann! How are you this fine Tuesday?"

I watched him greet the middle-aged businessman with his usual affable style. Lucky? I doubted Will felt particularly lucky at the moment.

BY TEN o'clock I was a jittery mess. My chat with George earlier made me anxious to act. I didn't have a solid plan yet, but I was done waiting for the right time. I untied my apron and waved at George, then glanced at my phone and scrolled through my missed calls and messages. I stopped at the most recent one from Benny. All in caps.

HEADS UP. DAD GIVING STATEMENT THIS MORNING. W IS MEETING MOM ON CAMPUS.

When?

NOON.

George lifted his hand and gave me a meaningful look that clearly said "Get your shit together, Randall" as I pocketed my cell and hurried out the door. I pulled out my phone again when I stepped into the Starbucks on the next block. My phone lit up with another round of messages. Most were from Tim, Cory, and Mike, and a couple from Ed.

It was more than I could deal with before a decent cup of coffee. I placed my order and waited at the far end of the counter. My gaze wandered to the flat-screen television anchored on the opposite wall.

"Gubernatorial hopeful Charles Sanders has released a statement in response to his stance on gay rights in light of a recently leaked story that his son was allegedly homosexual."

"My son is a talented musician with a bright future. He does not live a homosexual lifestyle. As for my campaign, I remain steadfast in my beliefs. I do not support the homosexual agenda. And neither does any member of my family, including my son."

A young woman in a floppy hat and yellow sundress looked up at the screen and shook her head. "That guy's a douche."

I nodded absently and picked up my latte just as my phone rang. Ed. "Hi."

"Man, I've been trying to reach you all day! Have you seen the fucking news? This shit is blowing up! One minute it's a rumor attached to a concert photo, and the next it's a political fucking headache! Will's daddy's people have been calling all morning, threatening to level us unless we drop your ass like a hot potato. He wants to destroy you, Rand. What the hell?"

My pulse revved ominously. I swallowed hard and made myself take a drink of my latte before answering. The ups and downs of fame and fortune, I thought without humor. I didn't have either yet, but I had people already trying to bring me down.

"What are you gonna do? Are you going to fold to an irrelevant political hopeful with a platform based on hate? Just curious."

"No. I'm not. Our deal stands. We sell you as bi and ride this shitstorm of free press. If anything, I've got to get you into the studio to record immediately. We need to up your release date and—"

"Not so fast, Ed. Look...." I walked toward the window and let my gaze wander to the traffic on the street. "I'm not going to lie. At all. I'm bi but I won't lie about Will. We can't win if we're like them."

"It isn't going to sell, Rand," he huffed impatiently into the phone. "You gotta distance yourself. Stay away from him. We'll make a statement of our own when the time is right, but—"

"No."

"Excuse me?"

"You heard me. I'm not staying away from him and I won't keep quiet."

"It won't sell," he repeated.

"It will. I've got a good feeling about this. But either way, it's a chance I have to take. In the meantime, I know how to get Mr. Sanders's team to back off."

"How? You got some shade to throw at him?"

"I do. Tell him you know all about Martin Kanzler, and if that doesn't ring an immediate bell, tell him to ask his wife. I'll talk to you later."

I TOOK a taxi home and had the driver wait at the curb for me while I grabbed my guitar. Lifestyles of the not-so-rich and not-yet-famous, I mused as I directed him back toward NYU. My plan was ill conceived… as in, I didn't really have one. The only thing I knew for sure was that Will was in the building. Everything else was a crapshoot. In times of stress, a musician always turned to his instrument. I was relying on Will to be predictable. If he was meeting his mom at noon on campus, he would be sitting at the same damn piano he always used to practice. He could lose himself in music and then surface to the real world when he didn't have a choice.

My cab pulled up behind a black Escalade idling near the crosswalk. I sensed trouble. I noted the news van parked at the corner probably wasn't a coincidence, either. Fuck, I felt trapped. I could only imagine how Will felt. I hefted my guitar case in my right hand and moved to the sidewalk, only to be stopped by a hand on my arm a moment later.

"You have no business here! What do you think you're doing?"

I turned to face Will's irate-looking mother. Mrs. Sanders was perfectly coiffed and beautifully dressed in a lightweight beige linen dress and a fashionable, chunky rhinestone necklace. She had a certain aura of authority about her, but my presence had obviously thrown her off stride. She looked a little… shaken. I gave her a cocky grin I assumed would piss her off and held out my hand. I chuckled when she left me hanging. I expected nothing less.

"I'm just a private citizen taking a walk on a fine day in New York City. And I'm here to see Will. You?"

"You have done more than enough damage. Go away and leave my son and my family alone. This ends now. Once he gives his stateme—"

"What statement is that?"

"The one cutting ties from you and your kind," she hissed in a low, menacing tone. "He is a good man from a good family and—"

"Only one part of that sentence is true. It's pathetic how people like you point fingers at others to hide your own sins. But it's really fucking sad when a mother does it to her son. You're exposed, Mom. I know all about you. I got your number. And Mr. Kanzler's."

Before she could respond, another woman approached from inside the building. She had the unmistakable look of a reporter. The bubbly type with an overly friendly "you can trust me" smile on her face. I didn't trust her at all.

"Hi there, aren't you the guy from the band?"

"I am." I gave her a devilish smile and offered her the hand Mrs. Sanders refused to shake.

"Do you have a comment for—?"

"No. He does not. We can resume this conversat—"

"What's the name of your band? What do you have to say about Mr. Sanders's claim that his son is not gay?" The reporter ignored her and kept a steady barrage of questions. "Is William Sanders your boyfriend? Are you a couple?"

With every question Mrs. Sanders was becoming visibly unglued. Her bracelets jangled noisily as she waved her hands, commanding the young woman to stop. I made my escape inside the building as the two women scuffled about the public's right to know.

OVER THE past eight months I'd come to know the staff manning the reception desk at the Performing Arts Center. Today it was Ray. He was a middle-aged African American man with graying hair and a beer belly that challenged the buttons on his light purple, short-sleeved shirt. He greeted me with a wide grin and a bro fist-bump.

"How you doin' today, Rand the Man?"

"I'm all right. Hey, would you mind letting Will know I'm here?"

"He'll be downstairs in a minute. He has to deal with that group over there." Ray pointed to two men and a woman at the opposite corner of the lobby near the glass doorway.

"Who are they? What's going on?"

"They all just got here. I think they're from a local news station, but I overheard them say they're moving to a nearby location to do a press conference when his mom gets here. I think they're trying to get a private quote from the young man ahead of the show. Vultures," he said, shaking his head in disgust.

"She's outside. Why are they allowed in the building? He doesn't want that kind of exposure, Ray," I whispered.

"As long as they're peaceful… what can I do? I warned him they were here. I thought he'd refuse, but he said he'd be down in a few minutes."

"Oh."

Ray was still talking. Family statement nearby. His mother. Scandal. Poor Will. Ridiculous mess. And they better take it elsewhere quick 'cause he didn't want them creating a riot on his watch. I tuned in at the last part and smiled. My first honest-to-God smile in days.

Ray furrowed his brow. "What are you up to, son?"

"Nothing at all, sir."

I slid my acoustic guitar from its case and strapped it over my shoulder. There was no time to waste tuning my instrument. I had to go for it. I strummed the first few lines of the song I'd just finished. Music by Will, lyrics by both of us. Ray gave me a curious look, but he didn't seem overly alarmed. He ran into artsy weirdos walking around playing instruments at all hours of the day. It was when I started singing that his brow furrowed and his expression morphed into alarm. I pretended not to notice as I raised my voice and sang loud enough to ensure I had the attention of every person wandering into the lobby.

"It's a dangerous kind of music. So beautiful but I'm haunted—"

"Rand, quiet down!"

I ignored him and wandered toward the middle of the lobby, then stepped onto a raised planter near the grand staircase. The added two and a half feet gave me a platform to be heard and the height required to see Will when he entered. I shifted my gaze between the doorway separating the elevators from the main lobby and the reporters watching from the corner. I sang loudly and projected my voice so it rang throughout the lobby. It didn't take long for my audience to grow. It was lunchtime and classes must have been getting out. Everyone loved a clown. For a minute or two anyway. I didn't have much time before Ray would be forced to call for reinforcements.

I ended the song with a sweeping motion across the strings. My small group of fans clapped wildly. I was about to start another when I heard a familiar voice.

"You're unbelievable."

I looked up and did a double take.

Will was beautiful to me always. Never so much as when he knocked me sideways by doing something completely unexpected. The blond, spiked wig, ripped jeans, and red, short boots were a surprise. And then there was the eyeliner and gloss. He was definitely not dressed for a normal day at school.

"You look amazing."

I pushed my guitar behind my back and hopped down from the planter. I couldn't stop my smile from taking over my face as I moved toward him, though I wasn't sure of my reception.

"I'm here to make a statement," he said with a cocky grin as I closed the distance between us. "You may want to clear out of here. A team of reporters will be here soon with my pissed-off mom. It might get ugly."

I gave him a brief once-over and swallowed hard. Fuck, he was fearless.

The crowd parted when the music stopped. I smiled at the few "that was killer, man" comments and caught Ray's relieved expression before he tottered back to his post behind the reception desk.

"The reporters are standing in the corner near the front. They look ready to pounce. And your mom's outside. She's gonna love you in that getup, by the way."

"It doesn't matter what anyone else thinks now. I'm doing things my way."

"I'm proud of you. I—I need a minute. Come with me."

I grabbed his elbow and pulled him with me toward the reception desk before he could protest. There was an alcove behind Ray's desk that was relatively private. For now. He gave me an impatient look but didn't say a word. We stared at each other for a long moment. I wanted to pull his wig off and wipe away the makeup so I could run my fingers through his hair and see his freckles. I wanted to hold him close and beg him to forgive me.

"Rand, I can't do this now. I want to give those reporters my statement first and—"

"What are you going to say?"

"I'm telling the truth."

I swallowed hard and nodded. "What's the truth?"

"I'm gay."

"That's all?"

He chuckled. "No, it's only part of the truth."

I quelled the urge to crush him against me and inclined my head. "What's the other truth?"

"I'm proud. I wish my dad success, but I'm not going to deny who I am to make that happen for him. I refuse to be ashamed for who I am anymore." He ran his hand over his wig with a lopsided grin. "Every part of me."

"Good."

"And I'm not taking second place behind anyone or anything. I'm—"

"I'm sorry."

"You said that. You—"

"I meant it." I set my hand over his mouth and pulled him against me. "Listen to me… please."

"I'm listening." He pushed my hand away and inclined his head in a manner that suggested I'd better make this good.

"You come first. I'm sorry I didn't tell you Leah knew about your dad. I told myself I was protecting you. I didn't want you to worry about her. Or them. Maybe there was a selfish part of me that just wanted to ignore the danger signs because I was afraid they'd fuck things up."

"For the band."

"No. For us." I bit the inside of my cheek and looked behind me to see how much time I had before people came looking for him. I had to take the chance while I had it.

"Rand, I—"

"No, please! Let me… try. I'm good at this usually. The words, the music, but—I didn't count on you, Will. I'm not the same man I was when I first came to this city. Nothing is the same. I'm not cold anymore. I'm not lost. And when I'm worried I might lose my way, I've got someone in my corner who knows the way home.

"When you told me you lied from the start, when you said you knew you'd fall for me… well, it wasn't like that for me. I didn't know

I'd fall for you. I didn't expect you, Will. I woke up one morning next to a guy wearing funny pajamas with freckles on his nose and glitter around his eyes, and I only knew I'd better pay attention. I don't know what I'm doing, but I do know this isn't a temporary feeling. This isn't going away. You're inside me now. I can live without fame or fortune, Will. But I don't want to live without you. I love you."

Will threw himself into my embrace and wrapped his arms tightly around my neck. I held him close and breathed in his scent. Everything around us faded. The students, the reporters, his mother waiting somewhere outside. It was background music. Not important. I pulled back slightly and waited for him to look in my eyes before I sealed my mouth over his. We let ourselves get lost in the moment, then rested our foreheads in silent communication. There was no need to question. No reason to hide. And fuck, it felt good.

"I love you too." His eyes glistened with unshed tears. "But what about the band, your contract? You can't walk away from all that. I don't want you to."

"We come first. Everything else will follow. It's gonna be all right. Do you trust me?"

"Yes."

I laced my fingers through his and tugged his hand, leading him out of the alcove. "Let's go. Your audience awaits."

Will chuckled, a sweet, musical sound that made my heart soar. "Are you ready for this?"

"I'm ready."

I was more than ready. Conformity of any kind was a lie of omission. Maybe it felt necessary at times, but I'd found it wasn't for me. It was time to shed the veil of ambiguity and be honest. It was time to fight for our truth by living proudly. No evasions, no uncertainty. Just love. The best kind of truth.

Epilogue

In a time of universal deceit, telling the truth becomes a revolutionary act.
—George Orwell, *1984*

THE LATE-MORNING sun reflected off the windshield, making it difficult to see for a moment. I adjusted my sunglasses and turned in my seat to check the traffic before merging onto the interstate. The radio was on low, but I was listening to Will reading the directions to me from his iPad.

"Babe, I got this. The car came equipped with a reliable navigation system. We're good. Just sit back and relax. No more backseat driving."

"Hmph. You're lucky I'm here or you'd be heading to Connecticut," he snarked.

"True. But we're out of the city now, and it's smooth sailing from here. Tell me about your day."

Will gave a half laugh and turned in his seat to face me. "You already know about my day. God, moving sucks. I'm glad we're getting away for the weekend. The designer said the install would be done by Monday, but I'll call her on Sunday to make sure. Worst-case scenario, we get a hotel room for a night or two. Or we can sleep on my old futon."

"Hell no!" My brow knit in mock outrage at the very idea. I went into comedic detail, listing the many things wrong with his suggestion while he chuckled good-naturedly.

Will officially moved into the Tribeca condo soon after he'd made his "statement" to the press. Six months had passed, but I knew I'd never forget that day. Or the look of absolute horror on his mother's face when she saw her son in full makeup, wig, and a glam outfit perfect for the stage but definitely eye-catching in the light of day. Priceless. Will's brief comment to the reporter said so much more about who he was than how he was dressed.

"I'm a gay man. I've been out for a while but only proud recently. I love my family, but I can't deny who I am for anyone's sake. I am not ashamed to be gay. I'm lucky. My lifestyle is no different from most college students'. I'm very ordinary. I just happen to love a man. That may be considered 'nontraditional' or even sinful to some, but I know it's a good thing. It's love. Not a different love. Just… love. I won't be moved by fear or convinced I'm wrong, and I refuse to deny the best parts of my life to make anyone else comfortable. Thank you."

Will had read his carefully chosen words and then looked up at me with a wicked grin that made my heart flip in my chest. He'd forgiven me before I'd apologized. Once again, I was humbled.

It took a strength of character far greater than the norm to stand up to the status quo. To insist you be given the right to be yourself. Your whole self. Acts of bravery aren't necessarily giant statements. Sometimes the most poignant ones came from those who live quietly but honestly. I wasn't sure I'd ever manage the quiet part, but I liked my life now. I was protective of what I shared with Will. It wasn't anyone's business, but it wasn't a secret, either. I was the lead singer of a hip, new band, who happened to be bisexual and lived with his boyfriend in New York City. If my sexuality was the only thing people focused on when they heard our songs, then they were missing the point.

Spiral's first single, "This Music," was released last September. It entered the charts in the top fifty and steadily climbed its way to number ten. When the second single went to number five a couple months later, it was clear that most people didn't really give a crap who I slept with or that my boyfriend's parents were radical conservatives. They liked the music. So far, so good.

Our burst into the limelight meant everything was about to change. Again. Traveling, touring, and endless radio appearances were part of our new normal. It was nonstop and frenetic, but I was enjoying the ride. It was outrageous to have this much fun doing something I loved… and get paid for it. The one thing I was adamant about was that my schedule meshed to some degree with Will's. Will couldn't take time off from school, but we managed to plan longer tours around his vacations. Yeah, I was greedy. I finally had a chance to have it all, and I wasn't backing down. The key was perspective. Will was my number one. Everything else followed.

It was weird to think about how different my life was now. A year ago I lived with two buddies in a tiny East Village apartment. Now my boyfriend and I shared a luxury condo I'd recently purchased from the owner. As I listened to him talk about the furniture and lighting the designer was installing while we were on this short weekend getaway, I knew without doubt this was what was real and important. Not the bright lights, the cheering audiences, or the ticket sales.

"So no futon?" he asked.

"Nope."

"What if your family wants to visit?"

"We'll get them a hotel room."

"O'Malley, you're a—whoa. Listen!" Will leaned forward to adjust the volume on the radio before turning to me with a proud grin. "Congratulations. You've made it!"

I laughed as the opening beat of our newest single blasted through the car's speakers. Will joined in and reached for my hand, pressing a small kiss on my fingers. "Golden hair, green flecks, and soul." Months ago I'd said hearing our music on the radio would signal the beginning of my dreams coming to fruition. Now I knew better. That was background music. The real reward was the journey, and the gift was having someone you loved along with you on the ride.

I am the oddest combination of a control freak and a free spirit. I want everything at once. I forget every once in a while to measure the distance between goals. Music gives me wings, but Will shows me how to fly. It's true I'm a little brash and reckless on occasion. I like getting my way, and I have a tendency to act without thinking things through. Call it an unfortunate family trait, an inflated ego, a heightened passion for justice, or gross immaturity in someone who should know better by now. I'm not sure I'll ever really change, but Will seems to get me anyway.

The geek and the rock-star wannabe. The loudmouth and the quiet soul who speaks through music. He is my measure of peace when I get away from myself... and maybe I'm his catalyst to encourage him to share his magic with the world. Some people may never understand, but it doesn't matter. This part of us isn't for sale. This is for us only. A simple kind of truth.

LANE HAYES resides in sunny Southern California with her fabulous husband and a very old Lab in an almost empty nest. Armed with imagination and a strong adoration for romance novels, Lane began writing MM a few years ago and has never looked back. She truly believes there is nothing more inspiring than a well-told love story with beautifully written characters. Her debut novel, *Better Than Good*, was a 2013 Rainbow Awards finalist. Lane loves reading, writing, travel, chocolate, wine, and spending time with family and friends. And if any combination of these can be done together, all the better!

Contact information:
Website: lanehayes.wordpress.com
Twitter: @LaneHayes3
Facebook: LaneHayesauthor
E-mail: lanehayes@ymail.com

A Better Than Story

Matt Sullivan understands labels: law student, athlete, heterosexual. He has goals: graduate and begin his career in law. One fateful night, Matt tags along with his gay roommate to a dance club and everything changes. Matt finds himself attracted to the most beautiful man he's ever seen. All labels go flying out the window.

Aaron Mendez doesn't believe in labels, and he's leery of straight curious men. He makes it clear that he'll hide his fabulous light for no one. While Aaron can't deny the attraction between him and Matt, he is reluctant to start anything with someone who is still dealing with what this new label means—especially when that someone has a girlfriend.

www.dreamspinnerpress.com

BETTER THAN CHANCE

LANE HAYES

A Better Than Story

Jay Reynolds has a crush on his project leader at work, but an office romance with Peter Morgan isn't likely to happen since Peter is straight. Worse, Jay soon fears Peter is homophobic, and his initial infatuation turns to loathing. But one fateful night, Jay is forced to acknowledge things aren't quite as they seem with Peter. Suddenly, his crush is back and unbelievably, Peter is interested too.

They begin a friends with benefits arrangement, which becomes difficult for Jay when he starts falling for his sexy boss. Peter's past issues keep him from committing, and Jay has to decide if he can be satisfied with friendship if Peter isn't ready to take a chance on anything more.

www.dreamspinnerpress.com

A Better Than Story

When Curt Townsend, a successful young DC lawyer, attends his first gay wedding, he doesn't expect anything more than a great evening out spent celebrating two lucky guys willing to commit to one another. He certainly doesn't anticipate meeting someone like Jack Farinelli. Fourteen years Curt's senior, Jack owns two businesses: a gay bar and a motorcycle shop. He's gorgeous and self-assured, but Curt is positive they have nothing in common.

Jack is comfortable in his own skin. He's attracted to Curt's quick wit and easy manner but most of all, to their unexpected mutual love of baseball. As they forge a friendship based on their shared enthusiasm for the sport, they begin a journey which reveals how their differences might be the catalyst behind a growing attraction. Both men have experienced their share of pain, but they realize they need to set aside the past and learn to trust in a future if they are to have one together.

www.dreamspinnerpress.com

A Better Than Story

Paul Fallon is a fashion advertising guru. He's a genius at dealing with difficult editors, art directors, and designers alike. He thrives on the chaotic atmosphere and constant challenges. But in his personal life, he's hoping for peace and stability. Settling down with a nice doctor or lawyer sounds perfect. Anyone but an artist. He's been there, done that, and he doesn't want to relive the heartache.

Seth Landau is a model, occasional guitarist, and aspiring painter. He's quirky, flighty, and wise beyond his years. Life has taught him some tough lessons, then given him opportunities he never dreamed of. He's learned to appreciate the fragility of life and to express it in his work. Seth's flare for the absurd combined with a supple mind and a beautiful body are too alluring for Paul to ignore. Against his best intentions, Paul is drawn to the younger man whose particular brand of crazy challenges Paul to accept that things aren't always as they seem. Sometimes taking a chance is better than being safe.

www.dreamspinnerpress.com

A Right and Wrong Story

Escaping an abusive relationship left Luke Preston anxious and spouting panic-induced poetry. Desperate for a fresh start, Luke accepts a job remodeling a tired old beach house for a professional soccer player and his model girlfriend. While his passion is literature, not sports, focusing on the renovations eases his anxiety. Until the job he signed up for turns out to be more complicated than advertised.

Sidelined with a serious injury, soccer star Michael Martinez decides his beach house is the perfect place to recuperate. Remodeling might be the diversion he needs to keep his mind off his busted knee. Falling for the pretty designer with some quirky habits wasn't on the drawing board. Unfortunately, Luke didn't build a big enough closet for Michael to hide in. Having a star-powered sports career used to be all Michael lived for, but he'll have to reevaluate his plans and find the right words if he wants to build more than a beach house with Luke.

www.dreamspinnerpress.com

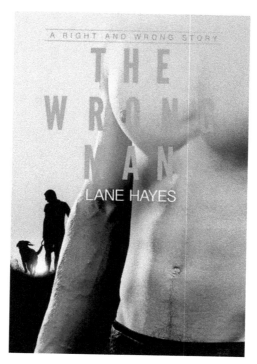

A Right and Wrong Story

Successful owner of an upscale boutique in fabulous West Hollywood, Brandon Good swears by his personal edict to "live in the present." After a bad breakup, he agrees to dog-sit to keep his mind off his ex. Never did he expect the dog to belong to a man from his past, the only man to ever truly break his heart.

When Jake Westley relocates to join the WeHo fire department, the last thing he anticipates is reuniting with his secret high school love. Thrilled with the prospect of reconnecting with Bran, Jake feels no guilt in using his charming old dog as an unwitting matchmaker. As he and Bran rekindle their friendship, it becomes clear the intense attraction they once felt is stronger than ever. But as hard as they try to leave the past behind, painful memories resurface. Bran will have to confront his fears and consider the possibility that the man he swore was absolutely the wrong one might be perfect after all.

www.dreamspinnerpress.com

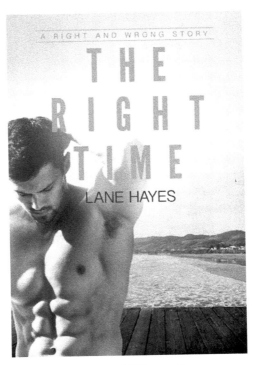

A Right and Wrong Story

Workaholic Nate Erickson is a successful real estate developer who thrives on long hours and stress. When a Los Angeles project prompts him to relocate to Santa Monica, he welcomes the change of scenery. Nate has always considered romantic entanglements trouble, but his sexy next-door neighbor isn't easy to ignore. Which makes no sense, because Nate is straight... or so he's always thought.

Alex Reyes is a retired professional soccer player turned West Hollywood business owner with an insatiable lust for life. He loves his family, friends, and work. But there's one life challenge left to accomplish: coming out publicly. Respect for traditional Latino values has kept him in the closet, but Alex begins to think he and his new neighbor might help one another combat their fears. As Alex and Nate forge a strong friendship, they soon realize facing their personal demons will take more courage than either man bargained for. The reward is immeasurable... if the timing is right.

www.dreamspinnerpress.com

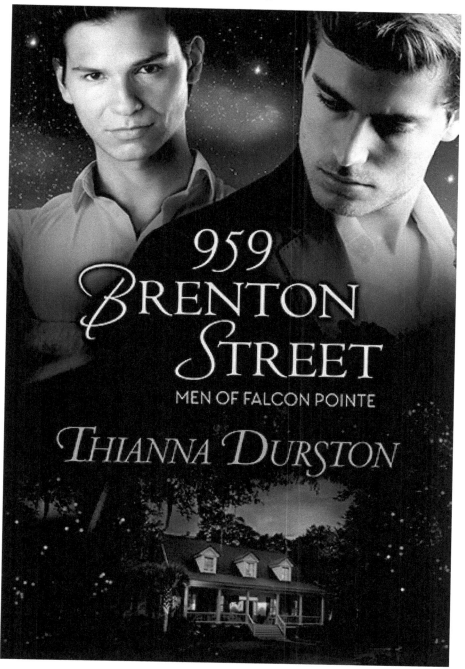

959
BRENTON
STREET

MEN OF FALCON POINTE

THIANNA DURSTON

Also from Dreamspinner Press

BEIGNETS

MICHAELA GREY

www.dreamspinnerpress.com

The CAGE

Catt Ford

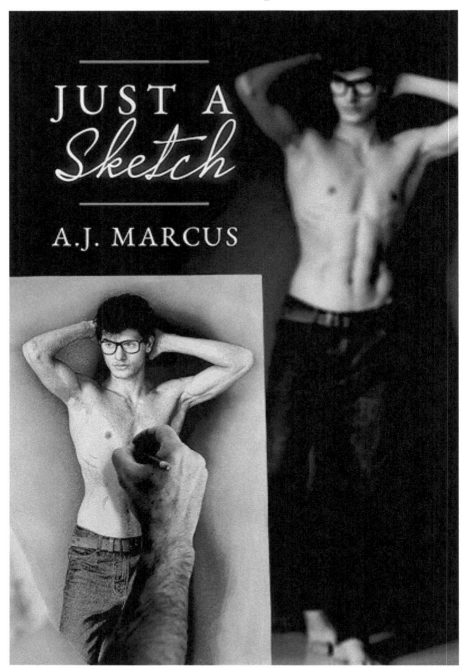

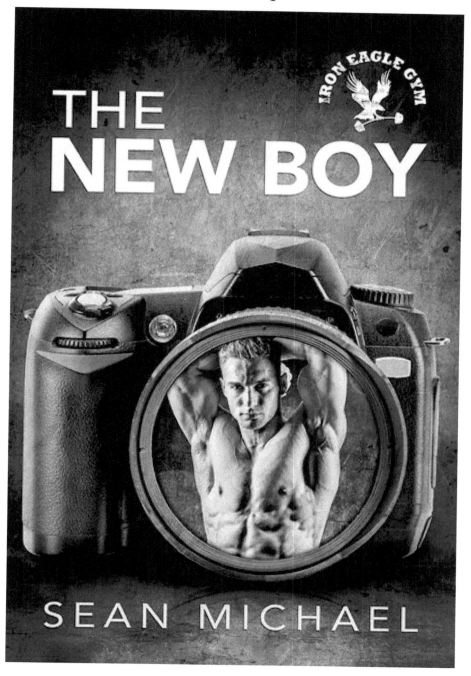

THE
NEW BOY

IRON EAGLE GYM

SEAN MICHAEL

CHARLEY DESCOTEAUX

CASCADES

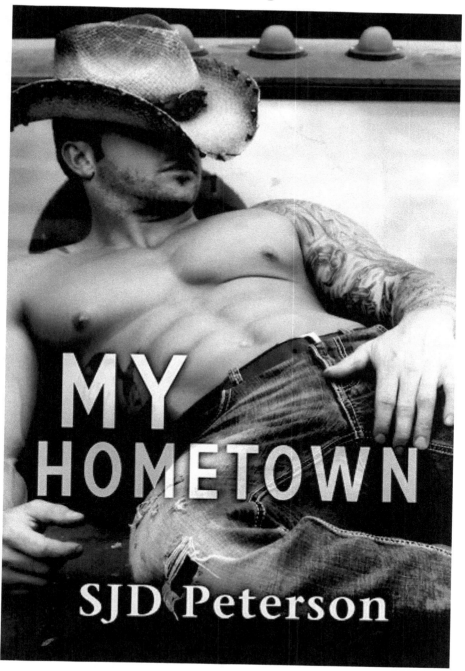

MY HOMETOWN

SJD Peterson

FOR

MORE

OF THE

BEST

GAY

ROMANCE

DREAMSPINNER
PRESS

dreamspinnerpress.com